W9-CQH-456

THE PENNY

THE PENNY

A NOVEL

Joyce Meyer
and
Deborah Bedford

New York   Boston   Nashville

This book is a work of fiction. Names, characters, places, and incidents are the product of the authors' imaginations or are used fictitiously. Any resemblance to actual events, locales, or persons, living or dead, is coincidental.

Copyright © 2007 by Joyce Meyer

All rights reserved. Except as permitted under the U.S. Copyright Act of 1976, no part of this publication may be reproduced, distributed, or transmitted in any form or by any means, or stored in a database or retrieval system, without the prior written permission of the publisher.

FaithWords
Hachette Book Group USA
237 Park Avenue
New York, NY 10017

Visit our Web site at www.faithwords.com

Printed in the United States of America

Originally published in hardcover by Warner Faith

First International Trade Edition: June 2007

10 9 8 7 6 5 4 3

FaithWords is a division of Hachette Book Group USA, Inc.
The FaithWords name and logo is a trademark of
Hachette Book Group USA, Inc.

ISBN 978-0-446-58188-2 (pbk.)

Alack, when once our grace we have forgot,
Nothing goes right; we would, and we would not.

WILLIAM SHAKESPEARE
Measure for Measure
Act 4, Scene 4, lines 33-4

You know, I just loved Grace Kelly.
She was a soft, warm light every time I saw her.
And every time I saw her,
it was a holiday all its own.

—JIMMY STEWART

To those who long to come out of dark places.
To those who yearn to find the One who is trustworthy.

Chapter One

There are two things I will always remember about summers in St. Louis. One is walking barefoot on pavement so hot that I could pop the tar bubbles with my toes. Pavement so hot that, by the end of July, the hide on the soles of my feet was as thick as my tanned-leather coin purse from Woolworth's and I could cross Arsenal Street without having to run. Every year, some photographer from the *Post-Dispatch* would take a shot of an egg frying sunny-side-up on the sidewalk and the paper would run it on the front page. HOT ENOUGH TO FRY AN EGG ON THE SIDEWALK! the headline would bellow. As if they were telling us something we didn't already know.

The other thing I'll always remember is the summer of the penny. At this point in my life, I'm picking up pennies all the time. But that wasn't the case back then. Not before *the* penny, the *important* penny, the one that led me to Miss Shaw at the jewelry store.

I learned from that first special penny how important the little things in life can be.

Because the penny led me to knowing Miss Shaw, and knowing Miss Shaw was what started things changing between Daddy and Jean and Mama and me.

Before the penny, if you'd have asked what I knew about Miss Shaw, I'd have shrugged and acted like you were loony. "I don't know *anything* about her," I would've told you, because girls like me had no reason to speak with ladies like Miss Shaw.

No one in the neighborhood knew much about Miss Shaw. For although my one friend, Marianne Thompson, and I had seen her greet her customers with a warm smile like she could tell something special about them, people like us never had any reason to set foot inside a jewelry store. So Marianne and I just wondered between ourselves: did she come from money or did she earn it? Did she grow up around here? How old was she? How did she manage to keep her hair dry on rainy days without using an umbrella? And because of that, because no one knew where she'd come from or who her parents were or how she'd come to have her own jewelry store, she was the most profound mystery along Grand Avenue. And you know how everybody likes to talk about a mystery.

"Now there's a woman up to no good," Daddy would comment whenever he happened to see Miss Shaw promenading along the sidewalk downtown with her pocketbook tucked beneath her arm. Daddy had a general distrust for all things to do with women bettering themselves. And he had a healthy contempt for Miss Shaw in particular. "That woman causes all the talk, anyway. She *thrives* on being talked about, or else she wouldn't stay tight-mouthed the way she does. Let me tell you, there's a woman who rides a high horse. Acting like the rest of us aren't good enough to know her."

Only one part of the neighborhood hearsay going around about Miss Shaw didn't match up with the stories of Miss Shaw's grace, beauty and superiority. Marianne Thompson made a vow to me once that she'd seen Miss Shaw sneaking around in the shadows of the town cemetery. She'd been hiding behind trees, Marianne insisted, and taking careful steps through the fallen leaves so as not to make any sound with her high-heeled shoes, and glancing around stealthily to make certain nobody saw her. She'd been looking around for a grave, Marianne said, and when she found the one she was looking for, it didn't have a stone. Marianne had seen Miss Shaw stoop to the ground and wipe the dead leaves from a smooth patch of dirt and place her gloved hand atop the dry mound. She held her hand

to the ground for the longest time, Marianne declared, like she expected to feel a heartbeat.

These are the things I knew for sure about Miss Shaw from my own
observance. She arrived at Shaw Jewelers before nine every morning, leaving plenty of time to polish the counters and arrange the
pearls on the headless necks in the window before the store opened.
She wore pumps that reminded me of the ones I'd seen once when
Mama took me to the A&P Supermarket, the pretend princess shoes
you could buy on the toy aisle, with plastic jewels across the toes and
soles so stiff and curved that they arched your feet like a ballerina.

Every time I saw her, I wanted to stare, seeing how she held herself. To this day, I'll bet Miss Shaw practiced balancing books on her
head while she walked around her house in those beautiful shoes.

And this one last important thing I knew about her. No one ever
saw Miss Opal Shaw without her white Sunday gloves on, tiny buttons fastened against the soft underside of her wrists. She wore her
gloves no matter if she was counting inky receipts or down-shifting
her Cadillac convertible or presenting diamonds to a customer.

What *you* have to know is this: South St. Louis is not a place you'd
want to wear white Sunday gloves on any other day of the week.

But I'd best get back to the penny.

I discovered Grace Kelly movies that summer, mostly because
the Fox Theater had refrigerated air. The sign proclaimed in frozen-
painted letters, AIR COOLED, with white x's to look like sparkles and
icicles hanging from the A and the C. The Fox was so fancy that,
after you paid at the box office, you got to pick any one of a dozen
gleaming doors to walk through.

We lived upstairs in a two-story flat on Wyoming Street, in a
neighborhood where the buildings had been wedged much too close
together. What had started as red brick, weathered and coated with
coal soot, was now the color of brown rust. When the hot air rose,

our rooms soaked up heat like an oven. The flat belonged to Daddy and we could have lived downstairs if he'd wanted, but he reminded Mama every time she asked that he could get higher rent by keeping the paying tenants in the cooler rooms downstairs.

My big sister's temper matched the heat that July. Jean paced the house, as restless as the lynx that prowled its cage at the zoo, and about as moody, too. You could almost see the room get darker when she entered the door.

Jean, almost four years my senior, had graduated early. There wasn't a fourth grade one year, so the school board made it up by dividing the smart third graders from the ones who weren't so well off in that department. Jean acted like she'd won a Nobel Prize or something, when all she'd done was show up and go where they told her. Still, if I'd been in that class, they would have left me in the third grade, and Jean knew it. She bragged about moving up all the time. I guess I understood why. Sometimes, to survive Daddy's meanness, we got along best by acting too big for our britches.

Jean's secretarial school would start in two months. Lately Mama had begun making off-handed suggestions about Jean taking me for an outing. "You go off to be a secretary soon, Jean, and you won't have time left to pal around with your sister," Mama would say as carefully as if she were tiptoeing on shattered glass. Even with that, Jean ignored me. She would slouch in the chair by the window and stare out with her arms crossed.

I guess my sister and I got along the way most sisters do. I always felt like I was living in her shadow. She told me later how it bothered her that I was always nipping at her heels. I told her she was wrong—I was just always trying to catch up with her.

On the day of the penny, Jean had gone into another brood because Adele Middleton had invited her to spend the night with her family in an air-cooled room at the Ambassador Hotel but, as usual,

Daddy had told her no. Daddy always said no to everything. Just because he was miserable, I don't know why he thought he had to spread that around to the rest of us, too.

Even when my sister was brooding, Jean was everything I wasn't: tall and willowy, with light brown hair and hazel eyes that flashed a hint of green. My hair looked like a fistful of cork grass when I wrestled it into a ponytail. Jean's hung straight down her back, as smooth as ribbon.

When she asked, "Why can't I go?" fear twisted in my throat the same way it did whenever Jean pushed it with Daddy. He would never change. And my sister seemed destined to be the one most willing to provoke his anger. I wanted to grab her and make her be quiet. But before I could, she blurted out, "Why not?"

My sister and I were many things to each other: sidekicks, rivals, accomplices, enemies. Some days we became an indecipherable muddle of all four. As I watched Jean stand up to Daddy, her bravery left me both aching with dread and reeling with love. I wanted to murder her for being so dim.

As Daddy ambled across the room toward her, his thick body moved with surprising agility. The anger in his pale green eyes looked like it could bore holes through my sister. A hank of his sparse brown hair, which he tried to keep combed across his balding scalp, fell forward onto his forehead. His thin, unpleasant lips curled.

"You talk back to me, girl, I'll knock you across the room."

"Jean." I picked up the goldfish bowl from the coffee table as he advanced on her. "Don't." I already knew it wouldn't help at all to go find Mama.

But Jean was too fiery for her own good. "You never let us do *anything.*"

And just like that, Daddy grabbed her by the hair with a hand as broad as a fence board and landed a stinging smack across her face. She staggered over the coffee table, trying to shield herself with her left arm, but Daddy's punch to the stomach sent her sprawling to the floor. She landed hard on her rear. When she lifted her eyes to him, he said, "We don't got money for places like the Ambassador Hotel and you know it. You stop wanting what you can't pay for."

Jean stared up at Daddy in hatred. I knew what she must be thinking by the flash in her eyes. *Well, of course we've got money. You spend money all the time.*

It was an invitation, I wanted to cry to him, but I didn't dare. *When people invite you to do something, they don't intend for you to pay.*

The window fan did nothing but move the stifling air from one spot to another. Since the heat began, hardly any cars or people had been in sight, not even in Tower Grove Park. Sirens wailed out in the street. And Daddy kept right on going.

"I'll knock you down every time you glare at me like that. You hear me?"

It might have been the wrong thing to think, but I kept wondering if anything would come along that would knock *him* down.

"Come on." Jean clutched my hand so tight that the knobs of my knuckles crunched against each other. "Might not have enough for the Ambassador, but we *do* have enough for a picture show, Jenny." I knew she was using me to shield herself against Daddy, which made me feel a little important and terrified me all at the same time. I felt important because I was helping Jean. I was frightened because Daddy could just as well beat me up next. "*Rear Window* is playing."

I tugged on Jean's arm and tried to make her look at me, but she wouldn't. If she met my eyes, one of us might have to admit that Daddy scared us. Nobody wanted to do that. It was safer to keep our minds filled with notions of Grace Kelly and Jimmy Stewart; we'd seen *Rear Window* twice already.

"And you won't be able to take your eyes off her glowing beauty," the voiceover on the trailer touted with bated breath. I'd seen it so many times, I had the words memorized. "She shares the heart and curiosity of James Stewart in this story of romance shadowed by the terror of a horrifying secret."

The delicate, sophisticated actress on safari with Clark Gable, the pioneer bride who protected Gary Cooper in a shoot-out, didn't seem all that remarkable to me. But the movies she played in about girls-winning-out pulled at my insides like the moon tugs at the Mississippi.

It was Jean who copied everything about Grace Kelly, from the hair she pulled into the shape of a dinner roll at the nape of her neck, to the dark glasses that made her look glamorous and mysterious at the same time, to the scarf she wore, as billowy as a spring cloud, knotted beneath her chin. Jean drove me crazy, the way she let thoughts of Grace Kelly dominate her life. Sometimes I thought I'd go nuts if she didn't stop talking about how Mr. Kelly's nickname for his daughter was Graciebird, or how her first commercial featured her spraying a can of insecticide around the room, or how, at the beginning, most directors she auditioned for found her too tall. I was sick to death of hearing the story of how, when Grace was a teenager, she stood on the front seat in a convertible and steered the car with her feet.

I was scrounging through my pocketbook, looking for my coin purse, thinking how my sister drove me out of my wits because she couldn't talk about anything besides Grace Kelly, when Jean came and dragged me down the narrow staircase. "Streetcar's coming," she said as I squinted against aching splinters of light. But she needn't have told me. The warning bell clanged as the door accordioned open and Jean shoved me up the steps. We lurched to the rear to buy tickets and fell into warm, hard seats. My sister crossed her legs at the knees, shoved her sunglasses up over her forehead and drew out a tube of Pond's Ever-So-Red lipstick. She drew a neat circle around her mouth and blotted. When she snapped open her purse to return the lipstick, I caught the beginning of what Jean's grown-up smell would be: a mixture of powder and faint-scented tissue and *Emeraude* cologne. The sweetness left my head aching and my stomach woozy.

When the trolley stopped in front of Woolworth's and we got off, Jean hurried across the street ahead of me to join the ticket line. Even from this distance, I could see the angry red handprint Daddy left on her cheek. She would be getting away from us soon. I couldn't breathe when I thought about Jean getting out of the house, going on to secretarial school.

"What are you staring at?" She plopped her hands on her hips. "Come on."

Often when we were by ourselves at home, when Daddy was gone, when Mama was outside and I was aching to share confidences with my sister, I'd catch Jean staring at me like she regretted knowing me. Maybe she didn't much like the idea that, due to the inopportune occurrence of my birth, she was tied to me for life. At times she almost seemed okay with having a sister. At other times, she made it plain she didn't like who her sister was. I couldn't do much to make it change, other than wish she'd try to see me differently. Jean's moods may have been a bother, I thought as we stood in the street outside the Fox Theater, but I wanted to stay on her good side. She was all I had.

That's when the streetcar clanged its bell and pulled away behind us.

That's the very moment I first saw the penny.

And that's the moment where this story really begins.

The penny lay wheat-side-up on the ground, so dirty as to almost be invisible. Like I said, I wasn't accustomed to picking up pennies at that point. A penny is such a little thing—it's never been worth much. I stared at it, stepped over it, and headed toward my sister waiting outside the theater.

Then the noise of Grand Avenue went silent. *Go back*, something inside me insisted. *Don't miss this chance.*

To this day I have to wonder: What if I'd stepped over that penny and left it where it was? Or what if I'd knelt to the ground and grabbed the penny the first time around without stopping to think, if Jean hadn't turned toward me from the box office to holler, if she hadn't bossed me ("Okay, Jenny. Jenny, come on—*don't*. That's disgusting, picking things up in the street. You're washing your hands before you're getting anything from the snack bar!"), would everything have happened the same?

But I *did* walk past the penny at first. When something whispered, *Pick it up, Jenny—little things make a big difference,* my heart almost paused in my chest. And I knew it without a doubt. As surely as if someone well trusted had whispered it in my ear.

This moment has something to do with your destiny.

It was only a matter of seconds before I went back. Seconds, I found out later, that would change everything.

The copper had melted its way clear into the asphalt. I bent over—I still see it in my mind's eye—and used my fingernails to pry the hot coin out of the roadbed. I remember straightening up, the penny branding my palm right there in the middle of Grand Avenue. And that's when the mystifying chain of events began.

It started simply enough when the Pevely Dairy truck braked to keep from hitting me, which sent bottles, full and empty both, toppling sideways. A dozen or so dashed to the street and shattered with sharp cracks.

Glass flew. Daisies of milk splattered on the street. The door of the five-and-dime opened, and a woman lugging her baby in a car bed stepped outside just as the last three bottles fell. "Oh my word," the woman said, swinging the car bed toward the building, shielding her child from what must have sounded like the Attack of the Killer Shards from Space. When she swung, she blindsided Bennett Mahaffey, who happened to be headed home with his favorite record, Elvis Presley's "That's All Right (Mama)," tucked beneath his arm.

The blow struck Bennett hard enough to knock the record from its jacket. When the disk hit the sidewalk, it wobbled on its edge and headed downhill toward everybody waiting in line at the Fox box office.

Bennett took off after his record.

He wasn't running exactly, because you can't run after something that's doing the platter thing—rolling in a complete circle, then a smaller circle, until it starts to clatter to the ground. He loped after it with his arms widespread and his knees bent, making a tentative grab every time it came close, as if "That's All Right (Mama)" could actually go wheeling around like that and not get a scratch on it.

Now here's something about Miss Shaw that I didn't know—I didn't find it out until much later. Each Wednesday just after five in the evening, no matter whether it was snowing in St. Louis or blowing up a gale or hot as a skillet, Miss Shaw rearranged her display windows. Shaw Jewelers stood two doors to the north of the theater, its front door shaded by a green awning with silver letters, the awning's scalloped edges lifting in the slight event of a breeze. Anyone who cared to watch could see Miss Shaw's gloved hands working, removing a necklace here, a bracelet there, angling a set of earbobs, pushing a ring closer to the center.

Miss Shaw worked dutifully for some length of time, arranging gems, aligning chains, matching colors. Occasionally she would step out to gaze at the displays herself, tilting her head, assessing her artistry. Each time Miss Shaw stepped outside, she carried a polish rag in her pocket and necklaces draped across her gloves, often glancing to see if one of them would make the display more appealing.

THE PENNY

On this particular day, Pete Mason happened to see Miss Shaw eyeing her windows from where he sat on a bench across the street. Indeed, he would say later, he had watched everything: the dairy truck, the swinging of the car bed, the crowd buying tickets for the picture show. He watched the stranger step off the curb, making a beeline for Miss Shaw. He watched the planned sleight of hand, the lifting of the necklaces from Miss Shaw's glove, and the bolting for cover into the box-office crowd.

"Hey!" Miss Shaw cried, too surprised for anything else.

That's how it happened that Pete Mason went into the crowd after the thief. That's how it happened that Bennett Mahaffey, who delivered appliances after school for Stix, Bauer and Fuller and who was the size of a small icebox himself, made a successful grab for his record just as the fleeing looter, glancing back to gauge Pete's distance, tripped over Bennett instead. Bennett let out an "oomph" of breath that sounded like a tire going flat. The looter somersaulted to the ground. Miss Shaw raced toward the Fox Theater box office in her slender-heeled pumps. The man behind the window shouted, "Any more for *Rear Window*?"

"These yours?" Pete scooped up necklaces from where they'd flown to the sidewalk. He wiped them off with his monogrammed hanky.

"They are." Miss Shaw held out a gloved hand. "Thank you so much." It all happened in front of me, unfolding like a dream, where nothing's tied together but, in the end, the pieces make sense some way.

"Did you see that?" I ran to my sister's side, knowing she must have noticed something.

"What?"

"The truck." I pointed in the direction of the shattered bottles in the street. "Miss Shaw and her necklaces." I pointed in the opposite direction toward the green awning. I closed my fingers over the penny, which had cooled in my hand. *A moment to define my destiny.*

That's when I saw Pete Mason nod his head toward me. Miss Shaw glanced in my direction and shot a warm, curious smile.

"Jenny Blake," Jean ordered, having missed the whole thing, "if you don't come on, we're going to miss the newsreels again." She sounded just as dour as always.

Chapter Two

*G*race Kelly is in love with Jimmy Stewart when *Rear Window* starts. Jimmy Stewart, playing a photographer, is stuck in his apartment for eight weeks because he broke his leg—flying metal smacked him while he took shots of a car wreck at the race track. Jimmy's got time to think about marrying Grace and he gets rankled over the dumbest things. She wears thousand-dollar dresses, and he's worried she won't survive as she follows him from one far-removed photography shoot to another, living out of one lone suitcase and dining on native delicacies that include everything from snails to sour berries to snakes for dinner.

"I wish I could be creative," Grace tells Jimmy.

"Oh, sweetie, you are," Jimmy tells Grace. "You have a great talent for creating difficult situations."

I balanced on the edge of my seat at the Fox that afternoon, penny in hand. I couldn't stop thinking that Jimmy Stewart got it backward. *He* was the one who made everything difficult. I wanted to shout at him, *Just give her a chance!*

I perched on the edge of the chair, the stiff plush indenting my legs. The cool, dry air felt magnificent. When Jean passed the popcorn, I dug in and wadded a fistful into my mouth.

On screen, Jimmy spied on everybody through their windows and noticed when a woman disappeared. "This is murder!" Jimmy insisted, only there wasn't a body. The police said the woman left early that morning by train.

In spite of how sick I was of hearing about Grace Kelly, I found myself rooting for her during this scene. She was the only one in the whole picture who believed in him. My breath caught in my throat when Grace climbed the fire escape to search for evidence that would prove him right.

Grace swung her skirts so she could climb inside the murderer's window and Jimmy realized, as he watched the murderer return to his apartment and apprehend her, that there was nothing he could do to help . . . and she mattered more than anything to him. I wondered how it must feel to have somebody believe in you the way Grace believed in Jimmy, when nobody else did.

When the lights came up in the Fox, and Jimmy and Grace had gotten together at last, we filed out, stunned and pleased again, shocked out of one storybook world and swept into another. The sun still smoldered in the sky, and walking from the cool darkness into the throbbing heat made me feel misplaced. Jean held her head at the same angle as the Lady Justice statue in front of the courthouse, her blue eyes pensive, her lips in a wry, slight smile, and I knew she pictured herself wearing those dresses, with hair in ripples like silk and a voice that sank lower to make everyone listen.

"You're not *her*," I said. "You'll never be."

Jean removed her tortoiseshell sunglasses from her purse. "I wasn't thinking I *was*." She sent me a withering look and slid her dark shades up her nose.

Oh, for glasses just like my sister's! I wanted to lace my statements with drama, too. "You want to come back tomorrow and watch again? I'll come with you," I said to the clouds above.

Just as we were stepping off the sidewalk, the box-office man, flat round hat, gold double-breasted buttons, came running after us.

"Hey!"

I glanced up at Jean, but she acted like she didn't hear him.

"I think he's talking to you." But Jean paid me no mind. "Maybe we left something." Jean checked her purse.

His shoes clattered on the pavement. "Hey! Wait a minute!"

I saw Jean touch her bruised cheek and leave her fingers there as if to hide it. "You mean us?"

"You." Mr. Box-Office pointed at me.

Jean dropped her hand from her face. I jutted my head partridge-like in disbelief.

He looked at me with such intense admiration that I didn't think I could bear it. I'd never had anybody look at me like that before.

"I've been waiting to talk to you for the whole length of the movie," he said. "Let me tell you, I stand in this box office all day watching folks go by, and I saw what happened out there. Does that happen to you often? I never saw anything like that before. You started off a whole string of events when you picked up that penny."

So I hadn't been the only one to notice it.

"It was uncanny, don't you think? Things like that just don't happen all the time."

I fingered the penny in my pocket, gloating that he would say this stuff in front of Jean. Maybe someday she'd have to admit that I occasionally knew what I was talking about.

"I've been standing in front of this theater for fifteen years and I've never seen a chain reaction like that before." He shrugged. "The Good Lord has a way of nudging me when I need to notice something. Let me tell you, I noticed *that*. You must be one special young lady."

Nobody had ever called me *special* or *young lady* before. There was nothing special about me. I stood at average height, a little overweight, with curly hair I didn't like and plain brown eyes that wouldn't make anybody look twice. But at his words, I felt like the world had tipped slightly beneath my feet. I straightened my back, stood a little taller. "My name's Jenny Blake."

"Nice to meet you, Jenny Blake. I'm Mr. Witt. You ever come back to the Fox, you ask for me, okay? I'll take care of you with tickets."

"You'd do that?"

"Sure, I would."

Aside from the Good Lord nudging his heart, his compliments and offer of free tickets made me skeptical. I couldn't accept he would offer me something purely out of kindness. "Why?"

"At the end of it all, you helped Miss Shaw. There's those of us on this street who place a lot of stock in things like that."

"You do?"

Jean was fumbling in her purse, searching for lipstick again. She snapped her pocketbook shut with an exasperated *humph*. Here I was, having the moment of a lifetime, and I'll bet all she wanted to do was get home and poke her nose into a *Picture Play* magazine again.

"Absolutely, I do."

I stared at him. "I don't know what to say."

That's when he extended his hand to me. "It's a pleasure to meet you, Jenny Blake."

I allowed him to grasp my hand, although I didn't really grasp his back. "Thank you." And later I thought how I should have said, *It's a pleasure to meet you, too.*

"You don't make yourself scarce around here, okay?"

"I won't make myself scarce," I assured him, daring my sister with my eyes to keep pretending that none of this mattered. "We come to see Grace Kelly movies all the time."

He touched the edge of his hat as we boarded the streetcar. I couldn't stop watching him from the window. The streetcar bell clanged and we started off and the last thing I saw as we rounded the corner was the glint of the gold buttons on his sleeve as Mr. Box-Office Witt waved us good-bye.

THE PENNY

The sun was a low, gold circle in the sky when we returned home, and our apartment was still sweltering. The aroma of ground-round and onion and ketchup seeped down the stairwell to meet us. Mama was making meatloaf for supper.

Jean had to set out the mashed potatoes the minute we entered the kitchen, and I had to bring the butter and the salt-and-pepper shakers and pour the milk into glasses. Mama worked with us in rapid, sharp movements to get the meal on the table, her apron knotted around a waist as slender as a dogwood limb.

We didn't talk much during the meal. We dined to the hum of the oscillating fan in the corner, which lifted the edges of our napkins, and the persistent *clink clink clink* of Daddy stabbing peas off his plate with his fork.

I couldn't get away until the dishes were washed and dried and Daddy turned on the television to watch *The Milton Berle Show*. I dug around inside Mama's sewing drawer and found the perfect box. I flicked open the tiny catch, spit-shined the clear plastic lid. Once I'd emptied the box of pins and padded the bottom with a cotton ball, I scrubbed and polished the penny with Ivory soap and a wash rag in the sink. Some of the grime came off and, with no small amount of pride, I saw I'd almost worked it to a gleam. I perched on the edge of my single bed, fingering the box, thinking, *I don't understand what happened today, but this penny had something to do with it.*

I wondered what could be behind all those things happening in a row.

Mr. Witt from the box office had said, "You must be one special young lady."

I stared at myself in the mirror, dissatisfied with my unruly hair and my eyes the color of the stale coffee Daddy always left at the bottom of his cup. I sat there for a long time, until Mama came up carrying a basketful of wet laundry and dropped it on the bed.

"Where's your sister?"

I slipped the box inside my pillowcase.

"I've got an idea to help cool you off. Lay down."

That's the way it always was with Mama. She never would say anything straight on to Daddy, but she would try to make things better behind his back. She did things that let us know she felt for us even though she wouldn't dare come over on our side. "It's not the Ambassador Hotel, but—" She held up one of my wet jumpers and laid it over the top of me. She followed with one of her slips on my bare legs, then a pair of pedal pushers. "Better?"

Just last fall, when Jean had begged Daddy to buy her senior pictures, Daddy said no. He had never let us buy school pictures, he told her, so why start now? What good would it do to have so many little rectangle photos of us when nobody cared what we looked like anyway? Jean knew good-and-well she would've gotten hit if she'd spoken up. For all the times I ached for her to keep her mouth shut, this time I wished she would risk the bodily harm. If it had been me I would have shouted, *I want something to trade, Daddy. If I don't have pictures to trade for other pictures, I won't remember what my friends look like.*

Five days later Mama came to Jean's room, slipped a Rexall Drug sack across the bedspread toward Jean, and out slid photo sheets— two dozen copies of my sister with shadows on her face, taken by a neighbor at the South St. Louis Easter egg hunt last spring.

"I wanted you to have these." Mama's expectant air didn't change as she waited to see what Jean would say. Jean stared at the photos, and I saw her throat working. The hope on Mama's face was so set that it looked like it had been chipped out of Missouri limestone.

I found the package just after Jean graduated, without one photo missing, hidden beneath her tangle of garters and nylons.

"What are you doing?" Jean stood in the doorway now, staring at us with that look on her face that let me know she was expecting something. As if in answer, Mama plastered me with another jumper and a wet blouse. Here she was again, covering up Daddy's contentiousness just as sure as she was covering up my arms and legs with soggy clothes.

The phone rang in the kitchen then, even though it was way too late for anybody to be getting a call. When Daddy answered and the person on the other end asked for somebody, that somebody was going to get it. Besides, any phone call wasn't ordinary, and Daddy didn't like out-of-the-ordinary things. We heard his heels strike the floor as he stood up. Mama yanked up two undershirts, a pair of boxers, and my white cotton skirt. Jean looked sick; I could tell she figured the phone was for her.

"Jenny?"

"Yes, sir?"

"You come take this phone call, and then we're going to have a talk with my belt."

When I held the heavy receiver to my head, I couldn't stop shivering. I leaned my ear into my shoulder and my voice scraped like a roller skate on pavement.

"Hello?"

"Jenny?" A woman's voice. A gentle voice.

"Yes?"

"You came to the movies this afternoon, didn't you? There was a girl who stepped off a streetcar. She witnessed someone trying to steal from my store. Could that have been you?"

Miss Shaw. I knew it immediately.

"It could have been." But that's all I would say. Daddy was standing there, drumming his large fingers on the Formica counter, and I knew if this took much longer, he would rip the line out of the wall. He'd done that plenty of times when he'd disapproved of Jean talking.

"It *might* have been."

"I wanted to thank you for being the person responsible for stopping the robbery at my store."

19

"But I didn't do it."

"Pete Mason and Mr. Witt said you did."

I don't know; it just didn't feel right taking credit for this. But Miss Shaw's voice was full of soft, warm light. I thought her voice was lovely—just listening to her made me feel good inside.

"I wouldn't have come to the movies if not for my sister. Her name is Jean Blake. You could talk to *her*."

Suddenly I discerned what sounded like uncertainty in her voice. "I don't know if you—"

I waited, as uncertain as she must have been about where she planned to take this conversation. *Why would Miss Shaw be calling me?*

"This may be a crazy question. But I kept asking myself all evening: *How are you going to know if you don't ask?* I don't know a thing about you, not really, but I was wondering—would you like a job in my store?"

I didn't know a thing about her, either. *Do you wear your white Sunday gloves all the time because you're afraid to touch anything?* That's what I'd heard Mama say *she'd* really like to find out about Miss Shaw.

"You want me to work in your store?"

"Would you be available to work for me maybe two days a week at the jewelers?"

I'd twisted my thumb tight inside the coils of the phone cord. I yanked hard, couldn't get it out. The idea of Miss Shaw offering such a thing made her immediately suspect. Why would a person who was practically a celebrity in St. Louis pay me any mind at all? I'd never dreamed Miss Shaw would offer me a *job*.

Jean loved bragging about her occasional lucrative baby-sitting engagements. If I had a way to make money, too, maybe my sister would stop lording her superiority over me. If I had a way to make money, maybe I could get away from this place.

But no way would Daddy let me do this.

"I might be very interested," I said with the most grown-up voice I could muster.

"Would you come next Tuesday? We could try it out."

My ear felt like I had shoved it up inside my head. As I untangled my thumb from the phone cord, I saw Daddy eyeing me. I wasn't at all ready for the "talk with his belt" that he'd warned me about.

"You got yourself a job?" Daddy had already unbuckled his belt and whipped it from the loops. He held it ready, folded inside one hand like leather reins.

I tried to nod, but I was frozen with fear.

But this time he couldn't have surprised me more. "That's fine by me. You make your own money, that's less I have to do to take care of you."

"Okay," I said in a breathless whisper, halfway to Miss Shaw on the line and halfway to the man who was threading his belt through the loops again. "Okay."

I hurried to the bedroom to tell Mama and Jean what had happened with Miss Shaw. There they were together on the bed, clammy and laughing, plastered with wet pedal pushers and Mama's blouses and an assortment of Daddy's T-shirts. I plopped lengthwise across the mattress beside them and added one of Mama's skirts to my chest, wanting to be a part of their laughter as the clothes warmed to our skin.

"You with a job?" Mama ran her hand through curls that had once been the same color as spun honey, but which had now faded to the yellow-grey of dried hay. She examined me pointedly. "What's your daddy going to think about that?"

"He said it's okay. He said he doesn't want to take care of me anyway."

Jean propped her head on her fingers like she was posing for a movie poster and I was the camera. She rolled her eyes.

I thought, *I wish you'd go away to secretarial school this very minute. It wouldn't make any difference to me.*

After Mama peeled the wet things off and carted the laundry basket downstairs, I watched out the window as she hung clothes in the moonlit yard, her fingers trailing the line as she clipped blouses together by the hems, their arms reaching for the ground. *Here I am with a chance to try my luck on something new*, I thought as I watched Mama outside, *and neither Mama nor Jean thinks it's anything out of the ordinary.* That can be a way of living, I guess. When nobody notices things you think are special, you start wondering if maybe it's *you* who isn't seeing things right.

But I had found a special penny, Daddy hadn't been too mean today, I'd gotten singled out for free movie tickets, and I'd gotten a job, all in a matter of hours. I looked out the window at the heavy blue arms on Mama's wet blouses, dangling outside downstairs in the moonlight. Those arms reaching for the ground reminded me of me. Seemed like I was always reaching like those arms, too, without knowing exactly what I was aiming for.

Chapter Three

*A*ll my life has been shaped by other people's hands. Daddy slapping me, Mama never hugging me, Jean pointing a finger of criticism at me. . . . I believe when you look close at a person's hands, they help you figure out who a person is on the inside. Jean's slender, unmarred fingers with her nails filed into the shapes of crescent moons, they tell me that if something looks imperfect or frightening, Jean doesn't like to see it. Mama's cuticles peeled raw and the empty finger where her wedding ring should have been if Daddy had ever seen fit to buy her one, they tell me that she keeps her unease inside and that she's long ago turned loose of expecting anything. Daddy's broad, calloused palms, his swollen knuckles, they tell me he uses the flat of his hand to get what he wants and that he hangs on hard to things he thinks ought to be his.

And there are my own hands. A miniature version of Daddy's—stubby fingers shaped more or less like his—but I know in my heart I am not like him. What clues do they tell everybody about me? That these are the hands of a girl who feels something unnamed waiting inside to get out, something bigger than she can hold? A girl who keeps hearing in her head that she might be asked to do something great in the world someday? A girl who has a deep desire to use her hands to help other people, but she can't see how that would ever happen?

Our flat on Wyoming Street sat uphill from the curb, the roots from the maple tree threatening to buckle the sidewalk. I felt a strange blend of dread and resolve every time I slid my hand up the wrought-iron railing that edged the steps and climbed steeply to the porch. The windows in the front were the prettiest things, rounded at their tops, with red bricks fanning out from the glass like eyelashes. In between the windows stood two doors, the right door leading up to a landing and our five-room apartment, the other leading to the families who lived below.

Often at night my daddy would stand outside on our front stoop and take stock of the constellations burning overhead, his thick hands, his stiff palms, flexing at his sides. From my bedroom window upstairs, I could see a moving red glow as he drew on his cigarette, the double-barreled flow of smoke as he exhaled through his nose, the glint of moonlight on the metal eyelets of his boots. He seemed small from where I stood then, his eyes as sad and sharp as a rodent's, and I marveled that someone like my daddy, who loomed so large and dangerous in my life, could appear undersized and exposed.

He didn't smoke often in our rooms, but sometimes after supper, he would smoke two, maybe three cigarettes in a row before he came inside to go to bed. More often than not, he swigged from a bottle, too. I would watch him staring into space with a hardened look on his face. Then he would finally give up, poke out his last Lucky Strike on the whitewashed stoop, and pitch it to the step, where he'd scrub it out good with the sole of his workboot.

He'd come in again and I would hear Mama and Daddy's careful voices. I never knew what Mama was doing all those times he stood outside, but I always thought she might be doing the same as me, watching him and wondering what was going on in his mind. Things were much more peaceful in the house when he wasn't in it, and she probably just stood there holding her breath, wishing it would last a little longer.

One of the most surprising things that had happened to me that year was when Marianne Thompson, my seventh-grade best friend, moved from the apartment below us into a quality-built home in St. Louis Hills. The only reason I could ever have a friend like Marianne with Daddy around was because she lived right downstairs. In St. Louis Hills, the *Post-Dispatch* advertised, the Thompsons found "country living in the city" in a land "swept by cool breezes." I knew I was being selfish but I couldn't help it; right now I wished Marianne wasn't being swept by cool breezes. I wished she still lived in the flat below.

After all the talking Marianne and I used to do about Miss Shaw, after all the conspiratorial stories she'd whispered about Miss Shaw skulking around in the graveyard, she would have shared my excitement and trepidation, I knew. I could have tied a secret message to the end of the rope I'd brought home from the lot by the gas station and lowered it to her window. (Once I'd intended to cut it up and make jump ropes, but it seemed more daring to use it for covert activity instead.) I would have waited until I felt the delicious tug from her end, which meant she'd read my note and tied on an answer. But Marianne was gone.

When girls at school tried to make friends by inviting me to do something, I didn't want to say, "Daddy won't let me." So more often than not, I came up with an even better excuse. "I don't like sock hops," I'd say. Or, "I don't like basketball games." Or, "You're crazy if you think I'd go to Katz Drug for a soda with you."

Nobody would ever know how badly I wanted to go do all those things with other girls. I couldn't let myself get close to anybody because Daddy was always there.

Once when Marianne Thompson had come upstairs and Daddy was home, I caught him staring at her with an expression that made my stomach pitch. I grabbed my friend's arm, feeling as if the world had just lurched sideways and become more dangerous. I dragged Marianne downstairs into the yard to see about tree-climbing or making mud cakes. At that moment, I sensed that if I didn't get her out of there, Daddy might do the same things to her that he did to me and Jean when he snuck into our bedrooms at night.

Which meant I ought to be grateful she had moved away to St. Louis Hills. No matter, though. I still missed her.

That morning, I pocketed my penny and went in search of my family. I found Jean filing her fingernails in the breakfast nook. "How come you're up so early?" she asked me. She held up a hand and examined her cuticles.

"I'm just excited about my new job. That's all."

Without being too obvious about what I was doing, I opened the refrigerator and took quick stock of the supplies inside. *Good*. We were short on things. I slammed the icebox hard enough to rattle bottles. "Where's Mama?"

"She's sewing me a new skirt for secretarial school."

"Where's Daddy?"

"Patching cement down the street."

Daddy used to have a night job—he worked as a truck mechanic for International Harvester. When he was gone in the evenings, sometimes Marianne came up to play cards. Now that he'd gotten laid off, Prozma Realty called him for odd jobs—hanging sinks, patching sidewalks, fixing screens. This made it much harder to predict when the coast would be clear.

I found Mama with her head bent over the presser foot of her Singer, feeding fabric to the needle with splayed hands. "I'll run errands if you want. I think Daddy said yesterday he wanted Royal Crown Cola and peanuts from the store."

"Oh, you want to go for him? Why don't you get us a Redi-Mix, too?" When she glanced up at me with her large, dark eyes and smiled, I could tell my mother must've once been pretty. Now she seemed as brittle as a dead twig, ready to snap in two. "Maybe I'll get in the mood to bake a cake."

THE PENNY

I stood still for one extra obvious moment, waiting for Mama's permission to dig into the flour tin above the stove. That's where she kept the spending money. I kept thinking maybe she'd stop sewing and look at me. But those stitches needed to be perfect, I guess, because she never raised her eyes from them. "Take only what you need, Jenny. And bring me back my change."

I dragged a chair across the kitchen to get to the flour tin and glanced at Jean. I didn't want her watching me do this. Yes, I was taking only what I needed. But I needed more than what Mama knew. I could have easily walked to the confectionery and gotten the groceries, but I needed streetcar fare, too. Which meant I would shop the A&P, which the ad in the *Post-Dispatch* told me would make me a woman of unequalled leisure and economy. I needed to share the story of the penny with someone who, unlike Jean, would try to understand the mystery of it. For me, the good thing about shopping A&P was that the streetcar would take me past Aurelia Crockett's house.

We kept to our own neighborhoods the way compatriots keep to their countries. The Italians lived on The Hill, the coloreds stayed to the east of Jefferson and Market and close to Tandy Park and along Labadie Street, and we kept to Wellston and Forest Park and Richmond Heights. Mixing people from two St. Louis neighborhoods, no matter what color, was like stirring water and oil. We were most loyal to the people who lived in our quarter. Daddy would have slapped me silly if he knew I sometimes headed down to the Ville.

I had made a promise to myself that I'd never talk to anybody at school again. It turned out being too much trouble, talking. I'd just get started making friends with other girls and they'd start asking questions I didn't want to answer, like whether my parents would bring refreshments to open house, or if I could meet after classes for a hamburger at Famous, or if I'd ever stayed awake all night (which meant they wanted to be invited to my house) for a sleepover.

So I told Cindy Walker and Rosalyn Keys they must be crazy thinking I'd be interested in doing anything with them, in a voice so rough that it sounded like I was chewing on my own words. As long as Rosalyn and Cindy were only acquaintances, I could keep them. But I couldn't let any friendship flourish with girls who expected to be invited to my house. Although Daddy had never threatened to hurt any of my friends, I had seen him hit Mama plenty of times. I had seen the way he looked at Marianne. I sure didn't want to chance Daddy doing something to anybody else.

So I told them not to ask to come over to my apartment because they couldn't.

The next thing I knew, after I told them they couldn't sleep over, there were notes stuck in my locker, folded in thick triangles like the flags I'd seen being handed over to dead soldiers' mothers, notes that said things like, "YOU STINK, YOU'RE STUPID." And other things I hated because Daddy shouted them through the house at me, words that made me feel like I was worth nothing, words like rocks falling that made me want to duck my head.

Aurelia Crockett came to Harris School at the same time that the school district brought in the portable classrooms. Every morning two dented, creaky Blue Bird buses pulled into the drive, and the colored people, both children and teachers, lugged their satchels and coats out of the buses and into the prefabricated buildings, which had been trucked in and set in place with hoists, for class. They had their teachers, we had ours. Our breaks and lunch came earlier than the portable-classroom kids' did. The only time we'd get to see them was when they'd start a broomball game in the field outside Mrs. Coleman's class and we'd watch them racing around the bases and shouting at each other out the window.

I met Aurelia the day I found the note in my locker from Rosalyn that said, "YOU EAT SLOP." If my resolve had been slipping about not talking, that note set me to certainty again. I was sitting on the steps as everyone stampeded past, waiting for those girls to leave the schoolyard so I wouldn't have to walk past them, the cold cement soaking up through my skirt. When I blew on the grass I'd threaded between my thumbs, the sound bleated like a duck call.

"You aren't doing it right, you blow as hard as all that."

My head jerked—I hadn't known anyone was anywhere around. My first thought when I saw her was this: it would have been easier for a red-tailed jackrabbit or a flying squirrel to start up a conversation with me than it would be for this individual who twisted her loafer sideways and waited for my answer.

My second thought was this: I didn't have to protect her from befriending me. Here was somebody I didn't have to worry about. Oh, Daddy would beat me if he found out I talked to a Negro girl, that was for sure. But this girl would never ask to spend the night with me. Someone like her would never expect to be invited to my house on Wyoming Street.

"Girl, you looking for a true B-flat, you've got to stretch the grass tighter."

In her hair were a dozen or more plaits that stuck out at every angle of her head like limbs on scrub brush. Each one narrowed to a plastic barrette in almost as many colors as she had braids. Once, Daddy had taken me hunting and I'd seen the whites of a deer's eyes. Its haunted, fluid eyes had stared into mine right before Daddy shot it. Her eyes were the same, aqueous and deep. I could see myself reflected when she focused on me.

From this low angle I also noticed her bosom, more voluminous even than Jean's. I thought, *If anybody gets to BE flat, it's not going to be this one.*

A boy appeared at her side, maybe a head taller than her. He made a fist. "What's wrong, Aurelia? She too good to talk to you?"

I turned away, blew the grass strand between my fingers as hard as I could. It sounded just as bad the second time.

"You think you're too good to talk to my cousin?"

This boy had another think coming if he thought anything he could do would make me show fear. I had become an expert at hiding how I really felt. I'd grown up around Daddy. I shrugged to the boy's face; I was too busy wondering just how his cousin could hear a B-flat like that. Maybe they listened to music in the portables all day, for all I knew about what went on in there.

"What's that mean?" the boy asked. "Shrugging like that?"

I shrugged again.

"You ever hear of the *Admiral*, the entertainment boat? My daddy's a trumpet man in the band," she said. "Sweet music for dancing because that's what the people like. He can run a scale about ten times in one breath. I'd say he can play pretty good."

She dropped her satchel and, as if her fingers could show me what she would someday mean to me, she cupped her hands around mine. When she did, I saw that the insides of her palms were lighter than the rest of her, brown-pink and warm. Her breath told me she'd been chewing Beemans gum.

I'd once found a lifeless cardinal lying in the street and I'd carried it home in my palm, hoping I could bring it back to life and rescue it. When I dripped water from the kitchen faucet over its head and it didn't revive, I gave a funeral and sang and buried it. The feeling Aurelia gave me, reaching out to me in genuine friendship, was the same feeling I'd had as I troweled rich soil over the redbird's carcass. I felt I'd been entrusted with something precious.

She focused on the grass between my fingers again. "Hold it tighter. Like this."

The boy hurried her—I guess I made him edgy—when the buses drove up. "You miss the bus, Aurelia, they'll skin you."

"Wait!" I called as she hopped over me and the last three steps, too. "You live in the Ville? Could I come see you sometime?"

She turned and nodded, swinging her satchel.

I blew again on my thumbs and the grass made a new, beautiful sound.

Even now, even after everything that has happened, I sometimes get scared calling Aurelia my friend. Because, used to be, every time I found a friend, I ended up having to give her away. I ended up having to give my friends away to protect them from Daddy.

This thing that had been born on the day of the grass reed grew into many afternoons, a series of quick whispers and giggles in which Aurelia let me in on details of her family. I felt like I had known Eddie Crockett and Aunt Maureen a long time before I met them. Aunt Maureen, who'd raised Aurelia from a baby after her mother had taken off, who wouldn't let you in through the front door before she tried to feed you. Aurelia's daddy, Eddie Crockett, who played trumpet music sweeter than Sarah Vaughan could sing.

That morning as I made the detour from the A&P, the sun already blazed so hot you wanted to stand under a tree and do nothing. I hadn't thought about it being Sunday until no one at Aurelia's duplex answered the door. From the porch I could hear a trumpet running scales, the notes as light and sweet as the early-morning dew that had fallen on Mama's laundry because she'd never taken the time to bring it inside. I stood for a minute, listening, before I rang the bell again and pounded so hard that the screen rattled. If Eddie Crockett was alone in the house practicing, he wouldn't hear me—I already figured that.

I heard boots tramping and the door swung open just as I was about to leave. Eddie Crockett stood with his trumpet in hand, his fingers entwined among the valves, his black hair with waves that lay over his forehead like they'd been pasted on. The stairwell still smelled of hotcakes. "Well, bless my soul," he said. "Look who we've got at the door again. You come to see Aurelia?"

I nodded.

"Don't you know it's Sunday morning? Sunday mornings, she gets all cleaned up and goes to church."

Aurelia had talked about the Antioch Baptist Church plenty to me; I'd passed it before, one of the prettiest churches I'd ever seen, across Goode Avenue on the corner of North Market, three blocks away from where the trolley off-loaded its passengers. It was built from Missouri clay bricks and chunks of limestone, rough blocks that met like right-angled fingers, like the corners of the building itself were interwoven, praying hands. On its east side, the church stood square, a castle turret against the sky. On its west end stood an archway and a broad wooden door where wedding parties gathered to throw rice, and brides floated down the steps in clouds of tulle to waiting getaway cars, a fine contrast of white nylon netting and dark skin. Every so often, Aurelia would talk about the messages she heard in church. She would say how the words lightened her heart, how they lifted her up higher than this world.

"You got time to wait for Aurelia, Miss Jenny?" Eddie Crockett held the screen open for me with his trumpet hand. "You're welcome to, if you want. They'll head back just as soon as they're done with the benediction and the supper they're serving to the folks who go there hungry."

"I don't really." Hugging the bottles of soda pop against my chest, I was thinking that, any minute, Daddy might come home and find me gone. I declined Mr. Crockett's invitation, feeling dismal because I'd snuck away and come so far and risked so much for nothing.

"Well, sorry you missed her, child. You know she always loves it when you got the time to come around."

I stood still, waiting for him to raise the trumpet to his mouth. I loved the way he held it when he played, like it had been a part of him ever since he'd been breathing.

32

He grinned, lifted the mouthpiece to his lips, wailed on his horn some riverboat sound, a tune I didn't know. Something started singing inside whenever Aurelia's daddy played his horn for me. I could still hear the sound of it, the notes big and warm and quick, even after I crossed Sarah Street three blocks away.

Try as I might, I couldn't pass Aurelia in that church, knowing she was close by, with me having so much to tell her. With the way Daddy acted about us leaving, I never knew when I'd be able to get over here again. I hid the grocery bag in a tangle of honeysuckle that clung to the irregular slabs of brick and moved with stealth from window to window, leaning up over the stone sills, trying to get a look inside. Every window I looked through was too dark, an impenetrable mosaic of blue and green and red glass. I was looking through pictures of ancient stories, the saints' long hair and sinuous robes, circlets of amber behind their faces. Then, all of a sudden, I got to a clear patch.

Later I would see that I had looked through the crystal wing of a dove, hovering over a manger.

A pulpit stood at the front of the pews, its wood as polished and whirly as the sateen in the choir's robes behind it. A purple banner that read HIS LOVE ENDURES FOREVER hung above the choir members' heads.

The singers rocked and clapped beside a man whose face was so dark he looked like he'd been burnished with Daddy's bootblack. Aurelia had told me once that his name was Reverend Monroe. He was a husky, short man, with hair that poked from behind his ears like clumps of kettle corn. As he gestured, the sleeves of his black vestments flapped like pennants in the halftime show at the Missouri Tigers football game. With every line he hollered, he swung his fist and shouted that he was throwing punches at the devil.

Sweaty people crowded the sanctuary, some of them applauding and shouting *Amen* every time the man said words about Jesus, some of them fanning themselves with cardboard pictures of lambs ("Smith's Plant Nursery. Negro Owned and Operated" the notation read. "Our Dedication to You. If we can't make it grow in your garden, then you don't want it growing anywhere."), others with their palms uplifted and cupped like they were trying to catch rain. Their pleading faces made me think I'd come across something too personal for me to see.

When I finally spied Aurelia, she was clutching the pew in front of her and her lips were moving in almost the same shape as Eddie Crockett's when he played his horn. Her cousins, Darnell, who I'd met at school, and Garland, who was much younger, flanked her on either side.

Garland fidgeted with a button on his suit sleeve. He wouldn't leave it alone. He kept twisting it tight and letting it go, twisting it again, until the threads must have split because the button flew off his arm and popped someone in the back of the head.

Aurelia's aunt, who'd been swaying with her fingers knit together over her chest, reached down without hesitation and laid Garland a good one, a sharp swat on the behind. Garland straightened up, just like that, and started flipping pages in the hymnal as if he were old enough to read. What surprised me most was the smile she tried to hide after she'd gotten him, as if she treasured his antics but couldn't dare let it show. I'd seen Daddy smile when he struck and it wasn't anything like that. He smiled like he'd be happy to kill you.

But then, a sharp smack on the behind didn't seem like much of a punishment to me.

Just as I poked my hand into my pocket to make sure the penny was still there, my eyes traveled overhead again to the window across the way. There, in a mosaic of golden glass over Aurelia's head, stood the image of a sheaf of wheat in a field. Maybe it was me rubbing the penny, thinking about the wheat in the window and the wheat on the coin beneath my thumb, that made Aurelia glance my way. All she could see through that piece of dove's wing was maybe my eyebrow, but suddenly she whispered something to her aunt and sidestepped Darnell. Next thing I knew, here she came, finding me outside, standing looking in the window.

"Girl, what you doing here?"

"Looking to find you," I said.

"You come on inside, then. You're gonna make me miss it."

"Make you miss what?"

"We got us a good place today, right beside the new Christians. That's the best seat in church when everybody starts confessing their sins." She grabbed my hand. "Come on."

I saw she wore loafers with brand-new pennies in them. I pointed toward her feet, "*That's* what we have to talk about," but she was too busy dragging me inside to hear.

The heat was intolerable. Darnell moved over and made room. Garland slammed the hymnal shut and stared up at me like he'd never seen anybody with a white face walk into his church before. Then I realized maybe he hadn't. Maybe I *was* the first one. I was the only person at Antioch Baptist wearing pedal pushers, too.

"Hey, kid. How are you?" I asked, giving his head a scrub with my knuckle. When I whispered to Aurelia, "I just want to tell you something important that's happened," her aunt glared down at me and, for a second there, I thought she was going to pop me one just the same as she'd popped Garland.

The windows, which could have blocked my view forever if I'd kept trying to peer through them on the outside, glowed with life and fire now that light shone through. A glass man in the window beside me stood with his arms outstretched for a hug (the thought of Daddy reaching toward me that way made my stomach queasy) and his cape was so red with the sun that you could almost taste the color. A cherry red, a ruby flash. A red better than a cinnamon stick.

At the front no one showed off, the way Mrs. Crawford did when she bellowed the National Anthem before the fireworks went off over the river on the Fourth of July. (Jean and I called her Mrs. Crawfish after that because, when she hit a loud note, she wagged her arms like a crawfish waggles its claws.) The music at Antioch was straight bluesy choir, voices blending smooth as bees as they sweated and danced and swayed.

I'd never seen so many people leaning from side to side or smelled so much pungent wood and perfume. "You've got a seed of greatness in you," Reverend Monroe bellowed with such forthright enthusiasm in his voice that, had I been anybody else and prone to jumpiness, I might have run away. His eyes radiated kindness, and his plainspoken manner made me listen instead. "You've got a seed of victory planted by God inside of you."

I already told you how I kept hearing whispers about greatness in my head. I'd be in my bed at night, after Daddy left the room, and I'd think about it so hard that I'd get a heavy tangle in the bottom of my heart. I'd hold on to that feeling so hard, hoping it would make everything else go away.

Someday you're going to do something great.

But I always assured myself I was stupid to believe that. *There could never be much good in me,* I thought. *Not as long as Daddy tells me I'll never amount to anything. Not with the way I let Daddy do those things to me.*

I looked over at Darnell, figuring maybe the reverend was talking to him. But, "Do not be afraid, you will not suffer shame," the man said, his sweet, kind eyes centered on mine. "Do not fear disgrace; you will not be humiliated. You will forget the shame of your youth."

If you only knew.

My shame will never go away.

It's my own fault I'm dirty and ruined.

My knees started to get wobbly, hearing these things and daring to talk back. I sat down, still clutching the pew. Neither God nor the preacher, either one, could know the remorse I felt inside.

THE PENNY

I held on to the penny in my pocket for dear life. I couldn't share the story about it with just anybody. It felt too precious; something about it made me want to keep it to myself. Except, telling Aurelia about it seemed different. But just when I thought it would be okay to show it to her—*This is it, Aurelia, this is the reason I'm here*—I saw she was waiting for me, hanging on to some basket that she didn't show any sign of passing along.

"What?"

She jiggled the basket at me. "Well?"

"Well, what?"

"Aren't you going to put that in the collection? Isn't that why you got it out?"

"No. Not *this*."

"Then why do you have it out?" She rattled the basket a second time.

"I wanted you to see this penny. That's all." But then I remembered Mama's money, the change from the groceries, in my pocket. I fished for coins and dropped a quarter and a dime into the basket so she'd leave me alone and hand it away.

Reverend Monroe was talking right to me. He said something that made me forget about money changing hands. He said, "The LORD saves his anointed; he answers them from his holy heaven with the saving power of his right hand. Those who look to him are radiant. Their faces are never covered with shame."

I wanted not to be ashamed that my daddy didn't think much of me. Nobody had ever made God sound like he was real and like he wanted to protect me. I'd only heard Mama talking about things God didn't want you to do, like turn somersaults in a dress.

I wanted my life to be like Aurelia's life, where people said kind words to you when you walked in the front door and it was safe to go to your room and close the door. And where hope followed you down the street like music, even if nobody was standing there playing the horn.

All of a sudden, I realized that me standing here in this church had everything to do with finding the penny, too. If I hadn't found that penny, I wouldn't have gotten a job. And if I hadn't gotten a job, I wouldn't have come over here to tell Aurelia about it.

Every time anyone said something about the heavenly Father to me, I figured that, like Daddy, God didn't think much of me either. But the way Aurelia's preacher was talking about God, he made me think maybe God could be different from Daddy, somebody strong who believed in me, who might be willing to listen to my side of the story.

Suddenly I wasn't thinking about the penny anymore—I was thinking about what was going on inside of me. My heart started hurting so bad that I thought it might burst open. Grace Kelly believed in Jimmy Stewart when nobody else did. Now Reverend Monroe kept saying that Jesus believed in me.

How could anybody believe in me when I was always telling lies?

He kept saying how, if you believed in Jesus, he could make the stains inside you go away.

The stains from what I let Daddy do had soaked deep, and nothing could fade them.

The ache in my heart grew into something much bigger than anything I knew how to put a name to. The only thing I had come here to do was tell Aurelia that if I hadn't paused for a few seconds and picked up that penny, nothing about my life would've changed. I got the chill-bumps up my arms. *If I hadn't stopped, I wouldn't be standing here now.* For the first time ever, I felt something gentle take my soul in its hands. For the first time, I forgot to listen to the taunts inside my head.

Maybe because the Crocketts stood beside me. Maybe because I held the penny in my palm. Or maybe because I had a new job or because I'd heard Aurelia say she felt like she was walking on air when she came out of this place, or because I was just too crazy to stop believing in *possibility.*

THE PENNY

I decided to do it when that Antioch preacher encouraged people to come to the front and pray with him. He called it the "prayer of salvation." In spite of all my skepticism, after I'd heard those electric words, and thought how I'd like to have my life move smooth like Aurelia's, and had seen that preacher orating like he wanted to hand me his whole heart in his hands because he knew what was going on inside me, I wouldn't have stayed in my seat for anything. I remember the heat in my ears as I walked forward, my legs moving of their own accord. When I prayed the words that Reverend Monroe prompted me to pray, my insides seemed to expand with every word. I invited Jesus into my heart, although I can tell you right now I had no idea what I was getting into. I asked him to take over my life and help me do the right things and help me trust in him because I sure wasn't doing very well trusting myself. I asked him to show me what he wanted to do inside me to make me great, because if something didn't happen to make that obvious, then I sure wasn't going to figure it out.

And when Reverend Monroe stopped praying and the music started up again and people started chatting and shaking hands and hugging around me, I kept praying a little longer. I added my own parts that I wouldn't tell anybody else about. I asked Jesus to protect me just like Reverend Monroe had said he would. I told him how I knew it was my fault and that I was ashamed of being so dirty and that I could handle all the hitting in the world if he would just help me do something to stop Daddy from coming to my room at night.

I opened my eyes to a whole bunch of Antioch Baptists waiting in line to congratulate me. I felt drowned in love and sweet perspiration and the smell of lemon ValMor skin-lightener. "You've made a joyous decision, child." The softest hands I'd ever known cupped my face. "The angels are singing now up in heaven." And I felt like singing right along. After all that, we ate a potluck lunch with all of them and I walked out of that place and headed down the steps to hug my A&P groceries against my chest, feeling like I'd been bathed inside, cleaned up and polished to a gleam and fresh-smelling like soap.

The Crocketts walked with me to the streetcar stop. I can tell you I was walking high the same way Aurelia said she walked high whenever she came out of church with an answer to her problems.

"I got a job just because I picked up a penny," I told them. "A real job. That's the reason I got that penny out to show you, Aurelia. It all happened because of that."

"Girl." Darnell took the groceries from me so he could carry them. "You tell the biggest stories I ever heard."

"It did. It got me a job." I snapped my fingers. "Just like that."

"Prove it." I'd learned from that very first day on the steps at school that Darnell was always skeptical.

And just like I'd known she would, Aurelia became my champion. "What do you know, Darnell? You don't even know how to make an ironing board stay standing. And you talking like you're the authority on everything in the world."

So I told them the whole story, about the penny beside the streetcar tracks and the dairy truck and the Elvis record and the robber—all of it. I told them about the Grace Kelly movie and Pete Mason giving chase and the man from the box office saying, "You must be one special young lady." Then I told how Miss Shaw had called my house on the party line.

By this time, I'd pulled the penny out of my pocket for the umpteenth time and was showing it around. Darnell, who was carrying my groceries in one muscled arm, scrubbed the back of his neck in disbelief. "I don't trust a word of it."

"So, drop the penny on the ground again," Aurelia suggested. "Let me pick it up. I want to try."

"What?"

"I want to see what happens to me."

"You have to find your own penny first."

"Drop that penny. Drop it and I'll pick it up and see if it works."

I shoved it under my armpit in horror. "Over my dead body, Aurelia."

"Why not?"

"I don't want to lose this penny. It's too important."

Aurelia's loyalty seemed to waver for a moment. I couldn't bear seeing her unconvinced. I hadn't finagled streetcar money and come all this way and snuck into a church and accepted Jesus for her skepticism.

"My sister was standing right there with me when it happened. Jean saw the whole thing." Even though I knew the last thing Jean would ever do was take my side. "You can ask her."

"What if it's not just *any* penny?" Aurelia pointed toward my armpit. "What if it's just *that* penny that changes things?"

"Then," I said confidently, "it's mine."

Aurelia stopped right where she stood and planted her hands on her hips. She aligned her feet at the same impudent angle as a dress mannequin in Sonnenfield's display window.

At that exact moment, Darnell's eyes went wide and his face sort of puffed out. "Aurelia. Look." He pointed.

We all stared. There beside her toe lay a penny, just waiting for us, as shiny as if it had been struck from the mint that morning.

"You *see*?" I gloated. "I *told* you."

"Pick that up," Darnell said, sighting along his finger. "Go ahead. Pick it up. See if something happens."

"What if it does what you say? What if it changes something I don't want changed?"

"Everybody gets their own penny, Aurelia," I said. "This one's got your name on it. You're going to miss out if you don't pick it up."

Somewhere along the line while we'd been talking, Garland had wriggled out of Aunt Maureen's arms. Aurelia dropped her mannequin pose and almost stepped right over her penny. "Who cares about such a small thing?" she asked.

"You ought to," I said.

Just as she finally stooped over to pick up the penny, Garland snatched it up instead.

"*Garland!*" You would have thought Aurelia had got the breath kicked out of her.

Beating wings surrounded us. Darnell, Aurelia's aunt, and I searched in every direction for the sound. The oak tree that shaded us disgorged a flock of crows, their wings thrashing the leaves before they rose on the air, dipping and swirling above our heads.

They rippled black against the heat before they circled and dispersed into the sky. I can still hear in my head the ruckus those crows made that day. Aurelia had missed her chance. And Garland skipped along ahead of us on the sidewalk, holding the penny aloft in his fingers, shrieking with delight.

Chapter Four

When I walked into our kitchen, Mama had the bowl and the pink Sunbeam Mixmaster waiting, ready to make the cake. She saw me coming and started tying on her apron. The heavy bag crumpled when I set it on the counter, bottles clanging. I began to load Daddy's RC Colas into the icebox, two by two.

"That took you half the day." Mama kept working at her apron strings. "That grocery sack looks like it's been to Chicago and back."

I set the cake mix beside the bowl and adjusted the package so the picture of the perfectly iced confection could be seen from the entire room. Putting the box to rights made our kitchen look like the one from *Time to Eat*, Mama's favorite cooking show.

"I didn't ask which flavor. I got us chocolate."

Jean was engrossed in the *Cosmopolitan Magazine* with Grace Kelly on the cover. "You know," Jean said, swinging bare toes which she'd painted fuchsia, "this says Grace's family let her go to New York because they thought she'd last a month and then come home. Did you know that she hated her Philadelphia accent because she thought it sounded nasal?" Jean flipped the page. "Did you know she bought a recording machine for her room and taught herself New British, perfect diction. Can you imagine a girl changing herself, just like that?"

"Jean," Mama said. "Scoot yourself around the other side of the table, would you? I need a towel out of the drawer."

"Maybe that's what I should do. Get a recording machine. I could speak French." My sister ran her hand through her smooth hair. "I'm so happy for her that she won Best Actress. Did you know that she paid her father back, tuition and board and everything, after she finished acting school?"

I'd left the money tin pulled somewhat forward on the shelf, its lid only halfway fastened. In a fit of contrite guilt, I climbed up, tilted the tin forward and returned the precious few coins. I saw Mama's neck straighten at the meager clink and I imagined she'd expected me to disappoint her all along. She cracked an egg and the yolk slid into the batter.

I mashed the lid shut and shoved the tin as far back as it would go, trying not to think about Grace Kelly and the moral virtue she'd displayed, repaying a fortune to her parents after acting lessons.

"You missed lunch, you know," Mama said as she flipped on the electric mixer and the beaters circulated batter into clovers. She let the bowl skim her palm, as if she couldn't quite believe an appliance could do its job without her direction.

But, no, I hadn't missed lunch. I'd eaten with the Antioch Baptists, three kinds of meat, mashed potatoes with gravy, green beans, and fruit salad with coconut stirred in. For dessert there had been peach cobbler and brownies and lemon pie.

Mama was flouring the pan, turning it every which way, giving it nervous little pats with her hand. "Your daddy made it home to eat, though. He was asking where you'd gone off to. I told him you'd gone after those RCs he mentioned."

"Oh."

She transferred the batter from bowl to pan in massive spoonfuls, then scraped the sides of the bowl with her spatula. "Only he said he didn't think he'd ever *mentioned* colas."

"Oh." Then, "I sure did *think* he mentioned them." I decided I'd better drop it, seeing as trying to talk my way out of it wouldn't get me anywhere. I was trapped again. You know the feeling you get when you have to pep talk yourself that, no matter what happens, you did what you had to do? All the way to Aurelia's that morning, I'd known what the risk would be.

"Jean, open the oven, would you? So I can slide the cake in?"

Jean sighed, slapped the magazine shut, and did as she was bidden.

When Daddy came upstairs, cement and plaster covered his shirt. He washed up with Lava Soap, scrubbing his knuckles while grey suds ran down his wrists in rivulets. He dried them on the tea towel and stretched to retrieve the money tin.

"Now, let's see what we've got here." His palm was big enough to pry the lid off with one twist.

"It cost me streetcar fare to get to the A&P." *Say it*, I begged Mama with my eyes. *Say you gave me permission to go. Tell him you said it was okay for me to take the streetcar money, too.*

But Mama's gaze skittered from mine. Some dumb idea, wishing she would speak up for me. She'd let me bear my retribution alone, the way she always did. Then she would wait until he was out of the house and try to make it up to me. At least she could have poured him a soda over ice or something.

Daddy shook the tin at me. Then he emptied it into his hand and sorted through the coins. I couldn't raise my eyes from his hands. I was at the mercy of them. They held me as surely now as they did when they were wrapped around my shoulders, pressing me down. "You lied to your mother when you said I wanted colas. She let you take grocery money, but you didn't stop at that, did you? Where is the rest of it?"

"I'll pay it back."

"Of *course* you will. Now that I've let you accept a job offer, you can be certain I'll expect you to pay your own way for everything."

I hated the quiver in my voice. "I will. I'll do that, Daddy."

"There's almost a whole *dollar* missing here. *Where is the rest?*"

As well as I knew him, I couldn't tell you which he would hate worse. Me stopping to visit the Ville, or me giving hard-earned money to a church. When I'd thrown the money in the basket, I'd been thinking only about saving my penny. I hadn't been thinking about giving to God. I hadn't been thinking about the consequences later.

With everything else I'd been doing wrong, I hadn't been thinking how I was stealing from Daddy.

"I put some in the collection plate at church."

He stared at me, his jaw clenched. My answer gave him even more pause than I expected. But it seemed like it wasn't the stealing he was worried about.

"You went to church?"

"Yes, sir."

He set the tin on the counter, the loose change still in his hand. "Who do you know who would take you to a church?" He always worked me around to something I had to think hard to answer.

"Nobody took me." And that wasn't a lie, either. "I went by myself."

Just like that, the money went flying all over the floor and he collared me. "You know what people who go to church think about?"

I had my own fists balled as if I could protect myself. I tried to jerk loose but he hung on tight. "I don't—"

"They think about being better than other people. They think about being better than me. That's what they think about. They don't do anything different than I do, but there they are at church, acting like they've cornered the market on living."

My staying quiet must have made Daddy madder than what I'd done, taking money in the first place. He turned the air blue for miles around, shouting at me. I guessed I deserved this. And at least he wasn't hitting me. Maybe Jesus had taken me up on my bargain after all.

THE PENNY

But when Daddy grabbed my hair and yanked my head upright, no powerful protector stepped in to intervene on my behalf. Nobody came to rescue me, not Jesus, not my sister, certainly not my mother, when Daddy punched me again. He shoved me away and I hit the wall and stared all that meanness right back at him.

Mama had disappeared the way she always did. When I realized she'd vanished from the room again, it struck me harder than any of Daddy's physical blows. *Why don't you ever do something to make him stop?*

Mama never stood up to him when we needed her most. She never stepped forward when we needed a safe guardian. She always appeared later, her help ill-timed and inept, the same way she'd tried to make it up to Jean by having secret senior pictures made instead of confronting Daddy that they needed to be done at a studio. The same way she'd tried to make it up by overlaying our bodies with wet clothes when Jean had asked to go to the Ambassador Hotel.

When I wiped my mouth, my wrist came away with a bloody smear. *Why don't you ever stand up for us, Mama?*

Jean's carnation fingernails alighted on the magazine like pink butterflies, her eyes darting away from mine. *Do not be afraid,* Reverend Monroe had said. *The LORD answers them with the saving power of his right hand.*

The only powerful right hand that had been flying around this place since I got home belonged to Daddy. The room stayed silent except for the *tick tick tick* of the pink-cat clock on the wall, its eyes shooting back and forth with the seconds, its tail swinging to the beat. Daddy towered over me. I got the feeling he was waiting on me to make one false move. Me, I was waiting for Jesus to show up.

What were you expecting, Jenny? I asked myself. *What did you really think was going to happen?*

A cord of disappointment, which had begun its slight tug at my heart, now cinched noose-tight and relentless around my chest. I sat silent in the chair, blood oozing from the cut in my chin, unwilling to wipe it because I liked making Daddy look at it. But Daddy's anger waned and he gave in to boredom. He left suddenly, shrugging his shoulders in disgust. Jean shoved her magazine aside and said, "You'd think you'd learn to stay out of trouble."

I glared at her as hard as I'd glared at Daddy. "Oh, why don't you go pretend to be some stupid movie star? Because, let me tell you, pretending is the only way you'll ever be what you want to be."

She glared at me as the kitchen timer buzzed. "I'm not just pretending. You know I'm headed off to school. Not many girls get to do that." Then Jean said, "The cake's starting to burn. Where's Mama?"

I wiped my chin down the entire length of my sleeve. "Who knows?"

"You're never going to grow up."

"Who said I wanted to?" I asked. "Who said I want to be anything like you?"

After Jean stalked out the door, I brandished the hot pad and rescued the cake so it could cool. I stood staring at the smooth slope of it.

No matter what, I wanted to hang on to that clean-scrubbed, white-fresh feeling I'd carried with me down the steps of Antioch Baptist. I wanted to take bottomless breaths and know that everything I'd been given was protected there inside me, ready for the right moment to burst open, mysterious and fragrant. I touched my hand to my chest. Once, I'd seen our downstairs neighbor Mrs. Shipley embrace her belly with one curved, careful arm before her baby had been born. I wanted to do the same thing. No matter what happened, I wanted to hang on to hope the way I'd seen Mrs. Shipley holding on to her baby inside her.

Chapter Five

On Tuesday morning, the first day I was supposed to work at Shaw Jewelers, I scrubbed up twice with castile soap and left a murky ring in our pink bathtub. I dressed in the most grown-up clothes I could find—a hand-me-down skirt of Jean's and a white blouse with a ruffled collar. I tamed my next-to-impossible hair by winding each strand around a finger and shoved it away from my face with the teeth of a plastic bandeau.

"Here. Stand still. I got an idea," Mama said when I stepped into her room to show her.

"What?"

"You just wait." The next thing I knew, she brandished a lipstick tube. "I sure do think a daub of this might help."

I stood in front of her bureau mirror with my feet planted apart and my face turned expectantly to hers. She unscrewed the tube to reveal a wand the color of cherry sherbet, which she lightly applied to the O of my mouth. After she stepped back to admire the results, she shook her head in dissatisfaction. "Something else. Just a minute." Mama rummaged in her drawer again and pulled out her face powder. She clicked open the compact and waved the powder puff. "The most important thing about getting out in the world, especially with somebody like Miss Shaw"—she patted and blotted the welt on my chin the whole time she talked—"is that everything's got to look right." She stepped back again and, this time, deemed my face acceptable. She snapped the compact shut and stood surveying me like she had wrought a miracle.

Daddy gave me a look, too, the minute I walked into the den and started straightening my skirt pleats. I knew from experience what he was thinking about when he looked at me that way. It was the same expression I'd seen him use when he first laid eyes on Marianne Thompson and he looked her good up and down. He was thinking how I belonged to him. He was thinking how he was the parent and he could make me do whatever he wanted.

"What you got lipstick on for?"

Mama said things needed to look right. It was her idea.

But Mama didn't say a word. She stood still, her eyes wide like she was the one who had gotten caught, and not me.

"You wipe that paint off your mouth right now." He yanked out the filthy rag he kept in his back pocket to wipe the sweat off his face while he worked, and it came flying through the air toward me. "You don't talk to nobody on your way down there to that job. Or on your way home, either, you hear me? Because I'll know. I'll know if you go someplace you're not supposed to go."

Although Mama had been lighthanded with the lipstick, I could feel the wax she'd applied to my lips now smudged on my teeth. Already, out of nerves, I'd done a fine job scraping my lips clean. I'd scraped plenty of skin off, too. I rubbed my mouth with the rag, which tasted sour and gritty. What lipstick remained didn't leave much of a stain. I threw it back to Daddy and he tucked it where it belonged.

"Jean," Daddy said, "you go get your sister when she's done. I don't want her in the street looking like a loose tramp."

The last thing Jean wanted was to be responsible for escorting me home. She wanted to argue with him, I could tell. For a split second, I saw anger flare in her eyes and worried she was about to start up the arguments again. The last thing she needed to do was get Daddy riled up right now and, knowing my sister, that's exactly what she'd do. I wanted her to hush up. I didn't want him to hurt her. I never could be sure of Jean. You'd think she'd have learned by now that the only thing she'd gain by goading Daddy on would be a quick kick to her rear.

Thankfully, Daddy never gave her the chance to get him wound up. He kept his eyes on me. "The first money you get from that job goes to pay me back the money you stole, you hear me, girl?"

I told him I heard him.

"The whole time you're in that jewelry shop, I want you to be thinking how you stole from me, you hear?"

I heard that, too.

"Don't you go stealing anything from Shaw Jewelers. Guess we all know how your mind works, don't we? You thought of how much you could make selling one piece of her jewelry—a bracelet or a ring? You'd make more doing that one thing than you'll make working for her all summer. You thought about that?"

How good it felt to get away from our flat, even with Mama waving me off from the whitewashed stoop, her gaze heavy. Her eyes bore into my shoulders until I reached the corner and turned. I glanced back and saw her in her apron shading her eyes and waving good-bye.

I knew Jean would do as told, loitering around the movie posters at the Fox, perusing every name at the bottom of the bill as it became smaller and less distinct and the letters ran together, things like "song lyrics by Ira Gershwin, produced by William Perlberg, written for the screen and directed by George Seaton," until I left the jewelry shop and she was forced to shepherd me home.

Stepping inside Miss Shaw's shop was like stepping into a sparkling globe of gold and cut glass and gemstones. The display cases buzzed with lighting, their metal edges warm from the bulbs. I couldn't find a thumbprint or a speck of dust anywhere and, for the moment, I felt giddy and unsteady, surrounded by treasure. In a voice just about as creamy as Mama's potatoes, Miss Shaw said, "I've been planning a great many chores for you, Jenny. Are you ready to help? I'll be sure to keep you busy while I have you."

For years I'd been hearing the rumors about the lady who stood in front of me, and Daddy's voice had been among the loudest of all. "That lady thinks she's God's gift to Grand Avenue." "That lady holds her nose so high, she can hardly see down it at who's below her." "That lady thinks everybody has to work twice as hard to be half as good as she is," he'd said, and I'd believed him. Last night he'd remarked, "Don't know what a lady like that would want with a girl like you."

But now I got to thinking that everything around Miss Shaw looked so fine and everything looked so perfect, people just got scared of her. And from the way she endured their whispers with her set-smile face, I guessed she liked to keep it that way.

I realized I was chewing my bottom lip sore.

She said, "You'll be paid fifty cents an hour. Does that sound fair?"

It sounded fair, and then some. I could pay Daddy back fast.

"It can be a good thing for a young lady like you to have a job," she noted in her practiced voice, as if she wrote the book on scales and we were starting a piano lesson. I kept thinking how she said "*a young lady like you*" and how she didn't know what she was talking about.

You got no idea, I wanted to tell her. *You got no idea at all what I'm like.*

"I had a job like this when I was your age. I ran a cash register when I was still so short, I had to stand on a box to reach it."

My ears perked up. This small hint of her past piqued my interest. *So Miss Shaw had a job, too?*

"Are you ready to begin?"

THE PENNY

Thinking about the whole thing, I was struck dumb with fright and self-consciousness. Even running my fingers over the penny hidden in my pocket didn't help. "Are you sure you want me in here?" I blurted. "I'm not good with this stuff. If you wanted to find somebody to work for you, you should have put an ad in the newspaper or a sign at the window. Plenty of folks would walk by here and see a sign if you posted one."

She held me under close scrutiny with her bright, mysterious eyes. It never occurred to me that her employing *anybody* could be as much an act of faith for her as it was for me. "Wasn't it you who stopped the milk truck and made the baby in the basket swing and knocked Bennett's record away?"

Of course it was me. I'd already answered that question over the telephone.

"Do you think you know better than I do how to run my shop?"

"No," I floundered. "I'm not trying to tell you how to run anything."

"You, Miss Jenny Blake, are the person I want."

I clamped my mouth shut. I'd just get myself into more of a mess the more I tried to talk her out of it.

"It doesn't make sense to interview a whole string of people I don't know and try to discern which of them will be trustworthy."

You don't understand, I wanted to shout at her. *I'm the least trustworthy person of all.*

She smiled at me. "Now. Are you ready to get to work, or are we going to stand here talking about this all day?"

She'd talked me into a corner again. I didn't dare tell her I wasn't ready.

Miss Shaw started me off with a box of tiny price tags no bigger than Chiclets, each fastened to a length of string. She had me practice my numbers with a black fountain pen, and when she was satisfied that I could inscribe small digits without smudging zeros and eights, she had me write down prices, affix each tag to the stem of a men's watch, and tuck each tag beneath each watchband to my liking as I arranged it inside the display case.

I thought, *No wonder she saved this job for me.* Tying string and writing eights and zeros proved easy enough for my small hands, but would have been impossible for Miss Shaw and her white gloves.

Miss Shaw made me feel guilty for even thinking I *shouldn't* be there. For a while, I didn't allow my mind to wander while I wrote numbers for her. But the second she placed me at the top of a ladder in the middle of the shop and instructed me to dust hundreds of dangling crystals on the chandelier overhead, my mind galloped off of its own accord again.

Here I was, standing at a dizzying height, the most untouchable and intriguing mystery in all of St. Louis counting the change in her cash register below me.

Rainbows darted across the ceiling as I took each piece of faceted glass and wiped it clean. I guess maybe I put too much stock in reading people by their hands, but I couldn't stop thinking about those white gloves Miss Shaw always wore. To me, they represented refinement and style that I would never have. Each time I saw Miss Shaw, those white linen gloves looked as pressed and fresh as if they'd just come out of the cellophane. They never had a speck of dirt on them.

I didn't know what she could want with me.

Each time I released a crystal on the chandelier, it tapped the others with a short, light ring.

"How often you going to want me to do this?" I asked Miss Shaw. It gave me the shivers standing up this high. It gave me the shivers thinking about Marianne Thompson's murmured tales of Miss Shaw visiting some unmarked grave and how they might be true. "You going to expect me to do this every time I come in?"

"I dust the lights every two weeks and the chandelier once a month. Not nearly so often as some of the other things."

"Well," I murmured from beneath my arm. "Guess it's nice of you to save it for me."

Her chin lifted at my impertinence. I wondered that she didn't tell me to climb down this minute and find my way home. When she turned toward the wall to set receipt books on a shelf, I saw the row of covered buttons go straight along her spine. I guess we were both testing each other.

"When you're finished there, I'll have you sweep the floors," she said.

For the rest of the afternoon, I followed the list of chores that she laid out before me the way she might lay out crumbs for a sparrow. She coaxed me along to the next duty only after she was certain I had fully mastered the one before. I wrapped several boxes in brown paper and tied them with string before Miss Shaw left briefly to carry them to the post office. I organized the gemstone rings according to color. Every so often, as I did so, I would cast a furtive glance in her direction and think, *I'll bet Marianne didn't make up the story about a grave. I'll bet she saw it. . . . I'll bet she did.*

Maybe I shouldn't have taken the job Miss Shaw offered me. Except for making money, I suddenly didn't want to get to know her. For all her talk about me being trustworthy, I sincerely doubted that I could trust *her.* I'd learned a long time ago that I couldn't rely on anyone. I couldn't keep from feeling, every time I glanced warily at her, that I'd almost caught Miss Shaw watching me covertly, too.

When I finished arranging the remainder of the gemstones, I stopped where I stood to test my theory. I wanted to know if she was studying me. Sure enough, without hesitating Miss Shaw asked, "Would you like something else to do, Jenny? Or do you want to call it a day instead?"

I lifted my shoulders and let them fall, feigning indifference.

"That's fine, if you want to go," she said to release me. "Now, when will you return?"

Well, she sure didn't have to ask me that. She'd been the one to assign my hours in the first place. I repeated my schedule faultlessly and she seemed pleased that I remembered. Just as I headed out, Miss Shaw called to me, "You did a fine job today, Jenny," as if it was important to her to compliment me.

"Thank you." My response sounded just as stiff and formal as she did.

"You'll be paid on the first and the fifteenth of every month. Does that sound acceptable?"

"Yes," I said. "Thank you."

Just before I turned away again, I got the impression she might want to say something more. Her gloved hand pressed flat against the glass countertop. She looked like she was trying to hold on to something that wasn't there.

"Do you need me to do something else?" I asked.

But she must have thought better of it because she shook her head and waved me on.

"You don't need me to stay awhile longer?" I asked.

"You're fine," Miss Shaw insisted. "Go on."

All the way home in the streetcar with Jean, I couldn't stop wondering why Miss Shaw had wanted to call me back. I kept wondering if she wanted to tell me something. Everyone said Miss Shaw had too many secrets.

All the way to Wyoming Street, I kept picturing her face, unsure of what she could want with me.

Chapter Six

It took me a while to figure out why Jean would walk into the kitchen the next day and bring up one of her old birthday parties again. She knew she had a captive audience, I guess, because she caught me in the middle of cleaning the goldfish bowl. I had to listen to her while the fish swam small, desperate loop-de-loops in the jar where I'd poured half the water.

As she chased the fish with her finger and I sifted through the brightly-colored rocks on the bottom, she brought up this ancient history. It was just her luck, she told me, having a party planned two days after President Roosevelt declared war on Japan.

This part wasn't new to me. I'd seen the photos of myself taken with Mama's Brownie camera—me only three months old, sitting buckled in a baby carrier on the table, wearing a sleeper. In the black-and-white pictures, I'm not even as big around as Jean's three-layer birthday cake.

"You don't have to tell me about it." I filled the bowl under the faucet and looked sideways at it, making sure I'd scraped all the silt off the glass. "I've heard all this before."

"Maybe you have," she hinted mysteriously. "Maybe you haven't."

I sloshed water on the counter. "What's that supposed to mean?"

"It means you might want to stop acting so smart, Jenny Blake. There might still be things you don't know."

"Like what?"

"Like what Daddy did that day to Mama."

So Jean had done it to me again. No matter how I tried to stand up against my sister, she always managed to find ways to pique my interest. "You never said a thing about that."

"That's what I'm trying to tell you, smarty pants."

As Jean related the details, I began to figure out she wanted to make sure *she* had secrets to reveal, too. She wanted to rub it in that I wasn't the only one privy to secrets, even though I'd started working for Miss Shaw.

"I've been around much longer than you have. That means I know a lot more."

"I don't see that's anything to brag about, do you?"

My sister recalled things in brief snapshots, the way every four-year-old remembers. Halfway through the party, the door opening. Daddy strutting in wearing a uniform with brass buttons. Jean asking him, "Who are you? You don't look like my daddy."

The way she described it, I could see Daddy turning in the center of the room so everyone would admire the uniform. He stood with his arms extended and his brimmed cap with brass insignia cocked to one side and the jacket wrinkling because he wore it buttoned clear to his hips.

The fight came after everyone had gone home, Jean told me as I poured the goldfish into its clean bowl and waited to see how it would adjust—after mothers of the guests had taken their daughters by hand and dragged them home. Daddy told Mama he had to join the army and leave us. He told her that if he went off to war, maybe that would make his own daddy proud.

Daddy never talked much about not being good enough to please his own father, but I'd always known, from stories like this that Jean told me, how Daddy hinted that he couldn't measure up, that no matter what he tried to do to make his father approve of him, his father never did. When he was a boy, Daddy came down with rheumatic fever, which damaged his heart. Even though he wasn't too weak to do handyman jobs and buy booze and support our family now, he'd once been too sickly to play football or walk far when his own daddy took him hunting or join in with the boys who chopped and hauled firewood in the fall. My grandpa, who I'd barely known before he died, had always acted slightly embarrassed about his son.

Hearing those stories made me think how hurt people are the ones who hurt people.

Daddy had let Mama grieve a good while the day of the party, Jean recounted, before he finally told her it wasn't true, that he wasn't joining the army after all. Mama cowered in the corner, and Jean was sure Mama was afraid he'd hit her if she admitted she wanted him to leave so he wouldn't beat her up anymore. Daddy laughed hysterically at Mama's bewildered reaction, saying how he'd wanted to impress everybody at the party but it was all a joke. He confessed that he'd borrowed the uniform to fool everybody. He confessed that he wanted to leave us all and go into the army more than he'd ever wanted anything else because it would prove something to his own daddy. He said he thought it was high time he lived some adventure somewhere because he sure wasn't living it around here. He said they'd turned him away from the army when he'd tried to sign up. They wouldn't take him to fight because, even now, years after the ridicule he'd endured from his own daddy, his heart was too weak; the army medics wouldn't clear him to go fight.

Jean told me everything she remembered about the borrowed uniform and her birthday cake and Mama crying after everybody left. And you know how it is when you're four years old. Jean said she never could figure out whether Mama cried because Daddy teased about leaving, or whether Mama cried because he wasn't leaving at all.

Word had gotten around the neighborhood that I worked for Miss Shaw. Even the Pattersons below and the Smiths next door had heard and so were anxious to share theories about her. Mrs. Patterson whispered, "Oh, yes. The grave is more than a rumor, for sure." "Since no one knows about her past, I'll bet she's running that business by ill-gotten means," said Ralph Patterson. "What I heard is that she's a lonely woman with a runaway lover," said Miss Mona Miner, Mrs. Patterson's best friend.

The largest amount of speculation besides the price of her car and the name of the beautician who styled her hair was over whether there truly *was* a grave in Miss Shaw's life and who, for heaven's sake, could be the person in it?

I heard as many notions as there were people. I could give you a list a mile long. "I heard it's her grandmother's, who she could never quite let go," said Mrs. Patterson. "A sister," said Mrs. Shipley, who accosted me one morning in front of our building. "It's her young man who went off to war but who returned after being dishonorably discharged," said Mrs. Smith. Add to that the list of suggestions Jean had managed to gather: a playmate, a husband no one knew about, her maiden aunt, a beloved housekeeper, a gentleman she had admired but never told.

As much as I distrusted Miss Shaw, I distrusted myself even more. *I'm not good enough to work for a person like her.* Yet, intrigue more than the fifty cents an hour she paid me kept me coming back.

The back room at Shaw Jewelers could be reached only by pushing aside a dark velvet curtain. When Miss Shaw asked, "Would you like to see where I spend most of my time?" I followed her through the opening to a shop bench lined with magnifiers and an Optivisor and scales and a gem scope. There sat tweezers and cutters and a set of screwdrivers so small, they might have belonged to an elf. A box of detached watch faces sat beneath a light with more joints in it than a praying-mantis leg.

I had at least a hundred questions about the bizarre items lined along the bench. I wouldn't ask them, though, because I was still so nervous around Miss Shaw. I rehearsed words over and over in my head until I got brave enough to say them. The only words I managed to blurt out were simple sentences as I bustled uneasily around Miss Shaw's shop.

"You want me to vacuum by the counter?"

"Is it okay if I move the ladder to get the boxes by the wall?"

"Is that the fly swatter you want me to use over by the shelf?"

Miss Shaw might have been formal, but she was also kind. I felt no small amount of guilt for not trusting her. Distrusting Miss Shaw seemed worse than not trusting Eleanor Roosevelt. All the same, maybe it was everybody talking, but something pushed me to ask questions every time I saw her.

Miss Shaw snapped the light on at her workbench, which made us both squint. "This is a true white, bright light that allows you to identify every flaw a stone might have. If you examine something with a regular bulb, you don't always see its true color. But in this"— she shoved the box of watch faces aside and picked up a gemstone with a pair of tweezers— "you see every facet. You see *inside* of something. And when you do that, you find out exactly what it's worth."

After she let me look at the cuts inside the tourmaline, she set the tweezers aside and showed me how she went about polishing metals. She applied something creamy from a pot and flipped the switch on a felt-covered wheel. She held a tarnished ring against the moving wheel and, next thing I knew, it wasn't dull anymore.

"When you finish arranging watches, you'll find a cloth beside the cash register," she said, peering at something else through her eye loupe. "I'll expect you to polish the cut-glass bowls each time you come in."

I knew I was being dismissed, yet I stood there a beat longer. "My sister talks about nothing but Grace Kelly," I offered. "She thinks she's going to turn out like a movie star, but all she's doing is going away to secretarial school."

Miss Shaw glanced up from the loupe. "You're going to miss her, then?"

Well, of course I wouldn't miss Jean. Why would I miss somebody who'd rather I disappear off the face of the earth than breathe air anywhere in her general vicinity? I'd only volunteered the information about Grace Kelly as a sort of barter. I'd offer Miss Shaw some tidbit about me and she might reciprocate, which meant I could return home with some morsel of valuable Miss-Shaw intelligence with which to antagonize my sister. Besides this job being a way to earn money, it was the perfect opportunity for a scouting mission.

Everyone on Wyoming Street would listen to me if I had something to say about Miss Shaw. I could explain the process by which she drove her Cadillac to the country and never came home with so much as a redbug on her grill. I could clear up questions about how she never wrinkled her crisp summer skirts nor nicked the heels of her shoes. I could unravel the mysteries of her birthplace, the source of her fortune, the fascinating circumstances that brought her to owning this store. And I'd have bet you my wages, all I could save of them, that her gloves would be clean as starched linen each time she came out of the workroom. Even though I'd seen the polishing rouge and tarnish rubbing off on them myself.

But except for asking if I'd miss my sister, Miss Shaw let my stories about Jean and Grace Kelly go by without offering so much as an iota of information about herself.

There are times when I think back and I can picture Mama happy. There are times I remember her moving along the clothesline in our backyard, pegging bedsheets to the wire with pins. I used to run through the sheets with my arms outspread, pretending I lived in billowy, white hallways. And Mama laughed with me.

It never occurred to me that someone else's mother might have scolded them for doing such a thing. Only later, when I saw Marianne Thompson's mother berating her for getting the clean laundry dirty all over again, did I realize that Mama could've found fault with the fun I was having. How lovely that she didn't.

The smell in the air on one particular sunny day was the honey-sweet of the neighbors' lopsided lilac bush and the bite of the sun and the clean of detergent. I felt free because Mama seemed happy. I came to the end of the row and stood with the hem of a sheet draped over my messy curls, and Mama shook her head at me and said, "Jenny, you remind me of a bride." Which made me stand straighter, even though I was little, because brides were always beautiful and tall.

"Were you a bride when you married Daddy?" I asked her.

Her fingers hesitated for a brief beat before she pinched the clothespin. "Yes, of course I was. I was a beautiful bride," she said.

"Was Daddy handsome?"

"Yes, of course. He certainly was."

"Is that why you married him? Because he was handsome?" I wrapped the sheet tighter around my head and began to hang on and twirl. I felt Mama's hands close over my shoulders as she began to unwind me again.

That was the day she told me she married Daddy because he drove in circles around the high school for hours, insisting she have lunch with him. That was the day she told me she married him because he threatened to beat up any other boy in the school if he so much as talked to her.

She talked to me about my daddy that day, but I believe fear held her back then, too. For many days after that, I clung to her happiness. I remember loving how the sun smelled.

The elm tree outside Jean's window had grown so tall that it rivaled the maple we used to climb in the front yard. Most of the time Jean didn't let me come in her room, so when she did, I felt like I'd been invited to visit one of the most elite places in St. Louis. After my first week at Shaw Jewelers, Jean decided on a whim to let me in. She was sifting through piles of her movie magazines, showing me her favorite issues, when I noticed limbs jostling outside her second-story window. The *tap tap tap* on the glass window sent my pulse speeding.

"Oh." Jean pushed her magazines aside and rose to her feet like this happened every day of the week.

"Who is *that?*" I hopped to my feet beside her, almost knocking over her bedside lamp. I caught the shade at the last minute to keep it from crashing to the floor.

"It's just Billy." She unlatched her window and slid it open. The boy who jumped inside was handsome, with earnest eyes, a dreamy square jaw, and sandy hair curling at his ears no matter how he'd tried to tame it with Brylcreem. He was wearing enough hair cream to asphyxiate everyone who lived in our flat, and then some.

Jean shoved her magazines back under her bed, made sure the cuffs of her jeans were rolled up tight, and slipped furtively into her sneakers. "We're going out now and you can't tell anybody," she ordered me.

"What?"

"You heard what I said."

If you counted on one hand all the things I knew about romance, you'd have at least three fingers left over. One thing I *did* know about love was this: Jean had never done anything like this before.

"Wait a minute." I didn't know exactly what I wanted her to wait for. I only knew if she left through the window and Daddy found out about it before she got home, I'd pay the price right along with her.

"Go to your room and read or something. Say you haven't seen me if Daddy comes looking. That's all you have to do." She shot me an expression that would have curdled milk.

"Jean. It's too *dangerous*."

"I'm going now."

"Jean, who *is* he?"

"I told you. Billy."

"Billy Manning," he said, following up for her, looking as uncomfortable as I felt, extending his hand.

I didn't take his hand to shake it. I was too distraught for that. He stood by the window waiting while we discussed his attributes like he was a specimen.

"I met him at the Fox, okay? One afternoon when you couldn't go because you were too busy working at your new *job*." Then, exasperated because she knew I'd insist she give me every detail or I wouldn't be satisfied, "It was that time I went to see *Mogambo* again, okay?"

Mogambo was the Grace Kelly movie about a woman who became dissatisfied with her life when she and her husband went on safari in Kenya. Grace was nominated for Best Actress in a Supporting Role for that one, and she should have been the winner, Jean often complained. It should never have been Donna Reed in *From Here to Eternity*. And of course, Jean told me, everyone thought Clark Gable must have fallen in love with Grace while they filmed the movie.

"It was the third time she'd seen it," Billy volunteered.

I narrowed my eyes at him to make him be quiet. Of *course* she'd seen it three times. Every Grace Kelly admirer had seen it three times. To my sister I said, "You can't just *run* like this."

"You weren't supposed to be here when Billy came anyway. He got here early." She rolled her eyes at him, making it clear this was all his fault. "If you hadn't been in here, you wouldn't even know I'd taken off."

"Yeah, but now I do."

"I wasn't going to tell *anybody*." She slung her leg over the window ledge and grabbed onto a branch. She wasn't taking anything with her, not her rhinestone-button sweater, not her purse, nothing.

"When will you be back?" I hissed.

"Maybe never."

"Is there a phone where you'll be?" I asked.

"No."

"Where are you going, Jean?"

"I don't have a place in mind."

I clamped my mouth shut. *Does he have a place in mind?* I'd been planning to ask. But I stopped myself, it sounded so ridiculous. How odd was this? Me, acting like a mother.

Chapter Seven

All that night, the walls of our flat jeered and sputtered with sounds I'd never heard before: walls shifting, bricks hissing out the day's heat like a sigh. I turned my pillow every so often, trying to find another cool spot. I gave up after a while and let it grow warm beneath my head. It couldn't have cooled off more than a few degrees outside since the sun went down.

Every crack of brush outside made my heart pound. Every creak of the floor inside was even worse. What if Daddy missed Jean tonight?

I strained at the slightest hint of noise. A lizard slipping through the grass became a footfall I needed to listen for. A rustle in the tree became my sister coming home.

The sheets weighed a hundred pounds on my legs. I sat up in desperation and kicked them off. It cooled me a little, freeing my toes.

I'd figured Jean would stay out all night and I wasn't wrong. I didn't know which frightened me more, that Daddy would figure things out or that my sister would come to some harm. Just before daybreak, I heard the stealthy scratch of Jean's window rising. I slid low in my bed like I was sinking into a bathtub with relief.

Presently, "Jenny," I heard her whisper at my door. She opened my door an inch, then lightly knocked, as if she suddenly thought I deserved privacy. "You awake?" As if I'd grown a little in Jean's eyes just by association with her because, after this one night, she'd achieved her own pinnacle of maturity.

I felt limp with relief. *"Come in,"* I whispered back.

That was all the invitation she needed.

"I've got so much to tell you." She sat down hard on my ankles, about wrenching them from the sockets. Her eyes, when she stared at my wall, looked way beyond what I could see. For once she wasn't talking about Grace Kelly. She wasn't going on about Grace's trip to Cannes or about the filming of *To Catch a Thief* with Cary Grant or about how Grace had said the South of France was her favorite location. It was a rare moment when Jean forgot to talk about Grace Kelly and told me about herself instead.

"Do you want to know what we did? Do you? *Do* you?"

I clutched the sheet to my chin, feeling amused because, after all the times I'd begged her to let me know what was going on, I could see I wouldn't be able to stop her now if I tried. "I didn't think you wanted to tell."

"We dust-bombed streetcars," she gasped. "You scrape all the dust by the curb into a paper sack and swing it around your head and let it fly when the streetcar comes by. All the passengers start jumping around and coughing and dusting themselves off. Some of them are dressed so fine and they *holler*—"

Somewhere beyond her words, the faucet began to run. We both froze. From the kitchen, we heard the refrigerator door slam, the rumble of a chair scooting on the floor.

Jean looked like a trapped rabbit. "He's *up?*"

I shook my head at her. *I didn't know.*

"Has he been up all *night?*"

I clutched the sheets clear up to my chin. I sure couldn't answer.

"I've got to get back to my room" is what she would have said if she'd had the time. But when she edged the door open and sidled out, I could see Daddy's silhouette against the far wall. I knew then that her sidling out was exactly what Daddy had been waiting for.

Sometimes not knowing what to expect felt worse than getting belted. I listened to the surge of their quarreling voices with my head in defeat against the wall.

"Where've you been?"

". . . in my room . . ."

"Don't lie to me."

I couldn't see Daddy's face, but I could imagine it. All twisted up like a rotted pear.

"You think I let anything in this house get by me? You think I didn't hear what time you came in?"

We'd learned to be cautious around Daddy, picking out the right words like we'd pick the right change out of a coin purse. Daddy always needed to control what went on—when we went to bed, what time we had to get up. He decided what television programs we watched, how much money we spent, what clothes we wore, what we ate for supper. I cringed when I heard the flippant way my sister answered him. Billy must've gone to her head, made her feel too important. Jean forgot to be careful.

I couldn't believe she'd lied outright to him. But then, in a fit of insanity, she told him the truth. "I met a boy and I was out with him," Jean suddenly challenged. She sounded like she expected Daddy to be impressed. "He liked me."

And just like that I heard something thunder across the floor and hit the wall. I heard her shriek—he must have grabbed her.

"Don't you let any boy come close to you, do you hear me?" I heard his fist strike and knew he must have doubled her over.

"You being loose with boys, aren't you?"

I heard her gasping for air.

"How many, Jean? How many have you had relations with?"

Another punch and, from the thud, he must have dropped her to her knees.

"Any boy gets close to you, I'll kill him. You tell them to their faces for me, you hear?"

With sheets wadded beneath my chin, with fists trembling, I waited to hear another blow. The flat grew quiet, as still as all the other dwellings that crouched along Wyoming Street. Then, as if the sound came from very far off, I heard my sister sobbing.

Our lives are never going to be more than this.

"You tell this to any boy who so much as looks at you, Jean. You tell him you aren't ever going to be free."

Jean didn't argue back anymore.

We'd learned never to argue back.

I pictured Daddy in the other room wiping the sweat off his upper lip with the heel of his hand. "You tell everyone who's interested, you hear?" he said. "You girls belong to me."

Miss Shaw decided to teach me the cash register. No matter how hard I tried to concentrate on punching the right numbers, my fingers kept hitting the wrong keys. The only thing more frustrating than trying to prove you're not good enough for a job is trying hard to do something right and messing it up.

When I tried to add tax to $53, the register kept ringing No Sale. When I tried to make change for a $20 bill, I gave back $22. When I pulled the arm to open the drawer, it stayed stubbornly shut instead.

I stood morosely by the front window looking out, my fingers in my pockets, trying to pretend nothing was wrong. Daddy's awful words resounded in my head. *Never going to be free.* The long night of listening for every crunch and clatter outside was taking its toll.

"Is that the one?" Miss Shaw asked.

She pointed at my palm. I looked down, too, not realizing I'd pulled it out. I tucked the penny away with false nonchalance. But not before she craned her neck to have a good look.

"You know what, Jenny?" she asked me. "The worst thing you can do is go into a day being afraid."

"Afraid?" I asked. "Why would you think I was afraid?"

"I think you're afraid that everything you do is the wrong thing. I think you're afraid of all the good things you are."

I'd learned to hold my tongue with my daddy. It wasn't quite the same with everybody else. "I don't know what makes you think that. You can't think that—you've only known me inside your shop."

"That's one of the things about Jesus," she said. "Once you know how to receive the love he's pouring into your heart, then all of a sudden, out of the blue, you start knowing whom to give it to."

My face shot up. It gave me a jolt, having Miss Shaw start talking about Jesus.

How did Miss Shaw know that, for one night, I believed all of Jesus' promises? How could she know that I prayed the words at Aurelia's church, but now I was starting to doubt I'd ever hear from him?

If there was anything I'd learned from Daddy, it was not to let anybody see me scared. He didn't go easier on me if I didn't let him see me afraid, but he didn't quite get so much pleasure out of hurting me, either.

"I'm not afraid of anything," I lied.

"Well, as long as you're standing there, would you mind helping me rearrange the windows once we're done here? I haven't been happy with them in a while. Since that man grabbed those necklaces from my hand." Then, "If not for you, Jenny Blake, I would've lost some expensive pieces."

If not for the penny.

So here we came to the penny again. It seemed like every time I forgot about it, and about how many things had changed in my life since I picked it up, something came along to remind me again.

Miss Shaw draped a watch over the black velvet stand shaped like an arm. I draped another. The watch's opalescent face and gold numbers glimmered against Miss Shaw's glove. My hand looked small and grimy compared to Miss Shaw's white gloves and perfect, refined gestures. I thought about how these timepieces were worth at least fifty times what Daddy kept hidden in the tin above the stove.

Miss Shaw must've seen me noticing because she laid her gloved hand across mine. "You know what I think? I think your picking up that penny was more than part of a random chain of events. I think God was giving you a message. I think he wants you to know that he's watching over you all the time, that he has a good plan for your life."

My eyes shot to hers. "You're talking about me?"

She nodded. "Sure, I am."

"Why?"

She began tucking each price tag behind each band so if a customer was interested, he would have to inquire. She ran her fingers beneath each clasp so every one lay at the same angle.

"Just a hunch, I guess." Miss Shaw slid the cabinet shut with a firm click. "You're a pretty girl, Jenny. Mind if I try something?" She opened her palm to reveal a sparkling barrette.

I nodded. *I mind.* I didn't want her experimenting with her fashion ideas on me. But she looked so disappointed, I yielded.

"Go ahead if you want. I don't care."

She slid my bandeau off and gathered my unruly hair in her fist. When her gloves brushed my neck, I got the goosebumps. I wasn't used to anybody being careful when they touched me. I wasn't used to anybody touching me in kindness at all.

"Here. Let me show you." She fiddled with my bangs, slipped the barrette in place and gave me a hand up so I could look in the mirror. "If you sweep it to one side, look there."

I stared at myself.

"Your eyes are the color of that penny you carry."

All I could see in the mirror was my chewed-up lips and too many freckles and a nose that looked about as sharp as a spout on a coffee pot.

"Copper comes from the same ore as iron, did you know that? Do you see that iron strength in your eyes? I sure do."

I squinted, looked a little harder. If she hadn't been Miss Shaw, I would've called her crazy.

"I see in you a determination that not everyone has."

I looked at her instead of the mirror.

"You have the strength to trust, Jenny. You hang onto that, because it's been given to you as a special gift. It's the kind of strength that's the most hard to find."

I examined the toe of my shoe in discomfort. "My sister says Grace Kelly hated her first on-screen performance in *High Noon*." Talking about Grace was the only way I could think of to redirect the conversation. "After Grace watched her own movie, she hired a new acting coach. Jean read it in *Photoplay* this week. Grace wasn't happy with herself because she said she could look into Gary Cooper's face and see everything he was thinking, but when she looked into her own face she couldn't see anything at all."

"With all the talk about Grace Kelly, it sounds like your sister wants to live someone else's life instead of her own."

"She's obsessed," I said, shrugging.

Then as if she'd given me free rein, I let everything go, all at once. "Lots of people want to live *your* life," I blurted. "You should hear the things they say about you. They say all the same things about you that Jean likes to say about Grace Kelly."

"Ah." I could see her face behind mine in the mirror. I hadn't expected this reaction. She laughed, but she sounded sad.

"They want to know why you always wear white gloves. They talk about how your manners are so good and how you lacquer your hair and how you put lipstick on so it never smears on your teeth. They all want to know about—" *The grave.*

"People have a way of looking at other people and seeing things the way they think them to be, not the way they really are. You've got to remember that always, Jenny Blake."

I'd taken Daddy's money for streetcar fare and lied to Mama about seeing Aurelia and ferreted out details about my new employer's life. If people knew what I'd done, there was no end to the bad things they could think about me.

It was easy for Miss Shaw to talk about messages from God and knowing who to love—her life had been completely different from mine. I would have bet she didn't have a daddy who told her she'd never amount to anything. I would have bet she didn't have a daddy who thought she'd never done anything right.

I'd give anything to live free like Miss Shaw.

Chapter Eight

I'd never seen anything like the Fourth of July Independence Day celebration going on in Aurelia's neighborhood. Up and down the street, flags flew beside awnings that had been scrubbed bright. People greeted each other from stoops or shouted through open screen doors. Women chitchatted as they shifted their babies from one hip to another. A stickball game had drawn a crowd into an empty lot, and umbrellas spun like pinwheels when revelers ducked beneath them for shade.

When Aurelia saw me, she stood still for a second, like she was blinded by the sight of me. Then she bounded forward, darting between about fifteen kin in her trodden-grass yard. As she wove toward me, I tried to figure out how to show my feelings, to show her how sad it made me that it took this many days to see her again. How if it were up to me, I'd be over here all the time, playing in the water hose, and leaving secret notes in the hollow of the elm tree in Aurelia's front yard, and devouring Aunt Maureen's hotcakes with butter and molasses dripping down, and carrying bottles to the confectionery store with her so we could trade them in for two cents apiece.

Maybe it was Miss Shaw and the way she'd talked to me about myself, but I couldn't stop thinking how Aurelia Crockett being my friend was like somebody giving me a present I didn't deserve. When she got there, I hadn't found any words yet. The only thing to do was to hug and laugh and hug again.

"Girl," she said, "I thought you'd *never* get over to see us again."

Miss Shaw said my eyes showed I had strength to trust. Aurelia was the one I thought I might be able to trust someday. Let me tell you, trust didn't come easy. Everyone I'd trusted before had hurt me.

"I don't have many chances. But I got one now."

Daddy had finally gotten a decent job from the real estate office—they'd assured him it might last three weeks. They'd hired him, he informed us, to break up cement and pull out metal posts. They'd told him they needed somebody with "arms of steel," he bragged.

Which meant, for a little while at least, we could count our lives as our own.

I'd used my very first Shaw Jeweler's wages to hop the streetcar to the Ville and visit Aurelia.

Above everything, I heard the crisp sound of Eddie Crockett's horn, its running tones and sharp style falling in pleasant chords on my shoulders along with the hot sun. I shaded my eyes to find Aurelia's daddy above me, his legs dangling from a window ledge on the second story, wailing on his trumpet to beat the band. I waved.

He took the instrument from his mouth and shouted, "How's the job going, girl?"

I shot him a thumbs-up sign, which he answered with three warm bleats of his horn.

When he began playing again, men in sweat-stained hats bobbed their heads to Eddie's song, staying one lazy beat behind the tempo.

The Ville smelled like stale cooking and strong coffee and old tire rubber. A swarm of boys raced toward me, playing a game of grab-and-go. Aurelia had told me plenty about how they walked along whistling, searching for the right spot, until they found a sign that said BEWARE OF DOG on a gate, and they'd grab the gate open and tear out of there faster than anything.

There was always something going on at the Crocketts' house. "We're burning stuff," Aurelia said, keeping hold of my arm.

"What?"

"Come see." She yanked me into a nest of cousins where Darnell was showing Garland how to hold a magnifying glass to catch the sun.

"Get out of the way!" Darnell shoved Aurelia's leg. "You're blocking it."

She grabbed my hand and pulled me down to my knees, where we both watched Darnell's two hands tighten over Garland's. "You keep fooling with it," Darnell instructed, "until you get the whole sun in one place."

Garland squinted up, peering into the sky.

"Not there, Garland. Down here. You're bringing it to the ground, like this."

No less than a dozen eyes followed the lens as Darnell slow-circled the magnifier. It snagged a glint of sun. Darnell adjusted the angle and, beneath it, a pinpoint of light fell on a leaf. "There." With a light jerk to Garland's hands, he released them. "Don't move. Hold right there."

Garland clutched the handle, trying hard. He sat so still for so long, sweat beaded along the edges of his steel-wool hair. Slowly, the point on the leaf turned brown, then black. Smoke spiraled from it. A flame burst forth.

"Look at that!" somebody shouted. But before we got any further, Darnell pounded the ground to get the fire out.

Aurelia held her hand out for the magnifier. "You've done it plenty, Garland. Let Jenny try it."

The screen door behind us swung open and here came Aurelia's aunt carrying a colossal watermelon. "You all get on over there and play ball. It'll do you good." Aunt Maureen set the watermelon down hard, quoting Scripture the whole way. She could rattle it off as easy as I could recount the alphabet. "Praise be to the Lord my Rock, who trains my hands for war, my fingers for battle!" she announced. To Darnell and Aurelia: "You keep teaching everybody to catch things on fire, this whole place will be gone by morning. As if that box of firecrackers you bought wasn't enough." Then, "Eddie, you get on down here and stop persecuting the neighbors. I'm not about to cut up this melon on my own."

Eddie Crockett folded his legs inside the window. Darnell poked the magnifying glass into the pocket of his jeans. It was clear who held the authority around here.

"Can I do some firecrackers tonight?" I had a way of talking to Aurelia that I couldn't use with anybody else. I couldn't tell Daddy what I was thinking, and Mama didn't respond—I tried to tell her things and she wasn't there even when she was. I'd open my mouth and she'd just stare at me like she wanted to be invisible, like she wanted to disappear from the room every time I walked into it.

"I'll talk Darnell into letting you do some black cats. I'll crack his head if he doesn't share them with the whole family." Then, in a voice of conspiracy, "Did your Great-Aunt Flo come visit yet? Mine did."

I didn't know any great-aunts. I sure didn't think I had one named Flo. And as far as I knew, neither did Aurelia.

"You know, Jenny. Have you fallen off the roof yet? It happened to me three times already."

"Aurelia, why do you keep climbing up there if you keep falling off?"

She kept looking at me like she thought I was missing something big. Finally she plain came out and asked it. "Did you get your period yet? Your Great-Aunt *Flo?* I did. That's what I'm *trying* to tell you."

Jean had bragged all about that to me once, too, a long time ago, and said how she'd become a woman and she had to go to the store for a belt and pads because she'd started her monthly courses.

"Oh, sure! Mama talks to me about all the girl stuff." Which was a total lie. I hated lying to Aurelia. Just another part of me I didn't see how I could be forgiven for.

"What does she say?"

"About what?"

"The girl stuff."

I clamped my mouth shut. I'd gone and gotten myself into a corner. "Mostly, that only common people talk about things like that."

When I made the comment about *common people*, I happened to be parroting Mrs. Blanchard, our nurse at school. She didn't seem too smart, but at least I could use her knowledge about this and give Mama credit.

"Aunt Maureen says that it's the way God made a woman to nurture babies. That it's pure, beautiful. A part of his plan."

Aurelia had no reason to peer so suspicious at me just then. I expected her to say, "Who do you think you are? Royalty?" But instead she said, "You know that's the first time you've ever talked to me about your mama, Jenny."

"There's nothing to say about her, that's all."

"What about your daddy?"

I was more than thankful when Garland rapped on my elbow at that moment with a tattered copy of *Henry Huggins* and asked me to read it to him. We found a place on the stoop and I'd gotten about five pages in when Aunt Maureen started rationing out melon slices and a pack of friends showed up to arm-wrestle Darnell. I kept turning pages and reading, my voice swelling louder, trying to ignore the ruckus and the banging on the garden table.

Garland finally gave up trying to concentrate, slammed the book shut between my hands, and went to take a turn at challenging his brother. Darnell let him win. When they finished, Darnell dangled his arm like it was helplessly mangled, like any minute it might fall off. "Garland, what you been eating for breakfast? You killed me, man."

Then Darnell's eyes found mine. "What about you? You picked up any pennies lately? You feeling lucky enough to beat me?"

"Luck doesn't have a thing to do with it, Darnell."

"That so?"

I straddled the lawn chair, rocking my weight from one foot to the other. "Sure is."

He scrubbed the floor with the toe of his left sneaker. "You sure?"

"Yeah." I sat in the chair and positioned my elbow for power.

Darnell spat and yanked his chair closer to the table. Next thing I knew, we were faced off, elbows planted, right hands adjoined, fingers braided, Darnell's black ones a great deal larger than mine.

"I have arms of steel," I told him.

"Ready. Set. *GO*."

He wasn't doing the fake stuff with me the way he'd done with Garland. He expected to win trouble-free. I caught myself starting to rise on my feet in counterbalance. But then I set myself and made headway. Darnell muscled his way back. If he'd expected to slam my arm down, I surprised him. I gritted my teeth so hard, I thought I might break a few off. No way was I going to let him win easy.

Suddenly, I caught the accusation in his eyes. The way he looked at me, I knew this wasn't all about arm-wrestling. It was something more, one force pushing against another.

"Don't . . . know . . . why you . . . always . . . come here." He spoke through clenched teeth, his eyes glued to our hands.

"I . . . don't." I pushed so hard, my mouth flinched. "Don't come . . . near enough."

His cheeks inflated with air. He looked like Howdy Doody in the pictures I'd seen at the A&P, only he was the wrong shade. "Makes . . . Aurelia . . . overstep . . . her bounds."

I quit. Just like that. Darnell slammed my arm down so hard he must have busted a wrist bone. He held on to his arm the same way he had after he'd wrestled Garland, but this time I think he really meant the helplessly mangled part.

"You got nothing to say about what me and Aurelia do."

I was so mad that even watching him rub his arm in pain didn't make me feel better. I goaded him about Garland. "Aren't you going to ask me what *I* eat for breakfast?"

He glared at me, still massaging his arm. "Why would I ask you a thing like that? *You* didn't win."

I knew in my heart he didn't like me coming around because I was white. "People are the same whether they're one color on the outside or the other," I said to him. Maybe I didn't accept myself sometimes, but I sure wasn't going to give Darnell the chance to heap it on me the way he wanted to. "There's not much that could keep me away from my best friend."

When he stood up and walked away, he was still hanging onto his wrist like it was tender.

"What's he so testy about?" Aurelia asked when she came out of the screen door carrying silver and plates to set the table. "You almost beat him?"

"I don't think so."

"You staying for supper? Aunt Maureen's got Gooey Butter Cake."

I stared after Darnell.

"Don't you pay him no mind. He's just jealous because you got a big-time job is all. All he does for money is put together boxes for the hatchery down the street. Folding and stapling boxes to ship chickens. He even pokes holes in them so the chicks can breathe."

"That's not such a bad job."

I cast about for my belongings—my headband and a coin purse. All of a sudden I got the feeling I'd stayed way too long.

"You were going to do black cats," Aurelia reminded me.

"I can't."

"Come on!" she begged. "We're putting on pajamas and climbing out to the roof to watch the fireworks over the river. We're going to watch every show they shoot off over the Mississippi. Can't you stay?"

"You're climbing out on the roof again?" I raised my eyebrows, teasing her.

By the way she grinned, she knew where I was headed before I got it out.

We were just two girls again, whispering indiscreetly about Great-Aunt Flo. We shook our heads and shrieked at the same time.

"Why do you keep climbing up there if you keep falling off?"

We got to laughing so hard, I forgot all about Darnell.

Chapter Nine

It was Aurelia's idea to sneak onto the entertainment boat so we could listen to her daddy playing the horn. They called their band the Six Blue Notes, and the more time they racked up playing weekends on the *Admiral*, Aurelia told me, the more impressive they became.

Playing the trumpet wasn't Eddie Crockett's only job. Weekdays, he ran a metal punch at the factory, punching out sections to build stoves. On weekends, I saw him use the scrap metal he'd brought home and shape it, at a workbench not much different from Miss Shaw's, into trumpet mouthpieces. Every musician I saw begged them off of him. Eddie Crockett told me it was a thing with horn-blowers. Every musician he knew worried with a sore mouth. He liked to build his valves very thin and very deep, to make it easier on a player's lips and give a big, warm, round sound at the same time.

He had a way of twisting and lightening the spring action of trumpet pumps so a horn would sound altogether different. One afternoon he even showed me how he could make the refrain of a song sound like it was a woman calling.

I got lots more time visiting with the Crocketts than I'd expected because, thankfully, Daddy's job pulling posts and breaking mortar lasted a full twenty days. They even had him working on weekends.

The humidity pooled over our town, and the sidewalk seared your feet and you felt like you were being steamed alive when you walked around St. Louis. But I felt happy.

Most mornings, I worked for Miss Shaw. She'd been so satisfied with my work that she'd offered me more days at the store. Daddy came home late every night and, when he did, he was so worn out from smashing cement in the heat, he was too tired to mess with us. And no matter how Darnell shoved past me when I showed up in the Crocketts' front yard, no matter how he hit toward me when we played stickball to show me I was a weak spot, or how he glared at me with the same sharp focus as the sun caught in the magnifier when Garland had about set the whole yard on fire, I chose to ignore him.

Nobody with such an attitude was going to take Aurelia away from me.

I saw plenty of liveliness those days in the Ville. I met people with names like T. Bone Finney and Chick Randle, and one of Aurelia's friends taught us how to dance. (*No need to jerk around like a house-fly, girl*, I remember she said. *Move like you're writing cursive on the wall with your backside.*) And Aurelia and I found a stray dog and fed it some water and a pork steak before Eddie Crockett shooed it away.

Every place I went, I kept finding pennies. I found one the day I played second base and the ball buzzed my head. Darnell had hit toward me again and I took off running, but I sidled back fast when the outfielder snagged it clean. Next thing I knew, the ball came soaring toward me. I leapt, bobbled it, and came down empty-handed in time to see Darnell make a standup double. And there in the dirt, of which I had a mouthful, laid the penny. I sat up, dusted myself off and turned the penny over in my hand, remembering that Reverend Monroe had said how much I was loved.

I found another one in my seat before I sat down on the streetcar and remembered that Jesus said I didn't have to be ashamed. I found one on the street when I took Mama's knives out to be sharpened by the scissor-grinder, and I remembered that God had planted a seed of greatness in me. I found one at the A&P while I waited in line with Jean to buy Lustre-Creme shampoo because Lustre-Creme was the kind Grace Kelly liked, and I thought how the preacher'd said if I put myself in the arms of Jesus, the stains inside me would go away.

One lady even dropped a penny right in front of us on the sidewalk. Aurelia was with me—and I promise you, she saw it. I left the penny on the ground and chased after the lady until she stopped in front of the Laundromat and set her clothes basket down.

"Excuse me, don't know if you noticed, but you dropped that penny down there."

"What?"

"You dropped that penny down there, ma'am. Don't you want to pick it up?"

She smiled halfway, as if she couldn't quite figure me out. And the story had gotten way too long to explain to her now. "No, child. You keep it. Being as you're honest and all. It's just a penny. You want it, it's yours."

"*God is giving you a message,*" Miss Shaw had said. "*He's watching over you all the time.*"

"Find a penny, pick it up," Aurelia chanted as I ran back to get it. "All the day you'll have good luck."

"No." I kicked a bottle cap full of dirt and it ricocheted off the curb. "Aurelia, I think it's more than good luck. It's a *message.*"

Lots of those pennies I picked up, I spent. But I kept the first one—the one that started it all outside the Fox Theater—safe and hidden in its box. Every so often, when the house grew quiet and I knew Jean wouldn't come in to tease me, I'd open the lid and take a look. I'd hold it until it grew warm inside my palm, then turn it over and check its date of issue.

Those summer days passed to the tone and brilliance of Eddie Crockett's trumpet crying. It didn't take much for even somebody like me to hear that Eddie Crockett's sound was just as good as anything Miles Davis could do. When Aurelia told him I'd said that, Mr. Crockett picked me up off the floor with his broad-beamed arms. For a minute, I went stiff as a cork, not knowing what he meant by laying hands on me. But he hugged me so tight I thought he might squeeze the air out of me, and I realized he did it out of fondness.

Aurelia danced around us, "I tell you, when it comes to blowing the horn, Daddy can really play it down."

And I felt nothing but wonder when Eddie Crockett treated me fine, the same way he treated his daughter.

He showed off, dancing with Aurelia, tilting his head back and playing to the sky. For the first time, I felt like I'd found a world where I belonged.

The S.S. *Admiral* had a brochure out that called it "a ship of luxury, of gaiety, of glamour." It promised a six-deck steamer with "clean, clear river breezes that make eyes sparkle and cheeks rosy-hued." The level rooftop guaranteed passengers "a taste of the South of France or Biarritz." Jean had been on it for her graduation dinner and she'd come home talking about the Three Ring Circus tea room with waiters dressed up like clowns and chairs made to look like lions, leopards, camels, and giraffes. Aurelia had told me plenty of times how playing on the *Admiral* meant something to her daddy. Not because he hadn't been featured on the bandstand at plenty of music clubs before. He had even played on the radio station. But Aurelia said that the *Admiral* was the first place they'd wanted him to read notes to get his job.

"When they've got an old piece of horn, most musicians learn to work that horn from morning until night," Mr. Crockett said one day while the heat bore down on us so hard, all of us wanted to sit in the shade and do nothing. "What folks got to understand is, St. Louis got genius all over the place. They say the blues and the rhythm come up the river from New Orleans, but the genius comes from right here." He pointed at the whitewashed step, right where he sat. "That's the ones that make it, the ones that spend crazy hours playing their instruments."

Aurelia was scraping the stoop with a piece of broken plaster, leaving scratches between her feet. "Daddy—don't know why you won't let us hear you play over on the boat."

"I told you, girl. You hear us practice any time you want over at Mr. Lamoretti's."

"If you're a genius"—I swatted at a mosquito buzzing in my ear—"how come you can't read music?"

"Ha." Mr. Crockett lifted his knee up and crooked his elbow over it. "She tell you about that? That's why we call ourselves the Six Blue Notes. Six of us went to show Mr. Streckfus what we could play, and I took one look at all those notes on pages he showed us, and I started feeling blue."

But that was Eddie Crockett for you. He'd gotten the job anyway. He went and figured out something to do to get around the rules.

Aurelia told me that, without telling Aunt Maureen what he'd done, he took his trumpet, invited his band members, paid Darnell fifty cents to go to a basketball game, and the rest of them showed up in Darnell's stead at his piano lesson.

"Take lessons in your nephew's place? I never heard of such." Mr. Lamoretti began to flip wildly through the pages of the music primer above his keyboard. "Mrs. Crockett has already paid the monthly fee, as you well know. Are you sure this isn't just Darnell trying to get out of practicing?"

"Look." Eddie Crockett placed the score in front of Mr. Lamoretti's face. "We just need you to teach us how to play the book, so we can go on the boat on weekends and play parts."

Mr. Lamoretti, not one to waste a minute if it was paid for, laughed, creasing the book down its middle seam with skepticism. "Well, since you're here, can you play that? Let's see what you can do."

So the Blue Notes took out their horns and ran a few scales for him, and the next thing they knew, he started ragging it up with them on the piano. By the end of the lesson, he was playing Tchaikovsky while they followed his finger on the page. And Mr. Crockett kept stopping him and saying, "Play that again, Lamoretti. Hear the harmony? You could get that on a horn and a sax; I know you could."

The *Admiral* advertised a four-and-a-half-hour Saturday cruise, and that's the one Aurelia wanted to get onto. It left in the afternoon and made a trek along the waters while tourists strolled the decks in their crisp, summer cottons and visited the modern fluorescent-lighted, chromium-trimmed popcorn and newsstand, and a snack bar selling hot dogs. For those who could afford it, the band played for dancing in the ballroom.

"We could do it," Aurelia whispered. "I could tell Aunt Maureen we're going to a movie. We could tell her what we're going to see."

"No movie lasts four hours." It scared me, how much like Daddy I sounded. "Your aunt knows that. She'll knock you up the side of the head when you get home."

Aurelia looked sideways at me. "No, she won't. She'd give me a talking to all right, but that's all. It'd be so different, seeing him play there, not in some dark, smoky place like the Windermere, or one of those bucket-of-blood clubs." They called them bucket-of-blood clubs because so many fights started up there, she told me. "And Daddy says on the *Admiral* he gets to wear butcher-boy shoes and suits from Brooks Brothers, with collars so stiff with starch he can't hardly move his neck."

"He can show you a suit any time."

"No, he can't. The whole setup belongs to the *Admiral*. He can't ever bring any part of it home."

THE PENNY

I let Aurelia convince me. I'd do it for her because, for the summer of 1955, we were playing the part of sisters. I'd never seen her want anything this bad before.

The gangplank of the *Admiral* rose from Laclede's Landing like a metal serpent. Above it hung a green-and-white striped awning, so in case those present had to wait outside to show a ticket, they could take cover under the shade.

It took a whole week's pay to buy our entrance before we could board. Ever since that lady at the Laundromat had insisted the penny was mine, "being as you're honest and all," I'd started feeling like I was being tested for something. I'd started wishing I could *be* honest, although it felt like everything around me fought to keep me from it. I kept thinking, *If God has something big planned for my life, then I'd better start acting like it!*

When Aurelia tugged my arm and pointed to the short, steep plank at the rear with the sign that read SERVICE ENTRANCE, I looked a bellyache at her. Helping her sneak away from Aunt Maureen was one thing. Sneaking onto the boat was another.

"You don't understand." She turned away with her arms limp and her shoulders square, like she thought I'd lost my mind. "This is part of it."

"Is not."

"It is."

I snapped open the black velvet purse Jean had passed down to me. "Look, I've got the money right here." But when it came my turn to step inside the booth and say, "Two tickets, please," Aurelia had disappeared from sight.

"Students?" he asked.

"Yes," I said. "Both of us."

"Don't get seasick. Don't eat too many hot dogs. Have fun!" He pressed two tickets forward and gestured with his head. "He'll tear those for you up the gangplank, just outside the door."

"Thank you."

When I stepped into the sun, Aurelia said, "Just give me my ticket." She tried to wave me away.

"You've got to get it torn."

"You paid for it—that's what matters. Meet me in there." Then in desperation she whispered, "*Somewhere*."

I didn't know what had gotten into her, but I had to let her go. There wasn't any reasoning, as far as I could tell. I waited to get my ticket torn, mixed in with a jumble of ladies and gentlemen, the ladies wearing gloves like Miss Shaw's and two-strand pearl chokers and skirts with petticoats so stiff they crackled.

The ladies wore corsages, too and, oh, how good the flowers smelled as they wilted in the heat! I saw Aurelia clamp her ticket in her teeth and, after she'd hidden beside the ticket booth for longer than I could have stood it, she took off. A number of what looked to be waiters had started up the back ramp, and I watched her skip toward them, drum up a conversation, and duck inside that entrance as easy as she'd been born.

She'd left me alone.

Suddenly without Aurelia, I placed my feet together side-by-side. I clutched my velvet bag in both hands, my fingers as straight and pointed as clothespins. Raising my chin, I stood like a fine lady going to a dance. I could have been Miss Shaw, or I could have even been Grace Kelly, standing among so many admirers, her eyes lit with stars.

Jean would've been jealous as a snake if she could've seen me at that moment.

At the thought of Jean, an ache flickered and began to grow, burst open to all that hollowness I hadn't known was inside me. Sure, my sister and I did our fair share of quarreling. We might have been rough as nails to each other on the surface, but deep down, we knew how much we needed each other. Jean had been slowly disappearing from me for a while, though. She hadn't even packed for secretarial school yet, and she was already gone.

When my turn came to climb aboard the *Admiral* and enter through the gilded doors, I searched for Aurelia, pressing past draped cardigans and dozens of arms and hankies erupting from breast pockets. The *Admiral's* foghorn warning blast reverberated clear to my toes. And just when people took up talking again, the horn deafened us all once more.

We'd cast off. I could feel the boat keeling to the west, the current moving beneath my feet, persuading me to move, too. Along with the one tide moving me, I'd been caught by another, set adrift in a sea of white faces. I couldn't breathe without them pushing against me. How different this was from the days I'd spent with Aurelia in the loud streets of the Ville, swirling with color in every shade—the vanilla bean of Aunt Maureen's face, the burnt caramel of Garland's, the soft velvet shine of Eddie Crockett's.

As if thinking conjured it up, I spied a face the beautiful color of maplewood in the throng, her hand poised on the chrome beside the snack bar, searching in every direction, just as I was. She shoved her way toward me, looking breathlessly relieved.

"I just didn't know what they'd say about me being colored. And look how it worked. Wasn't no problem."

"Well, it was a stupid thing to do. We might never have found each other in here."

"But we *did*."

I started off in the direction of the sign marked BALLROOM with an arrow that pointed to DECK B. I wasn't going to forgive Aurelia for at least fifteen minutes. She'd twisted my arm to come with her almost as hard as Darnell had twisted it trying to beat me arm-wrestling. And then she'd gone off and left me alone in a plan of her own devising.

"Wait! Don't you want a hot dog?" Aurelia asked.

"I'd like to get where we're going. It's taken us long enough, don't you think?"

Aurelia peeled herself away from the line faithfully. With no small twinge of guilt, I saw she already had money in her hand. "Never mind, Aurelia. If you're hungry, you go ahead."

"Lost my place in line anyhow."

I can't tell you how I knew something strange was about to happen. I just sensed it, the way I used to get goosebumps when Jean ran a duck feather along the underside of my knee. The purser trotted toward us, the one who'd nodded his black-patent leather cap brim at me like I was Grace Kelly as I'd stepped aboard. His arms swung with angry purpose, and his gaze pinned us.

"Come on." I touched Aurelia's shoulder. For the life of me, I couldn't figure how he'd picked out the one girl who hadn't followed the rules in this crush of people.

"What do you think you're doing in here?" He grabbed her by the scruff of the neck, the same way I'd seen Marianne Thompson's dog carry off its puppies.

"Aurelia, show him your ticket," I commanded, bristling with self-righteousness. "It's paid for, even though it never got torn in half."

"My daddy's in the *Blue Notes*," she insisted, pulling against him.

He didn't glance at me even once. He stayed focused on the side of Aurelia's face, which she'd averted from him in shame.

"Is that so?"

I wanted her to look him straight in the eyes. I wanted her to shout at him, but she didn't. "Yes." I could barely hear her whisper.

"Really?" he asked, like he didn't believe a word she said. Like he'd never believe a word Aurelia had to say, ever.

"Aurelia, *show him* your ticket." To him, "Mister, I *paid* for it."

He shot a fleeting glance at me. "It's okay, young lady. You're fine, ma'am. You go on ahead and enjoy the show."

The difference in his voice chilled me. When he spoke to me, he crooned with respect. When he spoke to Aurelia, it sounded like he was speaking to a stupid, dull person. "We're mid-river. I put you out now and you end up swimming. Current will take you clear down to Festus."

She said nothing.

"You'll have to stick with your daddy, then, out of sight. Can't have you running around on the boat like this. Only Mondays are for the coloreds."

"My daddy doesn't play on Mondays."

For a minute, after she spoke up to him like that, he looked like he wanted to throw her over the side of the *Admiral* after all. He looked like he had a good mind to set her to work washing dishes in the galley.

"Excuse me, sir," I said when he started to haul her off. Thinking back on it now, I should have talked with the same sarcastic respect that would have made Daddy belt me into the next county. But I was too bewildered. I knew what Daddy said about Negroes, but I thought that was because Daddy was mean as the devil to everybody. I had seen how the colored people didn't come to the Fox, but I'd thought it was because they had their own theater much closer by. I hadn't known coloreds didn't come because white people wouldn't *let* them. For the first time, hearing the purser's words, I started to figure out what those portable buildings meant, set up outside our school. I hadn't known that anyone other than Daddy thought folks from the Ville belonged in a separate place, beneath other people.

Gone was the impertinent way I'd stood at the gate with my chin uplifted and my pocketbook gripped in firm, certain hands. I guess the purser saw me in a different way now, too.

"You want to come with her?" He looked down his nose with disdain. "You follow me."

He led us into the stairwell, in the opposite direction from where I'd been headed. Our feet, in our dressy patent leather shoes, tapped like raindrops on the aluminum steps.

Chapter Ten

When we were first ushered into their dressing room downstairs, it took seconds for our eyes to adjust to the cigarette smoke curling in our faces. But not so long that I missed Chick's sharp glance at Aurelia's daddy when we stepped into the room. Mr. Crockett stood up, looking at his daughter with such immense concern in his eyes that I couldn't bear it.

"This is no family gathering." A cigarette dangled precariously from T. Bone's lower lip. "Don't know what you two think you're doing here."

"Jenny brought me," Aurelia told her father.

"I can see that," he said. "Does Maureen know where you are?"

Aurelia didn't answer; I guess that told him what he needed to know. By the way Eddie Crockett frowned at us when we turned up in that dressing room, I thought for sure he'd send us packing for home.

"Daddy," Aurelia said, "you can't blame us for wanting to hear you take the house down with your horn. You're the one always going on about it." And by the time he lifted his fancy hat and scratched the top of his head, even though he gave Aurelia a good reaming, I knew he had changed his mind. He let us help carry music stands (which they didn't need, but they had to pretend they used them) to the shadowy center of the stage, behind the curtain.

Chick set up folding chairs for us right before the show started. He slapped a drum fanfare on the metal seats. "You'll be just fine here, Miss Aurelia. You're my guest. If you have any more trouble, you come and get me." As if he could have done something about it. "We'll give everyone the what-for."

He put us against the wall, beneath a shadowed overhang where no one could see or disturb us.

"Back for another weekend aboard the *Admiral* . . ." The announcer's voice boomed, and I'll bet you could hear it, low and resonant, all the way across the river into Illinois. The red velvet curtain jostled and billowed from last-minute adjustments made behind it. The footlights came up. The spotlight blazed to life. The curtains parted with a faint metallic hiss. For a moment, the silence held. Voices hushed. Silverware stilled.

In spite of the unpleasantness we'd experienced getting on the boat, Aurelia ended up being right as usual. It was worth everything to hear the Blue Notes play.

Eddie Crockett lifted his trumpet to his lips with that air about him I loved, like you were about to hear something you'd never heard before in your life.

T. Bone Finney poised his big fingers over his guitar strings.

All the world seemed to be waiting when Chick, the rhythm man, finally tapped the downbeat on his hi-hat cymbal and the Blue Notes took off.

The gleam in Eddie Crockett's horn zigzagged like lightning. Dancers flooded the floor, their skirts twirling, their feet prancing, surrounded by hand-painted zodiac signs and little white lights that formed the constellations. Pullman chairs and chrome-and-glass cocktail tables decorated the mezzanine overlooking the floor.

Aurelia had spoken truth about the Brooks Brothers suits, too. If I'd passed this collection of musicians on the street, I wouldn't have spoken. I wouldn't have known them, they looked so debonair. T. Bone even wore a black hat cocked low over one eyebrow. Who would have known they could look so fine under the lights?

THE PENNY

The Six Blue Notes played all evening while Aurelia whispered the names of the songs to me. "Body and Soul." "Fussing All the Time." "Tuxedo Junction." "One O'Clock Jump." And it was more than hearing the music that filled me up and set my mind in a jumble. It was the heavenly scent of ladies' perfume and the quick bursts of laughter and the feeling that, out of the dark, smoky place where our escort had first taken us, Aurelia and I had been afforded the seats of honor.

I got to sit here with Aurelia, yet I was an unworthy person. No matter how many times I snuck away from Wyoming Street and rode the streetcar to the Ville, no matter how often I tried to flee what I had incorrectly thought or done, I suffered Daddy's reminders in my head. I knew everyone looked at me and did not like what they saw. I didn't deserve even one moment of the pleasure I felt, listening to Eddie Crockett wail on his trumpet. When wrong happened, it would always somehow be my fault.

If I thought running with Aurelia would allow me to escape my guilt, I'd thought wrong about that. The better I knew the heart of my friend, the more my sense of dishonor grew. Aurelia loved me in spite of everything. How could she be treated so shamefully ("We can't have you running around on the boat like this. Only Mondays are for the coloreds.") when mine would always be the heart colored by disgrace?

As Chick nodded his chin to the strokes of his drum brushes, he glanced up and caught Aurelia's eye. When the number ended and a gentleman dropped a handful of coins into the ashtray they'd set out for tips, T. Bone found us and winked. Curtis Jackson put down fifth-notes on the piano, rippling like rivulets in a stream. Eddie Crockett pointed his trumpet toward us and fingered a rift so unexpected, I figured he'd just taken off into his own personal jam session.

He aimed his music right toward our seats. There might as well not have been anybody else in the ballroom. He serenaded us like he was trying to blow the nails off the roof, running through all that music like it was nothing. It was like he wanted to tease us and teach us right from the stage with his horn wailing, *You'd better never do anything again that's not safe for you, young ladies, but since you're here anyway, guess I'll just have to demonstrate what you've been missing.*

By the time he finished his bebop rendition of "Bloomdido," Eddie Crockett had everyone in the ballroom on their feet. We jumped from our seats and applauded so hard that our hands stung. Up in the mezzanine, guests forgot about their filet of lemon sole and their lamb steak béarnaise as they whistled their appreciation. Dancers pressed toward the stage.

Aurelia gripped my shoulder. "Don't know why they won't let them bring those suits home. Everybody in the neighborhood ought to see. Don't they look fine?"

I nodded.

"They ought to play here every day of the week. Daddy wouldn't have to have any other job except this one." She glowed with pride. "This is the gig he wants. He would die if he couldn't play his horn. Aunt Maureen ought to see this. Listen—don't people just love them?"

I didn't answer. I'd been distracted by the sight of a man pressing a paper bill into Mr. Crockett's extended hand. His girl clung tighter against him than ivy clings to a trellis. She wore a vermillion pink dress with her full lips painted to match.

The man whispered to his girl and she giggled, swung away from him, tried to pull him away with her hand. But the Blue Notes had gathered at the edge of the stage.

I saw the man insisting. I saw the girl lower her chin in embarrassment and smooth her hair behind one ear. I saw Mr. Crockett shake his head.

T. Bone bent his microphone toward his mouth. "What's going on here is this fellow is making a request for the lady. He wants us to play 'Embraceable You.'"

A ripple of romantic appreciation ran through the crowd in the mezzanine. Contented and amused, they reseated themselves at their tables and took after their dinners with renewed zeal.

Not until then did I truly sense the danger. I saw the fear flash in Aurelia's eyes, and knew she expected it to come to the same end as I did.

"We take requests all the time. But see, 'Embraceable You' is a pop number. What we been doing up here for you is the bebop jazz."

Only seconds before, we'd been clapping, but now Aurelia squeezed my hand in despair. I imagined T. Bone trying to change the subject and then Chick saying, "No, sir. Sorry, sir. We don't know that song."

"That's not the kind of music Daddy *plays*," Aurelia whispered.

I pictured the man not taking no for an answer, grabbing the book off the stand, and thumbing through pages of music no more readable to the Blue Notes than a barbed-wire fence.

The man would say, "Sure you do. Every band does. It's right here," slamming the page onto the stand.

The dancers would turn on them. The rowdy applause from moments before would fade into shouts of contempt. "We want a real ballroom band, not a group that doesn't know music."

Eddie Crockett picked up his horn, narrowed his eyes, fingered his valves. Let me tell you, those valves were springy as a cat on a telephone line.

I touched Aurelia's shoulder. *Wait.*

"You got to know," he said to everyone gathered below, "when we play this song it's a change of pace. We're used to playing the free expression, where you get away from the melody line and let the instruments follow their own trails. You got to understand we may be a little raw with this kind of music. But I'd like to dedicate the song to this couple here, John and Annette."

"Do you think he can play it?" Aurelia breathed.

For years after that, I liked to think I read Mr. Crockett's lips when he turned to Chick. I liked to think I'd been the one to see him say the way he told us he did later, *"Lamoretti taught us these notes. No reason we can't pull it off, add a little hip rhythm to it. Have fun with it."*

That was Eddie Crockett for you. He wouldn't let himself be broken in front of Aurelia. He went and figured out something to do. I saw him tap his toe so T. Bone could catch the beat. I guessed he hummed a few bars so the rest of the Blue Notes could hear. He swung his arm and snapped his fingers like Lawrence Welk.

When "Embraceable You" started, the man held his girl's hand in a proud knot. I held Aurelia's hand. She clung to mine.

The couple pressed against each other, her arm folded against his chest, his nose against her ear so he could breathe in the scent of her hair. She laid her head beneath the jut of his chin. When she lifted her cheek to his, you could see they didn't care what song was playing. She wrapped her hand around the back of his neck and met his eyes, their hips swaying together in tempo. They danced in a world where skin color didn't matter and families loved each other no matter what. They danced in a different world than ours.

Chapter Eleven

The more time I spent with Miss Shaw, the more I wanted to find answers to the mystery of her. One day, when Jean and I stopped into Woolworth's after we'd gone to the Fox to see Grace Kelly in *Dial M for Murder*, I recognized Miss Shaw sitting alone at the soda fountain, and I froze. She sat there so distinguished, a careful, aristocratic tilt to her jaw.

Every time other diners came up, they stepped past the seat beside her, giving Miss Shaw a wide berth. Every time someone hesitated as if recognizing her, that person would pass by without saying a word. Which led me to believe that I probably shouldn't bother her, either.

Surely she was tired of me after seeing me so much at the shop. I was sure she was fed up with giving me instructions. When I tried to think of how to start up a conversation, I couldn't imagine a single appropriate thing to talk about with her. *If you spend time sitting at the grave of someone you love, Miss Shaw, why doesn't that grave have a marker?*

I stood in the aisle directly behind her, pretending to be fascinated by the boxes of cotton facial puffs, while she folded her plastic menu into thirds, handed it to the waitress, and ordered a tunafish-stuffed tomato. I perused Lustre-Creme shampoo bottles while the waitress brought her a Coca-Cola, which she sipped daintily through a straw. I read the backs of at least five tins of talcum while I watched the smooth fingers of her white gloves, and realized Miss Shaw had no intention of removing them even while she was eating.

The waitress set her plate down in front of her so hard that the lettuce almost flew off the plate. Jean appeared beside me. "Jenny, we got to get going."

"Not yet," I shushed, nodding in the direction of the soda fountain.

Jean followed my gaze. "Oh. It's *her*."

"Yeah."

Jean sighed. "She's beautiful, isn't she?"

"Yeah."

"How come you're standing here spying on her?"

"I'm *not*," I insisted.

"Then why are you whispering?"

"I'm not whispering," I whispered.

Jean heaved a sigh of exasperation. "Five minutes," she said. "Meet me at the front or else I'm going to leave you. I don't have time to baby-sit you anymore."

I grabbed an eyelash curler from the shelf and pointed it at my sister. Jean sure knew how to make me mad. "I don't know why not. I always have to wait around for you, too. I had to wait all night for you the time you left out the window with Billy."

She tossed her head, flinging her ponytail at me. "It's not *my* fault you come snooping into my life all the time."

Jean trudged off in a huff, and just when I turned to replace the curler in its bin, I saw Miss Shaw looking at me. My face burned with embarrassment. I hadn't wanted Miss Shaw to catch me scouting her.

"Jenny Blake," she said, coming over and touching my shoulder with her gloved hand. She'd left her uneaten lunch on the counter. "Are you interested in eyelash curlers? Who would have known? Do you want me to teach you how to use one?"

"Oh, I—" My words got tangled in my throat. Finally I said the first thing that came to mind. "I don't know why you think you got to be so nice to me," I blurted. "That's the biggest mystery about you of all."

She helped herself to the metal implement and demonstrated as if she hadn't heard a thing I'd said. "You open it like this and slide it in as close to your eyelid as possible. Then you press. Like this."

"I don't know why you think you have to help me with all these things."

"Every young lady needs to master the intricacies of an eyelash curler. Do you want to know one of my secrets?"

One of her *secrets*. Finally. I nodded dumbly.

"Move the curler out toward the tips of your eyelashes and press again. Just so."

I stared at myself in fascination in the small display mirror when she released my lashes. My eyes seemed huge. I could see the copper light reflecting in my pupils.

"There you have it. The fashionable wide-eyed look."

Well, surely that was one of the questions everybody asked about Miss Shaw. *How does she get that fashionable wide-eyed look?* At least I knew the answer to *something*. In an instant I realized how much I wanted to trust this woman. Maybe Jean went bonkers over Grace Kelly because Grace was the sort of person every girl dreamed of being. But to me, Miss Shaw, in her mystifying graciousness, was the daily embodiment of the same thing.

"Thank you for teaching me how to do this," I said, lifting my curled eyelashes toward her.

"Will I see you at the shop tomorrow?" she asked, as if she was almost afraid I wouldn't come. Once again, I marveled that no one had seen fit to pause and chat with her. I thought of her picking at the tuna and the tomato while no one so much as gave her a smile or asked her about herself or said hello.

"Of course I'll be there," I promised, "but I've got to go now." Jean was already heading toward the door.

I had to race to catch up with her.

The more pennies that kept turning up in my path, the heavier my pockets became. And the heavier my pockets became, the more I wanted to help people the same way that God was helping me. I would never let go of that very first penny I found. But I did give away a lot of the others. Everywhere I looked, I saw plenty of people who I sensed were sad, lonely, hurting, or in need of encouragement.

One day in the Ville, Pruett Jones (who rode the Harris school bus with Aurelia) took a ball to the forehead and I pressed a penny into his palm, telling him I hoped the ball didn't make too big of a bruise.

When I saw Mrs. Shipley dust off her toddler after he'd taken a nasty fall, I wrote a secret note to her ("You have a nice way with your boy"), taped a penny to it, and stuck it inside her mailbox.

I gave away pennies to everybody because I wanted to help people the same way God kept helping me.

When I observed my last-year's teacher, Mrs. Martha Dahlberg, sorting through fresh fruit at the greengrocer's store on the corner, I placed a penny on the grocer's scale so she would find it when she weighed her purchase.

I even swallowed my pride and gave a penny to Cindy Walker when she showed up on our landing, trying to earn a Girl Scout badge by asking if there was anything in our underprivileged neighborhood that she could help us with.

"You've got to have this," I said expansively. "Go ahead and think I'm stupid if you want to, but I'm giving you this in hopes you'll see all the good things that keep dropping into your life."

When people like Cindy looked at me like I was nuts, I wondered if my small acts of kindness were having any effect at all. Several times, I thought about giving up, but I didn't. Maybe I'd never see anything come of me passing along pennies. But reaching out to hurting people, even in a small way like this, helped me feel better about the hurts in my own life.

I was crossing Grand Avenue later that same week, headed toward the streetcar stop after work, when I heard someone call, "Jenny?" and I glanced back to see Miss Shaw's blue convertible rolling along behind me. "Would you like a lift somewhere?" she called, her gloved fingers gripping her steering wheel. "I closed the shop early so I can visit the hairdresser. Don't you live in the direction of Chouteau Street? I go right past there; I certainly wouldn't mind driving you home."

Instinct told me to decline even though the Cadillac dazzled me with its gleaming grille and its rockets protruding from the chrome on the front of the car. "I ride the streetcar every day," I explained.

She pulled her scarf tighter and lifted an eyebrow as if she didn't think that mattered one jot.

"I've never ridden in a convertible before."

She patted the white leather seat beside her. "Well, it's about time you tried it out, wouldn't you say?"

"Really?"

"Sure."

"You really want to give me a ride?"

"Of course I do. Hop on in."

I think I forgot to breathe as I climbed in beside Miss Shaw. I shut the door behind me and pressed my spine against the leather seat in amazement. The seat felt so low and broad, it made me feel like a giant held me in the palm of his hand. The minute Miss Shaw popped in the clutch and we sailed up the street, the wind caught my hair like we were flying. I cupped both hands overhead and tried to capture the air as it raced by. On the sidewalk, gazes followed us as we zoomed past. Miss Shaw switched on the radio. After a bit, when the tubes warmed up, we had music.

I gathered my hair in my fist, trying to keep it out of my eyes, to no avail. Miss Shaw tapped her fingers on the wheel in rhythm to the song.

"Did you know Grace Kelly showed off to her friends in a convertible?" I announced. "When she was a teenager, she stood on the front seat and steered with her feet." I wasn't trying to elicit information from Miss Shaw this time. I was just feeling chatty.

With her gloved fingers rapping against the wheel she said, "I suppose that means your sister would like to drive a convertible with her feet."

"Probably. If she got the chance."

I loved the way Miss Shaw arched her perfectly drawn eyebrows. "I have to tell you, Jenny—I wouldn't give her the opportunity."

Sitting back in my seat and feeling conspiratorial, I said, "Neither would I."

Out of nowhere, Miss Shaw started talking about herself. I can't tell you why; she just erupted into conversation, and I did, too. She asked if I'd fiddle with the radio and find KMOX because she wanted to listen to St. Louis jazz. I told her about Aurelia and Eddie Crockett, the horn man, and how he amazed me every time he played. She told me she liked to arrive ten minutes early at the salon to sort through hair magazines and make sure she wasn't missing any new styles.

She said it had taken her six tries to get the convertible top up the first time it rained. She told me she loved a good chocolate soda. I confessed that I hadn't meant to spy on her at the lunch counter at Woolworth's, but I hadn't been able to help myself. In another burst of vigor, she told me how her old house was much too big to manage on her own and she'd hired a housekeeper to assist her. She told me how she ate at Woolworth's often because when she ate at home, her maid served her meals alone.

I guess it was her talk about maids and a big old house and eating meals alone that finally helped me get my nerve up. Facing straight into the wind, I announced, "You know what folks all over town say about you? They say you store your shoes in separate velvet bags so they won't scratch each other up, and they say that you sleep with cold cucumber slices on your eyes at night, and they say they've seen you in a cemetery sitting on the ground beside a grave without any stone. It's crazy, isn't it, all the things people say about you?"

I was too busy feeling free and important to check her reaction. I took her silence the way I wanted to take it, as absolute denial. Then I realized I'd been so busy listening to Miss Shaw, I hadn't realized when we'd started passing street corners I recognized. We were coming perilously close to home. For these few precious miles, Miss Shaw had shared her freedom with me. But as her car zipped around corners and I began to recognize the flats slipping by, my glorious feeling of liberty began to vanish. My heart chilled. The easy banter died in my throat.

"You don't have to drive me all the way to my flat. You can let me off and I'll walk the rest of the way." I didn't want Miss Shaw to see the grubby, coal-stained building where I lived. I didn't want anyone along Wyoming Street to see *her*, either.

"I don't mind, Jenny," she insisted.

All too soon we arrived at my neighborhood with its darkened bricks and its weedy yards, with its dented trash cans at the curbs and its sidewalks buckled from tree roots. Our brick flats hunkered together like sentries, shoulder-to-shoulder. I gripped the door handle in mortification. "You can let me out here."

"I won't let you drive the car with your feet," Miss Shaw said, paying no attention to our surroundings. She didn't seem to notice either my gloom or the wretchedness of my neighborhood. "But sit up a little higher, prop yourself on the armrest or something, and see how it feels. I want you to have a real ride in this thing before you go. I want you to know how fun this can be."

When I did as she told me, the wind whipped my hair into my eyes. I thought, *This is it! This is it!* as Miss Shaw pressed down on the pedal and I had to gasp for breath. Front yards and tree trunks rushed past us. *This is what it feels like to escape*, I thought. But I wouldn't be escaping. In a moment the car would slow and she would drop me off at the curb and I would have to return to my own life again. By the time she hung a U and I directed her to pull up beside the buckled sidewalk, I didn't know whether to be grateful to her for giving me a taste of her freedom, or to be angry at her for making me want something I could never have.

"Is this where you live?"

I barely nodded as my hand slipped to the car door. "You'd better get out of here," I told her, my voice grim.

"Is everything okay?"

I didn't answer or look back.

"Jenny?"

I slammed the door resolutely behind me.

"I had fun," she said.

But I ignored even that as I mounted the steps.

"Thanks for letting me drive you home!"

I didn't wave or anything. As I heard the sound of her convertible driving away, the windows of our flat stared at me like knowing, accusing eyes. I couldn't bear to think what Miss Shaw would say if she ever found out what went on behind them.

Chapter Twelve

Then came the day when I walked into our flat and knew something had changed. Three weeks had gone by, and Daddy's job had ended.

I could tell by the way Mama tiptoed through the hallway. I could tell by the way Jean started blaming me for things I didn't do.

I'd messed with her blue eye shadow, Jean accused, and I'd ruined the brush. I'd snuck money out of her purse. I'd shoved aside hangers in her closet and now her skirts were wrinkled. Jean always came at me on the attack, with sergeant-square shoulders. She wanted to fight the world, it seemed, and I was always the first prey she encountered.

Mama never talked about what went on with Daddy, the fear he must've laid on her, the threats he made and carried out. Sometimes I'd walk into the kitchen in the morning and find her leaning over the sink, staring down the drain with her face grim, her eyes dry. When I tried to hug her, she'd pull away.

I'd tasted liberty only to have it stolen again.

How I dreaded Daddy's return the evening of his last day on the job. Every step Daddy took toward our sweltering flat pushed me farther away from Eddie Crockett and the Six Blue Notes, and from Aunt Maureen's constant need to feed me pork steak or Gooey Butter Cake ("Eat this, honey. It's good for you!"), and from the routine contentment of seeing Aurelia. ("Where was King Solomon's Temple?" she'd asked as we rode home, surrounded by trumpets and oboes and drums in the back of Chick Randle's pickup. "On the side of his head." "What kind of capsule do you take to make yourself feel way out?" she'd ask. "A space capsule!")

Daddy's walk went heavy in the heels. He'd thump through the house on our wooden floors, getting more reverberation out of them than Chick got from his bass drum. I heard Daddy heading up as I set the table for supper, his footfalls staggered. I could tell he carried something heavy up the steps.

When he swung the door open with his backside, we saw he'd bought us an air conditioner from Sears. He hefted it over his head like a world-champion wrestler would show off his trophy belt, and for one breathless moment, I thought he meant to throw it at us. Instead he said, "Look what we got."

He was trying too hard, his words sharp and overzealous. I made up my mind not to let him impress us.

"Get this thing plugged in," he ordered. "We'll be more comfortable than anybody at the Ambassador Hotel. What do you say, Jean?"

There were occasional times like this when he tried to do something nice, but it was always short lived. Often we would freeze in our tracks, thinking we'd get slapped for doing something as simple as dripping water on the furniture, but Daddy would let it pass instead. Another day, one of us would spill water on the couch and get slammed into the wall. Never knowing what to expect next was one of the hardest parts of my life.

My sister stared at the appliance in terrified fascination.

"Let's hook this thing up. What do you say?"

Daddy put the unit in the kitchen window. After he pulled out the pane, he went to find a piece of plywood to cut into shape. Mama sat down hard in a kitchen chair, staring at knobs marked HI MEDIUM LOW and at the spotless white vents that could be removed and rotated to send air rushing in different directions.

"Well," Mama said, "aren't *we* moving up in the world?"

THE PENNY

When Daddy finished the installation, I tested the stream of air with my hand, not certain it would ever turn cool. When the air finally became as cold as winter water, Jean adjusted the vents and inclined her head so the breeze poured over her hair. She raked her fingers past her ears, pretending to pose like Grace Kelly for a *Life* magazine shampoo advertisement. I looked at her with her hair flying and, for the first time, I saw my sister as beautiful.

I don't think she saw me at all.

Above the slight hum of the air conditioner that night, I heard the sound from Jean's room that always awakened me, the omen that always terrified me, that always sent the expectation of evil running in chills along my spine. A faint cry . . . the murmured growl of Daddy's voice.

The flat stayed silent as I lay listening in the dark, trying to convince myself that, maybe this time, I'd only imagined the sound. I wanted to push the idea away forever. I couldn't get rid of the feeling that I'd been cast adrift, the same sensation as when the *Admiral* departed its dock before its rudder caught the current.

Every time I sank off to sleep, my mind awoke with perilous tales. I dreamed the soft click of a door latch. I dreamed the muffled heel-heavy footsteps in the hallway. I dreamed of someone looking for me, the footsteps stopping outside my door.

I waited a long time before Daddy came in.

My mattress bowed when he sat beside me. I closed my eyes, willing my body to stay still. Maybe he'd think I was sleeping and he'd leave me alone. Maybe he'd be too tired. Maybe, this time, Mama would come in and stop him.

That was how it always began. That was how Daddy ruined me, took me away from myself, one step at a time. In the darkness, I wasn't dreaming as he placed his hand over my mouth and began to whisper. I wasn't dreaming as he pulled back the covers and held me down.

In the morning I found my sister at the kitchen table with Mama's pinking shears. She'd turned the air to HI and the blowing stream of it ruffled the pages of the magazine beneath her hands. It must have been about forty degrees in the kitchen, almost cold enough to snow.

Jean didn't look up when I turned the air conditioner off. She'd been carrying an issue of *McCall's* around since last week. She'd bought it at a newsstand because it touted pictures of Grace Kelly leading the United States delegation at the Cannes Film Festival.

Three times already, she'd showed me the pictures reprinted from *Paris Match*—a lavish photo spread from Grace's meeting with His Serene Majesty Rainier Louis Henri Maxence Bertrand de Grimaldi, from the small principality of Monaco in the South of France. "A *prince*, Jenny. Do you think he wants to find a princess for his kingdom?"

Jean made me look over and over again at the shots of Prince Rainier escorting Grace around the palace, through the gardens and his small, exotic zoo. *This meeting almost did not take place*, the movie reel had blared at us the last time we went to the Fox. *The power went off in Grace's rooms that morning and the prince arrived an hour late for their meeting.*

"Do you think he might fall for her?" I'd asked.

"Anybody would," Jean answered.

I wasn't quite as impressed as Jean. I didn't think Prince Rainier was as handsome as a prince should be. I didn't like his craggy eyebrows, his thick-chested, short-legged stature, the cleft in his chin.

That morning I thought Jean intended to use Mama's shears to finally cut out these pictures. She could tack them to her wall or put them in a frame and quit carrying the dilapidated magazine around with her. But when I sat beside her, I saw that wasn't her intent at all. She powered the shears through thick piles of pages, working so hard that the scissor handles pressed ferocious red notches into her hands.

Jean was not selective. She slivered the Grace Kelly article, the interview with Bob Hope about his mother-in-law, the Chrysler convertible advertisement, the cigarette ad that read HAVE YOUR COFFEE WITH A KENT. She shredded the Betsy McCall paper-doll pages and the article titled "The Hospital Gave Us the Wrong Baby." Magazine strips drifted to the table like confetti.

"Jean!" I laid my hand over the shears so she'd stop. "What are you doing?"

She didn't answer at first. Then, "There's just all this stuff—things I'm trying to forget." She stared down at the tatters of what she'd done. When she said that, I knew she wasn't talking about the stories she'd been reading in magazines, but about her history with Daddy.

"What stuff?" I demanded. "Say it, Jean. What are you talking about?"

The air between us hung heavy with what was known, what couldn't be spoken. Jean couldn't be consoled. She couldn't do anything except sit and cry.

Several times, when Daddy seemed preoccupied with tasks like cleaning his rifles or tinkering with the car, I attempted to sneak out of the house and go see the Crocketts. I gathered bottles to trade in, thinking the trip to the A&P would be an excuse to visit the Ville. But, "You know you get the same money for those at the confectionery," he said. "Don't let me find out you went farther than that."

I fabricated an invitation to Marianne Thompson's house in St. Louis Hills. But, "If she wants to see you, she can come here," he said. "That's what she gets for moving out to the boondocks. That's what she gets, thinking she's too good to live on Wyoming Street."

Every plan I invented, he thwarted in the same taut voice. Then, "You see this?" He broke a rifle open over his knee and began polishing the gunstock with an oil-soaked rag. The smell of the linseed oil stung my nostrils, made tears burn my eyes.

"Maybe things happened I didn't approve of while I was out working. I'm the only one making sure this family survives. Did that boy come around to see Jean? You'd tell me if he did, wouldn't you? And what did *you* do with all your free time?"

I clamped my mouth shut. I was terrified he could read my mind at times like that.

"You know why I'm polishing up this gun, don't you? It's to keep people away from this place. People I don't want to see. You tell Jean I said that, why don't you? What's his name? Billy? You tell your sister if that boy comes anywhere close to this house, he's going to get shot."

I nodded, but I was lying. I wouldn't tell her. I did not want to ruin one of the few things in life that Jean looked forward to. Daddy could tell her himself. I wasn't going to let him use me to hurt somebody I loved.

Chapter Thirteen

The year before, our vice principal, Mrs. Iris Connor, suspended Charlie Bidden and Andrew Scott for sneaking out of class and climbing up to peek through the high windows at the kids in the portables. Rumor circulated that if Charlie and Andrew hadn't gotten caught, they'd have made good their plans to raid the place and set off cherry bombs underneath the bathrooms.

There had also been stiff punishment for students who ran to the windows to stare at the assembly of rally marchers when they started up. The demonstrators had moved onto the front steps of Harris School for more than a week, men and women, mostly colored but some white, too. They paraded with block-lettered signs and shook them at us. They raised them toward the street every time a car passed. TAKE YOUR PORTABLES, the signs read. INTEGRATION DOESN'T MEAN SEPARATION. Any student caught gaping was sentenced to writing "I will not stare out the window" a hundred times.

But when I thought of returning this year for eighth grade, I didn't care what punishment Mrs. Connor might dish out for me talking to Aurelia. I knew school discipline was a whole lot easier than anything I had to deal with at home. These last few weeks of summer, I missed Eddie Crockett's horn playing almost as much as I missed my best friend. Impatiently, I counted the days (thirty-nine) and the hours (eight-and-a-half) until I would see Aurelia and Darnell at school again. I planned on talking to Aurelia as much as I could, no matter what Mrs. Connor's punishment might be.

Early September might as well have been an eternity away. And I was certain Darnell would use thirty-nine days to his advantage. *"See—I told you, Aurelia,"* he'd say. *"She had a little fun over here is all. She didn't really think you were good enough to be her friend. Good riddance now."*

Until school started, I kept myself busy at Shaw Jewelers. It seemed like everything Miss Shaw did, from the minute I walked in the door of the shop in the morning to the time I signed out in the afternoon, was intended to make me feel good about myself. She insisted I try on jewelry and kept telling me how pretty I looked (although all I saw in the mirror was a downtrodden face with muddy, unlit eyes). She showed me a Grace Kelly two-strand choker and offered to sell it wholesale if I wanted a going-away gift for Jean, somehow knowing I already felt my sister's absence in ways I couldn't explain. She solicited my opinion on everything from how to best arrange receipts in the cash drawer to how to best display brooches so the stones would glimmer beneath the spotlights. She occasionally asked if I had found any more pennies and wanted me to recount the story of the first penny that led me to her. She reminded me that God was trying to show me that he loved me and was working in my life.

But every time Daddy came to my room again, I knew that in spite of everything I did in Miss Shaw's store and all the nice things she said to me, I had no right to the confidence she placed in me.

I operated the cash register with sullen indifference, pummeling the keys with angry jabs of my finger. I went after the workroom floor with a punishing broom, thwacking metal shavings and dust out of my way. When customers were in the store, I plastered a smile on my face because I knew I needed to, but inside I was not smiling at all.

When the bell tinkled over the door one morning and two gentlemen entered, I happened to be out of sight, rearranging the watch display because of the new Timex wristband collection we'd gotten in. The two men couldn't have looked more different; one wore a brown summer suit with a fedora to match, and the other wore dungarees and a shirt dusted with cement powder. Miss Shaw didn't hear them, I guess. Her buffing machine kept purring behind the curtain.

The one in the suit lugged a heavy box which he set beside the register with a satisfied *humph*. The man in dungarees yanked the folded hanky from his friend's breast pocket and used it to scrub his own brow. Mr. Suit retrieved his handkerchief, shook out the wrinkles, folded it into thirds, and returned it where it belonged. He caught a glimpse of himself in the mirror and adjusted his hat with great care.

"You fixing that hat won't make your face any different," Dungarees said.

The other tugged at his jacket hem to straighten out the wrinkles. He cocked his knees, moved his jaw to and fro in the mirror and scrubbed his fingers in a V against his chin, looking for stray whiskers.

"Not going to get her attention doing that Creature-from-the-Black-Lagoon imitation, either," Dungarees taunted.

Intrigued, I switched my weight soundlessly from one haunch to the other. After everything they'd said, it was too late to rise from my hiding place and ask if they needed my assistance.

They exchanged boyish jabs even though the one in dungarees looked older than dirt—older than forty.

"You got to stop making things up in your head, Joe. What makes you think I'd want to get Opal Shaw's attention, anyway?"

"That thirty-dollar suit from Boyd's makes me think so. I've known you thirty years, Del, and you've never owned a suit like that. You never even had a suit like that before your wife died."

Del brushed off the lapel like he was brushing off his friend's comment. "I did, too. I had a nice suit when I married Camille."

But Joe kept going on. "One minute you're yammering on like a tree jay, and next thing I know, here comes Miss White Gloves looking like a *Life* magazine cover, and you clam up like you have wallpaper glue on your tongue."

"I don't clam up, Joe—" the widower said. Then, thinking more of it: "But I don't yammer on, either."

Joe wasn't near finished. "That, and the dozen times you've come in here buying charms for your granddaughter's bracelet. Last time, you let Miss Gloves talk you into buying a charm of the Eiffel Tower. How could an Eiffel Tower be the thing for Donna? You're supposed to go to Paris to get an Eiffel Tower charm, not Grand Avenue in St. Louis."

"Can't come in her store and not buy anything." Del examined his hat in the mirror meant for customers trying on pendants. He practically had to fold himself in half to see into it. "What if Donna never gets to Paris? The world is full of people dreaming of things they never get to have."

"Like you. Dreaming about Opal Shaw and not doing anything about it."

I was new to the world of love and sure hadn't learned much from watching Jean and Billy. I wasn't much for romance, anyway. After what Daddy had done to me, I didn't figure anybody would ever want me. But the idea of Del being sweet on Miss Shaw introduced a whole new realm of possibility. I remembered the lonely way she'd picked at her lunch-counter tuna while folks who must've recognized her made a broad circle around her. I recalled the faint regret in her voice when she mentioned that she often invited her housekeeper to eat with her so she didn't have to eat alone. Picturing Miss Shaw running a gloved hand over a grave, I imagined she might have lost the only person who had ever cared for her.

Miss Shaw gave me rides in her convertible and taught me how to use eyelash curlers. I may have made up my mind not to fully trust her, but even so I couldn't help wanting her to find true love. Hearing Joe and Del talk made me suddenly ache to help Miss Shaw find someone to stand beside her the way she kept trying to stand beside me. It made me ache for both of us.

"Since when did you get to be such an expert on women, Joe?" Del asked.

Joe poked him in the ribs. "Since I was born, I've known more than you."

I laid out a Timex with a linked gold band and waited for one or the other of them to thump the small counter bell to get her attention. From the back, we could all hear Miss Shaw humming in rhythm with her buffing wheel—a familiar song, although I couldn't remember where I'd heard it before. She warbled like a bluebird. Even then, when she didn't know anyone was listening but me, she didn't hit a wrong note.

Joe said, "And why do you think a woman would ask you for a box of bricks? What would anybody need with a box of bricks in a jewelry store? Could be she's interested, too."

Del gave up on his hat. He ripped it off his head and held it like a steering wheel between his two hands. "She asked for the most historical Laclede bricks I had in my possession." When Del talked about his bricks, his voice took on more authority. "What I got in this box represents the last hundred years of St. Louis."

"You've got to do something about this. I hope you see it." Joe stood with his hand poised over the bell. "Now, let's find out if that Boyd's suit will do you any good."

"I'm not afraid of Opal Shaw, Joe. I *respect* her. That's two different things."

"You ought to ask her to a nice dinner. Maybe take her to Rigazzi's for Italian. I'll bet she'd like that."

With no further ado, Joe thumped the bell.

"Wait. I'm not ready."

"Time to get the show on the road."

"Joe."

But it was too late. The bell had summoned her. The singing and the sound of the buffer subsided in the workroom. Miss Shaw emerged as if she were stepping through the curtain at Carnegie Hall.

"Well, *hello, you* two," she said with genuine warmth. Del had gone stiff as a stork with his fedora gripped in both hands. I couldn't tell whether he was going to present his hat to her as a peace offering or use it for himself as a shield. Quickly, he plopped it atop his head at a slant more comical than any he'd tried in the mirror.

"What about you, Delbert? Did you bring me my bricks?"

From the way Del's face went scarlet, his tie must've gone tighter than a bassett hound's choke collar. He worked his finger inside it as if he were close to suffocating.

"He sure did, Miss Opal," Joe answered for him.

I saw her quick glance at Del's red ears. Del cleared his throat again and straightened his tie. Miss Shaw met his eyes briefly, then nodded toward the bricks on the floor. "I could have picked those up at the brickworks, you know."

"No, you couldn't have," Joe said with gusto, obviously exasperated by the silence. He heaved the whole box onto his shoulder, a regular he-man. "Wouldn't do for any lady to carry something this heavy, especially not a lady like you."

Del shot Joe a look laden with resentment. *What? You showing off your muscles?* If Miss Shaw hadn't been fidgeting with the ruffles on her blouse, she would have read the whole thing, too.

"Wouldn't have you mess up that suit, Delbert," Joe said pointedly and hefted the box higher. "Now, where do you want me to put these for you?"

"In the back by the bench, please."

She pointed toward the workroom, and while Joe lugged the bricks away, Miss Shaw and Del faced off across the cash register. For a very long time, they said nothing. Each seemed to be waiting for the other to speak up first.

That didn't work. After several beats of silence, they spoke at the same time instead.

"How are—?"

"You been—?"

Silence again. He darted back into his shell like a turtle that's been poked with a stick.

"Thanks for bringing in those bricks," she prompted. "I know you must've wondered what on earth I could be using them for."

"Yes," he said, tugging the wrinkles out of his jacket self-consciously. "I *did* wonder. What on earth?"

"I'm using your bricks for my display cases. The brickworks are such a part of St. Louis, and necklaces will be beautiful draped over them in the windows. That, and the sense of irony, I suppose. Robbers throw bricks to smash and steal. And here the bricks will be untouchable, in lighted vaults for all to see."

In a rush, Del asked, "You think you might be willing to help me pick out another charm for Donna? She liked the Eiffel Tower well enough. Maybe I ought to get her the London Bridge."

"Why, Delbert, *another* one? That girl has so many charms, I'm scared she'll pop her wrist out of joint when she wears that charm bracelet. If she ever fell into the river with that thing on, she'd sink straight to the bottom."

He picked up the placard of gemstones beside his elbow. "Maybe we ought to start on her birthstone then. Let's see. April. May. It says right here, June is alexandrite." He set the placard down and it toppled over. He had to set it up twice to make it stay. "That's what she needs. Alexandrite."

"Maybe your granddaughter would like a pair of roller skates or a paint set or a walking Ginny doll. Something that doesn't come from a jewelry store."

"Yes, but—"

"Yes, but *what*, Delbert?" She leaned so far across the cash register toward him, I thought she was going to ring up a sale with her belt buckle.

"Then I wouldn't have any reason to—"

"Any reason to *what*, Delbert?"

He seemed caught between her question and a deep Ozark gorge. I could almost feel his terror from here. I wanted to jump from my hiding place and shout, *Say it! Say, "Then I wouldn't have any reason to see you again."*

Miss Shaw opened the register drawer with a light *ding* and immediately slid it shut again. She stood for a long time, waiting, pressing the drawer with her gloves.

When Joe returned from his task, he made it clear he felt as frustrated with Del as I did. "The silence is killing me, Del. I'm leaving. You ever decide to tell Miss Opal what we were talking about, you can let me know."

"I knew you'd do something nice with those bricks, Miss Opal," Del said. "You always think of nice things."

"Why, Delbert. What a lovely compliment."

"Right." He slapped his thigh in agreement, narrowed his eyes at her. They both spoke at the same time again. "Well—"

"Well—"

Del turned to go, took another three steps and stopped. He stood stock still, neither turning toward her nor proceeding toward the exit. The seconds ticked past.

She pressed, "What did Joe mean, 'what you were talking about'?"

When Del said, "Nothing much," it was everything I could do not to jump from my hiding place and shout, *Tell her you like her! Tell her you want to take her to Rigazzi's!* When Del said, "Guess we'd better get going," Miss Shaw exhaled a deep breath and I could hardly stand it, either.

That was the first time I realized you could be left alone by someone who admired you just as much as you could be left alone by someone who thought you weren't worth much. That was the first time I realized there are plenty of different kinds of loneliness.

"Of course," she said, standing in a pond of isolation. I could feel her disappointment clear from my lair in the display case.

Chapter Fourteen

We shared a party line with the Smiths, who lived opposite us upstairs, and the Pattersons and the Shipleys, who lived below. The telephone rang in our kitchen only when someone dialed Parkview 7-5768. But every so often when Mama or Jean or I wanted to dial out, we would pick up the receiver and roll our eyes—cut off from the world once again by the prolonged and delicious conversations of Mrs. Ralph Patterson and her best friend, Miss Mona Miner.

That afternoon, Jean stood with her arms crossed and passed the time, shifting her weight resolutely from one hip to the other, the receiver cocked against her ear. She initiated long sighs loud enough to be heard as far away as DeBaliviere Boulevard. Then she shifted her weight again and flopped her wrist against her forearm, her jaw extending ostrich-like with irritation.

All of that, and the chattering women still ignored her. At last Jean said, "Excuse me, but there are other people who need to use this line. Could you *please* finish your conversation so *others* can use the telephone?"

That was the problem. The conversation never quite finished. From across the room I could hear the babble of apology as the two women assured my sister they were just winding up, that they'd hang up in a minute or two, that she should have let them know sooner if she'd been waiting.

So Jean hung up and waited some more. I watched her hold down the switch with one finger while she stealthily lifted the handset to her ear. In a silent motion, she released the switch. If Mrs. Patterson was still on, she didn't even hear a click as Jean joined the conversation. Jean listened for a while and then said as loud as she dared, "Is someone *still* on this *line?*"

"What could they be talking about for so long?" I asked when she gave up and returned the receiver to its cradle.

"Nothing much," she said. "Mona Miner's brother got picked up for siphoning gas out of someone's car last night. And Mrs. Patterson didn't like the chuck roast she bought at the butcher's this morning. He trimmed it wrong and left too much fat."

Although these specifics did not appeal much to my imagination, the idea of eavesdropping did. It gave me a feeling of power, knowing I could listen in any time at my discretion.

I learned the skill of party-line snooping from my sister. Like Jean, I kept my finger on the button while, phantomlike, I lifted the earpiece to my head. Like Jean, I lifted my finger off the switch with the stealth of a spy.

Mrs. Patterson's daughter had problems with breast-feeding her baby so she'd given it up and tried Similac. Miss Mona's family reunion was next week and they made her promise to bring a caramel pie. Mrs. Patterson's arthritis had flared up. Miss Mona's brother's wife had told him she was leaving him after the gas-siphoning incident.

Poor Billy had been trying to call Jean for a week, and every time he managed to get through on the line, she hung up on him. But I didn't blame Jean. Who could tell who else might be listening? Our eavesdropping adventures always reminded us that we could never be too careful. It would be as easy as pie for Daddy to catch wind of things.

Both of us learned so much over the party line that summer, you'd have thought I'd have heard about the man who got his arm cut off, too. But, I didn't. Daddy made me go to the barbershop, and that's the first time I heard about it.

Daddy said I was way overdue for a haircut. He said he didn't like the way I kept brushing my bangs to one side and pinning them back with a bobby pin. He thought it made me look fast and too old for my age, like I wanted to chase boys.

I didn't dare tell him that Miss Shaw told me I looked amazing that way, that she'd showed me in the mirror how it brought out the shape and color of my eyes.

I took my seat in the high brass chair, and Daddy's favorite barber, George, tied a black plastic cape under my chin. George raised the chair with three pumps of the pedal. He got the comb good and wet, tapped it on the sink's edge, and went about untangling my bangs. He worked on them until they were sopping and stuck flat as a flounder to my forehead. "How's that look to you, Mr. Blake?"

I couldn't see because of the water in my eyes. My bangs dripped clear down past the tip of my nose. I heard the perverse pleasure in Daddy's voice. "Take as much as you can off the top, George. Make her look more like a boy."

The newspaper must have belonged to Mr. Cyrus Pete, the man who warmed the shaving cream and fetched towels and polished up the barber's pole by the front door, all sorts of tonsorial duties, because the newspaper was the edition for St. Louis colored people. I'd just wiped my bangs out of my eyes with the intention of fighting to the death for my hair when the headline caught my attention. My bones chilled.

"Can I see that?" I didn't wait for George or Daddy or Mr. Clyde to answer. I grabbed it up and started skimming the article.

"Hey, sit still," George threatened. "You go to jumping around like that and you'll be lucky if you don't end up bald."

The story told about a punch-press operator who'd lost his arm when it got caught in a press at American Stove Company. He'd been reaching into the press to remove some metal when he accidentally stepped on the foot pedal. The limb had come off clean. No breaking first or dangling or wrenching in two. Just *snip*, like the metal he'd been cutting, and there it lay, a part of him, beside him.

THE PENNY

The man had been rushed to the hospital for surgery, that's what the story said. I figured there were plenty of Ville people who worked at the stove company. Whoever it was, it wouldn't be anybody I cared about. Besides, I didn't care much about anybody down there anymore.

"Isn't it something?" George asked when he followed my gaze to the story. "Cut his bone right through. Sliced it clean off, just as easy as I'm trimming your hair."

If this was a trim, then so was the bulldozing going on in outlying St. Louis County. Mama had told me how everywhere you looked, some construction company was plowing under old trees and knocking over farmhouses for more "quality-built" homes like the ones in St. Louis Hills. "No down payment! G.I. loan!" the advertisements hawked.

So was the bulldozing that had taken out the entire neighborhood of Mill Creek earlier in the year because the flats were all falling down and the City of St. Louis intended, in the name of urban renewal, to build a large housing project for working families, both white and black. *Progress or Decay*, the headlines had blared. *St. Louis Must Choose.*

I endured the bulldoze of a haircut with the same suppressed dread with which I endured everything from Daddy. When George stepped aside so I could see, I couldn't have been more horrified. I gripped the arms of the chair and half-raised myself out of it in shock. I felt bare, and so ashamed. The barber hadn't left enough for me to even comb flat. So many times I'd explained away Daddy's actions to myself. So many times I'd decided that what happened to me must be okay because I wasn't worth much—I must have done something to deserve it. Staring at my likeness in the mirror, I felt like I was staring at a stranger. A stranger who had been totally betrayed.

"Oh, my," Mama said when we walked in the door and she saw my new coiffure. "Jenny, what happened to your hair?"

"Well, maybe if you had taken me to the beauty parlor yourself, it would have turned out better," I accused her with a fling of my shorn head.

Daddy's mistreatment and his cruel words drilled over and over into my head how dirty and ugly I must be. Miss Shaw kept trying to show me during all those hours at Shaw Jewelers that I wasn't as I saw myself. But no matter how she tried to coax me with her stories of iron-strength in my eyes or my uncanny aptitude for numbers or my adroitness at coming up with ideas, I still didn't believe her. Especially when she told me how pretty she thought I was. I felt ugly inside and out, and I was so ashamed that I wanted to die. I respected Miss Shaw too much to tell her to her face that she was wrong about me. But when the time came to prove my corruptness to myself once and for all, it came in a way that even *I* couldn't have expected.

When Jean flew into the family room that day, I held my finger over my lips so she wouldn't say anything. I had the receiver to my ear. If she blurted one word, Mrs. Patterson would hear us and we'd both get caught. As my sister pantomimed for me to hang up the telephone, Jean looked like she was about to erupt with news.

When I hung up the phone she said, "Now you're going to get it good."

"What?"

"Jenny, what were you thinking?"

"It's our party line. If we have to share it with everybody, I have a right to listen."

"Not that." Jean's face was fraught with drama. I knew it was something big because she didn't breathe one word about my missing hair. She didn't even seem to see it. "You get yourself down to the yard."

I took the steps two at a time, not having any idea what my sister could be so worked up about. But the minute I shoved open the door, I understood. The roots of the maple tree in our front yard had grown so old and thick, they'd turned sideways. There beside the lumps in the sidewalk stood Aurelia, her feet planted just as firm and stubborn as the tree trunk that towered over her beside the curb.

My whole insides felt torn to pieces. If I'd ever been scared before, it had never been anything compared to now.

Aurelia had a puzzled look in her eyes. She'd come all this way. She must have pictured me racing out to greet her.

I froze on the stoop above her, standing my ground beside twists of wrought-iron railing.

Receiving Aurelia at my house would be a perilous mistake. She had no idea how dangerous this was. If Daddy found her here, there was no telling what he would do to her.

I hissed at her, mean as a snake, so she'd get the point and go away. "What are you doing here? You got no right coming over like this."

"Why don't you get over to my house anymore, Jenny? One minute, you're coming every day and the next thing, you don't show up at all."

Standing there in the yard, Aurelia seemed to shimmer from the heat. Everything else remained motionless, from the bees that hovered beside the white hawthorn blossoms lacing Mama's flowerbed to little Scott Stinnett down the street who'd given up on his scooter with the bell on the handle and left it propped against a brick wall. Even the breeze, which had been fretting the leaves high among the branches, held its breath.

A posse of boys who'd spent most of the morning acting out the details of the next war (all of us were already thinking there would be another war soon—"*Buzz-zz-zzz, I'm a German warplane. You can't shoot me down.*" "*Ra-tat-tat-tat-tat. Fall down. I killed you.*") had disappeared for Kool-Aid inside.

Aurelia pleaded, "You going to invite me in or anything?"

"No. I'm not. Only place you ought to be invited in is a loony bin, if you ask me. You got no right." I glanced over my shoulder at the

Shipleys'. Depending on where Mama sat at the Tupperware party, she might see Aurelia out the window.

Daddy had taken off walking a good half-hour ago, headed to the electric company because he wanted to argue the bill. He'd taken one look at the BTU's drawn by the air conditioner he was so proud of and he'd unplugged the unit for good, after which he'd cursed at all of us, pulled out his favorite rifle, and threatened to shoot anyone who tried to start it up again. No matter if it topped 110 degrees tomorrow, he ranted, that air conditioner was going back to the store.

"You haven't been around in almost two weeks. I come to find out why. We miss you."

I advanced toward my friend in distraction, one hand hanging loose and the other knotted at my side. Someone had started up the street. Even though the figure was only a dot, I knew it was Daddy coming.

"Aunt Maureen even made buttermilk biscuits one day, she was so sure you'd come around. She was quoting Scriptures and *every-thing*—" She stopped mid-sentence. "What did you do to your *hair*? It looks like you got attacked by a buzz saw."

"You go away. Right now," I blurted out, ignoring her critique of my coiffure.

There could be no mistaking the resentful swing of Daddy's arms or the resolute cadence of his steps as he strode up the street. Even from here I could tell he was on the warpath. They must have made him pay up on the electric bill.

When I thought back to it years later, I realized that desperate moment was the first time since Antioch Baptist Church that I had prayed. I was so reckless from worrying about Aurelia, there wasn't time to worry that God wouldn't hear me or that he would see me the way Daddy saw me, that he wouldn't think I was good enough for him, that I was too damaged or vile to speak. Out of the corner of my eye, I saw Daddy halt. He bought us blessed seconds by giving the Stinnetts the what-for about their boy leaving his scooter where someone could trip on it.

Aurelia knew only the arms of a father who wrapped her against him because he held her dear. She knew only the arms of a man who made up his own music and played it down anytime the idea struck him. Eddie Crockett played for love, and those who heard him— from casual listeners to maestros—would come to the bandstand and ask, "Where did you learn to play like that?" Eddie Crockett loved music and beauty and people. My daddy disdained all of those same things.

I jammed my hand in my pocket to find my penny, but it wasn't there. I'd left it lying on the table beside the telephone.

Dear Jesus, help her please. Dear God, help her get home safe.

"Darnell says you think you're too good for us. He says that's why we don't see you no more. Is Darnell right, Jenny? Is that it? You think you're too good for visiting anymore?"

I couldn't have told you I was crying. I didn't know until later when I ran into my room to hide and felt my wet face.

"It doesn't make any difference what I think. You can't just go showing up like this."

"You got no idea what it was like getting here. Someone stopped me and said I'd better be coming someplace to work—I'd better be coming to scrub steps or wash windows, and not just catting around the neighborhood. That's what the person said to me. She said I had no business here. She sounded like you."

It jolted me that she thought she knew what I was talking about. She thought she'd figured out what was going on. I read it in her eyes just as clear as I'd seen it the afternoon on the *Admiral* when the purser yanked her arm and said, "You'll have to stick with your daddy, out of sight. Can't have you running around on the boat like this. Only Mondays are for the coloreds." She'd said, "My daddy doesn't play Mondays."

I had the chance to set her right. Maybe I should have tried to explain how mean Daddy would be. In those few seconds I could have yelped, "He'll hit you, Aurelia. He'll beat us both up, but good." But back then I had no vocabulary, other than shame. The least I could've done was tell her she didn't have any more sense than a Thanksgiving turkey, that she didn't know what she was talking about, that I loved her.

If I could be an expert at hiding how scared I was, I could also be an expert at hiding how I felt about Aurelia, for her sake.

The Daddy-speck coming up the road loomed larger. He was growing into a square, dangerous tower of a man. I could see him good now, his face steely, his chest bloating out of his T-shirt. I leaped off the steps and did the only thing I knew to do. *Please Jesus, let her get away.* I shoved her.

"You go on back to your neighborhood!" I shouted. "I'll just see you at school."

"You ashamed, Jenny? You ashamed to be called my friend?" She started in on me, saying I didn't know how it felt to be her, that I couldn't know how it was to always wonder if what's happening is happening to you because you're colored. "How could you possibly know what that feels like? How could you possibly know?"

"Go." I shoved her again. Hard. I stomped at her to make my point even clearer. "Get on out of here."

I watched her back away with hollow eyes and willed her to cut between the two flats across the street, to disappear from sight. I wished she would vanish like a small dark shadow along the sunburned stretch of grass so, not having to look at her, I wouldn't have to look at myself.

"He can't play his horn, that's what I come to tell you," she said, turning back. "Not with the Six Blue Notes or anybody. Chick had to go out and hire somebody else to be the bandmaster."

I stared at her, not understanding what she meant.

"It happened at the stove factory. You know, none of us wanted him to have that job anymore. We wanted him to play on the *Admiral* all the time. He could have gotten plenty of gigs if he hadn't been thinking he needed to take better care of us."

"What are you talking about?" I dared her to tell me that newspaper article had been about her daddy. I dared her.

"Aunt Maureen's taking care of him good as she can. He forgets his arm isn't there. He wakes up trying to play music because he's got something in his head. He could use some cheering from you, but I'll go back and tell him, no, I guess not. I guess you won't be over anymore."

"No," I said. "I can't. Now get out of here before my daddy sees you."

The hurt in Aurelia's eyes hit harder and cut deeper than all the meanness my Daddy had ever flung at me. Just like that, the self-reproach I'd carried so long ripened into anger at my father. I thought, *Today is one more day I'll never be able to forgive him for.*

It did not occur to me that God had answered my prayer when Aurelia slipped away unnoticed. I made it clear to the porch rail before Daddy came stumping up from the neighbors'. Mama stood beside me with her Tupperware loot. With Mama on the porch and Daddy on a lower step, they stared at each other from the same height. "What have you gone and bought now? We can't afford junk like that."

"It keeps sandwiches fresh. It makes lettuce last longer."

"How many heads of lettuce would we have to save to make up for what you're spending on that?" I hated Daddy even more for beating Mama down when there was nothing more at stake than burpable plastic. I hated Mama, too, for letting him do it. "Now you go on inside there and get your money back."

Mama did as he told her. When she returned from the Shipleys' this time, she was empty-handed.

That night, I did not sleep. Eddie Crockett had never taken me to see the inside of his workplace, but I pictured it something like

Aurelia's preacher had described hell. I saw endless metal shapes moving along a conveyor belt overhead. A furnace roared and singed everyone's faces. (Did they have furnaces in a stove factory? It seemed like they would.) There wasn't any escaping the heat. Every time I closed my eyes, I heard the deafening clang of metal, saw the glinting sharp edges of what I imagined a punch press would look like.

I couldn't stop picturing Eddie Crockett's hands forming mouthpieces so thin and light that trumpet players waited in line for them. I couldn't stop hearing the way those musicians in the Ville begged him to bring home extra stove tin.

My throat stayed clogged all night with something I couldn't swallow. What must it have felt like for Eddie Crockett as he stood there bleeding in the noise, with metal pieces moving all around him?

I pushed my old wounds deeper inside, and forced myself to grieve solely for the fresh ones, for Eddie Crockett's music and for what I had done to Aurelia. I wondered until the sky began to turn to soft grey velvet outside my window, *Is it different when life gets taken from you moment by moment than when it gets taken all at one time?*

Chapter Fifteen

I showed Miss Shaw the anger, pain, and darkness of my heart with every task I undertook. I wiped the displays with vicious circles of the rag, leaving wide patches of dust. I placed the tie clips in their case in a jumble without bothering to arrange them. I left the assortment of silver piggy banks and baby rattles in their boxes for someone else to take care of. But no matter how awful I acted at times, Miss Shaw remained the same with me. She was always kind and respectful.

Miss Shaw tried to draw me out, but I answered her with stern silence. She talked to me about everything from James Dean's smoldering eyes to the army hearings of Senator Joseph McCarthy, but I remained aloof. She asked my advice on everything from how to arrange brooches in the front window to how she might convince Del Henry to stop in more often, to which I raised the dust rag like it was a battle flag and proceeded, with great intensity, to polish shelves.

On the day Mrs. Stella Fordyce came to look at belt buckles for her husband's birthday, I let her wait so long that, had she been a silversmith, she could very well have hammered out a belt buckle on her own.

"Mrs. Fordyce." Miss Shaw rose from her desk at last, sidled past with a confused glance in my direction, and offered the woman assistance because I wouldn't do it. Once Miss Shaw helped her with prices, Mrs. Fordyce made a decision in no time. When Mrs. Fordyce asked if we offered gift-wrapping, Miss Shaw thrust the buckle at me. "Of course we do. Jenny, will you take care of this, please?"

Ordinarily I loved wrapping packages. All summer I'd taken pleasure in adorning small, elegant boxes with paper and ribbon. I'd taken pride in my perfect, mitered corners and my flawless fluffy bows.

When I ripped off a piece of birthday paper today, I took great satisfaction in tearing it from the roll. I wadded the buckle inside some tissue and smashed the box lid on. I went heavy on the tape, cut the ribbon with sharp snips, and tied knots so tight that Mr. Fordyce would have to go for a kitchen knife to get the thing open. When I handed it over, Mrs. Fordyce peeked in the sack and exclaimed, "My, but what a wrapping job. How creative."

Miss Shaw stood beside me and watched while Mrs. Fordyce made her way outside. When she disappeared around the corner, Miss Shaw laid her hand on my shoulder.

"Jenny, what's wrong?"

"Nothing."

Miss Shaw had plenty of paperwork left at her desk, but she followed me to the corner where I'd left the broom. She eyed me with concern.

"If there was anything I should know about your life, you would tell me, wouldn't you?"

"I would," I lied.

"You promise?"

I promised and went back to punishing the floor with stinging smacks of the broom. When Miss Shaw looked at me again, the lines around her eyes got deeper. She stared at me with such interest that I was tempted to relent and blurt out how dirty I felt. But ever since I'd chased Aurelia away from my house, I didn't carry my penny around anymore. I'd stopped placing stock in what Miss Shaw said a penny represented. Miss Shaw's life seemed so *right*. She would never understand. And I was tired of her telling me about God's plan for my life and that he was watching over me every minute. I'd had plenty of hope once. Maybe I didn't believe a word of it anymore.

My job with Miss Shaw had become so important to me, but I believed I was destined to lose it, just as I lost everything else that made me feel good.

"STUPID. STUPID," the notes that Rosalyn and Cindy put in my locker had read. I thought, *I was stupid, all right. I was stupid enough to think that anything in my life would ever change.*

But here's the thing about Miss Shaw: she surprised me. She was different from anyone else I had ever met. When I took my anger out in the jewelry shop, she didn't react the way I expected her to. Anybody else would have seen that I was no good for a jewelry store and would have fired me on the spot. I waited all day for her to chastise me, but she didn't. She didn't sit down and say, "I'm not satisfied with your gift-wrapping, Jenny," or, "You need to look the customers in the eye when they enter the store," or, "Could you be gentle with the cash register, please? I'd hate to have to send it away for repairs."

I know now that God was giving me unconditional love through Miss Shaw—I just didn't know what it was.

The day Jean left for secretarial school blew in with a violent windstorm. The wind blasted down the street with such force that you almost couldn't stand up in it. Gusts came so hard that the old dilapidated walls along our street began to totter. Mortar crumbled. Chunks of our flat fell to the ground and shattered. Just walking outside with your neck bent into the weather, you ran the risk of dust blinding your eyes and trash clobbering you and bricks coming loose and randomly dropping on your head.

"We're not driving to the bus station in this weather. I'm not getting the car out in this," Daddy hollered each time he stormed past Jean's door. "Doesn't mean a thing to me if you miss going to school."

She didn't seem to hear him. She went right on folding her stockings and her nylon slip and her scarves. Piece by piece, she set them inside the round red travel case Mama had bought her at Kresge's. It had a zipper all the way around its edge and a handle Jean could drape over her wrist like a handbag.

I watched my sister pack up her room and thought about the pictures in the *Post-Dispatch* of the ladies elected to the secretarial board—the scariest pictures I'd ever seen. There sat all the secretaries at their bimonthly meeting, the officers of the secretarial society—president, vice president, and secretary (would you want to be voted secretary to the secretarial board when you were already a secretary?)—with sharp, self-possessed smiles, glasses as big around as drink coasters, and white carnation corsages the size of small bunnies fastened to their collars. I tried to picture my sister in the midst of a scene like that, but I couldn't.

I stood in the corner, moving when she needed something behind me, trying my best to stay out of her way.

"Got you a going-away present." I held it hidden in both hands behind my back and bounced against the wall because I was so nervous about this. "You want it?"

Jean kept stuffing her belongings inside her bags and boxes. She stood a fistful of vinyl records inside a box that also held picture frames. My sister was taking her collection of Grace Kelly photos and all of her favorite male movie stars, too. Jean locked the tone-arm and needle into place and latched the lid to her record player. She yanked the plug from the wall and coiled the cord around the handle.

"Well?" I stopped fidgeting and stood up from the wall. "Do you want a going-away present from me? You have to say if you want it or not. If you don't, I won't give it to you. It doesn't matter to me."

"Okay." A great sigh of forbearance. "I want it."

"Do you? Do you really?"

"Didn't I say so, Jenny? Yes. I want it."

After that, I couldn't give it to her. I just stood there, waiting.

Jean zipped up the red travel case with great relish. "Never mind, then. If you don't want to give it to me, you don't have to."

All the times Miss Shaw had offered to let me buy the two-strand pearl choker for Jean at wholesale price, I told her I didn't want to. But when my sister started clearing her room of belongings that week, the sorrow hit so deep and made me so breathless, I felt like someone had socked me in the stomach.

"What are you thinking?" Miss Shaw asked when she saw me looking at the choker one day.

"Even wholesale, I don't think I've got enough money to buy it."

"You're thinking about that again? Have you changed your mind?"

I nodded.

"So, your Jean is leaving this week?"

It was something about the way Miss Shaw said "your Jean." I couldn't get rid of the tears that welled up.

"You know what I'm thinking, don't you?" Miss Shaw said.

"What?"

"That you and I can work something out." She laid her gloved hand on my shoulder and the warmth of her touching me soaked clear down to my toes. "Let's get the files and go over some prices, what do you say?"

To this moment, I'm not sure how she came up with the exact figure. Miss Shaw located the necklace in her paperwork, showed me the certificate of authenticity, and scratched so many numbers on a notepad that I couldn't follow her calculations at all. The next thing I knew, she circled a figure at the bottom of the paper that matched exactly the amount of the paycheck she'd handed me that morning, sales tax and everything.

"You want to give it to me, or don't you?" Jean demanded, pulling me from Shaw Jewelers back into Jean's cluttered bedroom.

I handed over the narrow box which I'd wrapped myself. Jean gave the ribbon a cursory tug, like I was forcing her to do something she didn't much want to do. I heard her breath catch as the choker spilled into her hand. You could see every shade of opalescent white glimmering in those pearls as she strung them around her neck and examined herself in the dresser mirror. She'd probably never use that dresser again.

When she struggled to fasten the clasp, her elbows jutted up over her head like wings. I saw the shine on her face and knew she liked them. Although I also knew she'd never tell me.

"They're like—"

"—Grace Kelly's. I know."

I stared at our reflection in the mirror. Two sisters, one taller than the other but not by much. One with a glamorous hairdo and one with a pitiful scalped head. I'll bet it surprised Jean how much we resembled each other in spite of all that.

She said to me in the mirror, "It'll grow back."

I said to her, "I'm *glad* you're going. I'm *glad* you're going and leaving me with him."

Neither of us moved.

For one last moment, we fell into our pattern of contention. Challenging each other came so much easier than admitting we needed each other.

"Well, I'm glad you're glad, Jenny, because nothing's stopping me."

"I'm not trying to stop you," I said.

Outside, a burst of wind trapped itself between our building and the one next door. Unable to escape, it became a whirlwind in the corner and picked up everything in its wake. Some empty cigarette packages. Dozens of leaves. A napkin left from someone's picnic. All of this swirled and tapped against Jean's window as if it wanted inside.

Another brick came loose and shattered on the patio.

"That's going to be a mess for somebody to clean up."

The treetops bobbed together as if they were worshiping the windstorm. Flickers of lightning swept past, but the wind bore it away before the clouds could even threaten us. I asked her if she'd ever told Mama anything about what Daddy did to her.

Jean reached behind her neck to unfasten her pearls. She stashed them in their box and shoved the box inside her red travel case. I didn't know whether to be disappointed or happy that she didn't want to show them to anybody else. I wondered if she'd even heard my question at first. She said, "I'm going to marry the first boy who asks me. Daddy says I'll come running back for help, but I don't want any help from him."

A whole stand of trash cans had blown over outside. They ratcheted to and fro in the street every time a gust got them, thundering hollow and loud.

"It took a while for me to get up the courage to talk to Mama, do you know that? When I finally got brave enough, you know what she did? She got all confused and teary and went right to Daddy and asked if it was true. Daddy flat-out told her I was lying. He told her my imagination must be running away with me. He told her I was spending way too much time listening to my friends' gossip about *their* lives. And that's the crazy thing, I don't even have any friends. There's nobody I can talk to but you. Daddy made *me* feel guilty. Daddy made *me* feel like I'd injured *him*."

Maybe Jean could hold her ground against the wind outside when she left, but I suddenly felt like it might carry me away. It terrified me to think of stepping outside in it.

"I don't know if she really doesn't believe me or if she just doesn't *want* to . . ."

The trash cans made so much racket, like somebody was out there hitting them. I couldn't say anything. I saw the pain behind Jean's words, and I couldn't have felt more betrayed. Mama was supposed to take care of us.

"She walked in on us once, while he was in my bed. You were still so little. She saw us, turned around, and walked out of the house. She came back in two hours and never mentioned it. Mama seemed different after that. She avoided me as much as possible and even seemed to resent me at times. After that I never said anything again."

We both jumped when Daddy showed up in her doorway just then. We'd been concentrating on her words, so neither of us had heard his footsteps thumping down the hall. If he caught us talking about this, he'd kill us.

"I'm not getting the car out in weather like this, Jean. Not getting the Packard out to get it sandblasted by this dirt or dented by a brick. The whole sky's falling out there. Everybody's so busy building in the outskirts that nobody's thinking what the city needs anymore."

Jean mouthed off, "If you won't take me down to that bus station, I'm going to call a taxi for myself."

Yesterday that would have provoked him to hit her. Today he stood in her doorway and took it. "Nobody's got money to get you a taxi, Jean. Nobody's got money to do anything like that."

"I do," I said.

"If you've got money, then you owe it to me," Daddy blustered. "You know I didn't let you take that job so you could amuse yourself. I expect you to chip in and pay your own way. I expect you to buy everything you need because I'm sure not doing it anymore."

After he stomped off, I took my sister's hand. I expected her to yank it away like she'd done a hundred times before, but she didn't. She turned and held both my hands so tight I thought she might break my fingers off. "I bargained with him; do you know that? I told him I'd never bother Mama again if he just didn't start doing it to you, too."

Then, "Is he doing it to you, Jenny? Did he keep his promise to me?"

I stood and stared at her in awe. It took long, precious seconds for the realization to sink in: Jean had tried to give herself for me.

Maybe Miss Shaw had been right; maybe things weren't always what they looked like. All this time when I'd thought I didn't amount to anything in Jean's eyes, my sister had been trying to take care of me.

I hated to tell her, but I couldn't hold it back. "I guess Daddy doesn't keep many bargains."

Her face crumpled like a paper bag.

"You got to go soon. You'll miss your bus."

She let go of my hands, and the next thing I knew, pedal pushers were somersaulting through the air toward me. "Fold those, okay? And you can stick those socks in that overnight bag, too."

Not until she'd zipped up the last suitcase and filled the last cardboard box did she glance in my direction again. "Jenny?"

"Yeah?"

"All those things I said—how I told you I wished you'd never been born? How I told you I hated you?"

"You can't expect her to be interested in everything you're interested in anymore," Mama had said when I asked if she knew why Jean and I were drifting apart, if she knew why Jean treated me the way she did. When girls grow up, they start needing time to themselves.

"It didn't matter what you said," I lied.

"All those times I quit talking to you."

"Yeah, I remember."

"I couldn't stop thinking—if you hadn't been born, I wouldn't have had to worry about you getting hurt, too."

I found another pair of socks under the bed and gave them to her.

"I couldn't stop thinking I should have been able to do something to protect you."

Those last few minutes I bustled around Jean's room in a bitter-sweet fog. After today I'd be alone with Mama and Daddy, but that didn't matter right now. What mattered was this: I'd thought I lost Jean a long time ago, but I hadn't.

Jean had to chase Mrs. Patterson and Miss Miner off the party line so she could call for a Yellow Cab.

"If you need money to get there, I'll give you everything I made this summer," I volunteered.

"You keep your money." Her voice relapsed to its huffy tone. She'd turned snotty on me again, and this time I understood she did it because it was the only way to keep a safe distance, now that we were saying good-bye. "I got some saved up."

She toted everything downstairs to wait for the taxi. Every time she opened the door, the wind blasted her skirt around her legs. Every time she came back inside, her hair looked like somebody had taken an eggbeater to it.

I lugged her record player down for her and set it beside the cardboard boxes with the records. When the taxi honked its horn, I ran to help the driver load the trunk for her. The wind plastered Mama's blouse to her chest. She wrapped both arms around her middle like she thought the wind wanted to rip the blouse completely off. Even from where she waited at the porch railing, gusts blew her hair sideways and she could hardly open her eyes in the blowing dust. The Shipleys came out to wave Jean off. No telling where Daddy had gone to.

"Good-bye," Jean called to everyone. "Good-bye," over and over again. I'd never seen my sister so happy as when her cab pulled away. "Write," she mouthed to me through the glass.

"I will," I mouthed back. I couldn't stop waving, even after the Yellow Cab started creeping up the hill. I held on to my own shirt then, too.

Shards of brick lay in the grass at my feet. Dirt pellets and tiny rocks pelted my legs as I waited at the curb and waved my sister off. I jumped around to keep them from hitting me so hard.

Oh, how I'd dreaded this moment when Jean would leave us for good.

I braced myself against the wind, letting the air-bound dust and pebbles sting my legs. I couldn't bear the thought of going inside.

The time had come when I had to face life with Daddy alone.

Chapter Sixteen

*E*verywhere except on the thermometer, the hottest-summer-on-record seemed to be fading from its own heat. "Back-to-School Togs for the Fine Men and Women of Tomorrow!" the *Post-Dispatch* advertisement blared as I read it across the streetcar aisle. "Petti-coats! The Perfect Autumn Accessory for Your Newest Dark Cotton Frocks!"

As the trolley made its regular jog to the south between Sarah Street and Delmar, I pressed my nose to the open window, thinking I was going to die before it ever cooled off. We passed a red Pontiac convertible crouching on the side of the road, overflowing with young people. Maroon and gold crepe-paper streamed from the antenna. The colors of Jean's school: Central High. In another year that school would be mine.

The streetcar clanged its bell, and tires squealed as the driver floored the red Pontiac, smoke pouring from the pavement. The teen girls screamed from their perch on the back and hung on to each other as the car took off. The driver looked sideways then forward, sideways then forward, his tongue clamped between his teeth, as he pulled abreast of us. Two boys in the front seat twirled shopping bags in the air, the girls egging them on as they aimed and let the bags fly.

When the bags sailed in through our windows, they exploded in clouds of dust. Babies screamed. Flying dirt seared my nostrils and stung my eyes. Women coughed and tried to fan some of it out the windows. Businessmen brushed off their suits and shook dust out of their newspaper pages. The conductor swatted at the clouds of dust with his hat. The woman beside me tried to wipe off her glasses.

The car sped beside us, the girls shrieking with hilarity. I wondered what we must look like to them as we jumped and fanned and complained inside the trolley, trying to get away from the dirt.

"Hey, Billy!" I heard one of the girls holler as she leaned forward and grabbed the driver by the neck. "What time's the next one come along?"

"Any minute, sweetie," he bellowed back. "Don't be in such a hurry. Enjoy this one. Look at all those people in there."

The girl positioned her chin atop his shoulder.

Just then the streetcar slowed. With both hands, I lifted myself until I was standing inside the open window.

"Billy Manning!" I screeched, and it surprised me plenty that my voice carried so far. After the tales Jean had told me, I knew without a doubt which boy would partake in *this* activity. And I recognized him from the night he'd come tumbling into Jean's window. "Billy!" I shouted. *"Billy!"*

He turned and looked my way, dislodging the head of the glamour girl who tried to stay plastered against him.

"I'm Jean's sister!" I shouted louder, leaning out the window and waving frantically. "I'm *Jean's sister!*" I declared to passing cars and pedestrians along the Hodiamont right-of-way and the passengers in the convertible flying Central's official colors. My whole being wanted to jump out and join them, they were so carefree.

"Oh," Billy shouted. "Oh, hi!"

"Hey," the girl slapped him on the shoulder. I'll bet she asked, "Who's Jean?"

And then they were gone. They zoomed past. We were forgotten, the next trolley targeted. Still I hung out the window, calling after them. I called to the skyline of St. Louis and beyond.

"I'm Jean's sister!"

Because calling out her name like that was the only way I could give credit to her, the only way I could make sense of the horrible bargain she had wrought with Daddy, trying to protect me. Jean and I belonged to each other. All those years I'd thought I was on my own. But now I knew my sister cared about me after all.

I couldn't have guessed how much I'd miss Jean after she'd gone. Every time I walked into the house, I expected her sullen voice. Every time I passed her room, I expected her judgmental glance.

Only now that I knew what had elicited her ill-temper, her absence left a gaping hole in my chest. I felt so lonely sometimes without Jean and Aurelia, I thought I might die. Whenever Jean phoned us, which wasn't too often, I hung onto the receiver with both hands as if I were hanging onto my sister instead.

The details of my sister's new life sounded spectacular, and I'll bet even Mrs. Patterson was listening in. Jean had taken a Saturday job at a dress shop to make spending money. Every day at school they had timed drills in typing, and yesterday she'd clocked in at 47 words a minute with only two mistakes. Her roommate, Sarah, had spent a week in Chicago once, and now Jean thought she might look for a job in Chicago after she got her typing certificate.

Running across magazine articles about Grace Kelly or hearing reports about her on television made me feel worse than ever. Every time I heard Grace Kelly's name, it reminded me that Jean wasn't around to share movie-star stories with me. I started gobbling up the gossip magazines by myself instead, knowing the words would make me feel twice as alone when I read them, but reading them anyway. That's how I grieved my sister's leaving, I hung onto the details of Grace Kelly's life the same way I would have left my feet planted too long on the searing pavement, knowing the hurt would be there, waiting for it to start soaking through.

When I picked up the party line to listen in one afternoon, I caught Mrs. Patterson in the throes of a conversation with Miss Mona about asking Daddy if he'd be willing to refurbish her scratched floors. She ran through at least three piqued imitations of my father.

"He said, 'Now those aren't my floors to worry about, are they?' Can you *believe* he said that, Mona? 'I'm not the one who has to walk on them.' He said, 'If you fix those floors yourself and make them all nice, I'll have to raise the rent on you.' Can you *believe* it?"

On the other end, I heard Miss Mona Miner laugh occasionally during this tirade. "Some people like to control everything, Lily. Just feel sorry for that man's family."

"I know," Mrs. Patterson said. "Can you *imagine?*"

Listening in on the party line was yet another activity that kept me feeling closer to Jean. Just as I reached to silently disconnect myself—this certainly wasn't a topic I hadn't eavesdropped on before—the chitchat veered in a direction that made my hand pause. Miss Mona said, "Oh, I hear Opal Shaw was at it again at the cemetery. Sitting on the ground the other night and weeping over that grave like she thought nobody could see her."

"Maybe she doesn't think it *matters* if anybody sees her," Mrs. Patterson said.

"Well, of *course* it matters. Why else doesn't she talk to anybody about it? Why else doesn't she put a marker on that grave? I tell you, everyone says it's the most unsettling thing, seeing her kneeling in the dirt there and not knowing who on earth she's having a visit with."

"Well," Mrs. Patterson commented drily. "It isn't anybody *on* earth, is it? It's someone *in* the earth."

"Yes, Lily." An exasperated *humph*. "I stand corrected. *In* the earth. It's obviously a grave, you know. It's a mound like all the others."

"Is it easy to find?" Mrs. Patterson asked. "After hearing all the gossip, I'd like to go take a look at it sometime."

"It's down at the cemetery beside Lafayette Park. Beside the church where she goes. It's the plot just past the huge cedars there."

"Have *you* been to see it, Mona?"

"Me? *No.* I'm just telling you what I've heard. Why would *I* go down there and be a busybody? *I'm* certainly not going to go prying into other people's business. This much I know, though. She may be one fashionable woman, Lily—she may wear her white gloves to every important function and she may drive a car better than the one belonging to the mayor of St. Louis—but I tell you, there's more to that woman than meets the eye. She keeps too much to herself. I don't blame *anybody* who wants to avoid her."

I flicked the button and hung up the receiver. Miss Mona's words echoed in my ears. Maybe I butted heads with Miss Shaw in her jewelry shop and tried to give her reasons to fire me, but it infuriated me to hear these women going on when they didn't have any idea what they were talking about.

I thought back to the time I'd given Miss Shaw the chance to set me straight. I'd taken her silence for denial: This graveyard gossip couldn't be true. It made me plain mad, hearing these two whispering about nothing.

Daddy could punish me all he wanted for leaving. I knew just where I could go to disprove the gossipers.

The cemetery grounds stood groomed and quiet before me. Each tilting stone had its own shadow to cast, its own story to tell.

As I stood at the cemetery gate in the pretty neighborhood that bordered Lafayette Park, I thought about how certain I was that

THE PENNY

I wouldn't find the grave Miss Mona described over the party line. I might constantly try Miss Shaw's patience in the jewelry shop, but she never gave up on me. Miss Shaw's steady, unswerving faith in what I could do left me with a growing, grudging respect for her.

I *needed* Miss Shaw to be the person she had shown herself to be, not the person I heard everyone else describing.

When I finally worked up my nerve, the gate swung open easily on well-oiled hinges. I stepped inside and made my way along a stone path. The remnants of a fish pond, where once a small hollow of water must have stood and fish must have risen to feed in the bubbles, had decayed into a chipped, hollow basin. A yellowed marble statue of a shepherd boy stood with his arms gesturing to the sky.

Oh, how I wanted to trust Miss Shaw. Oh, how I didn't want her to be hiding anything from me.

The farther I walked without finding anything suspicious, the more confident I became. And the more confident I became, the higher my heart began to lift. Until I spotted the open stretch of earth beyond two tall cedars in the distance. Then my pulse started to hammer in my throat. With one more step, I saw a plot with no ornamentation, no marker. This might have been the corner of any park, where a family would picnic, a child would play, except for the way this one square of earth had been mounded up and cleared of any leaves fluttering down. I knew then that I'd discovered something Miss Shaw wouldn't want me to see. I couldn't have been more certain if she had been there herself, leaning over it.

A grave site with no stone.

Maybe I can't trust anything Miss Shaw has ever said to me. Maybe she didn't tell me the truth about myself, either.

I have no idea how long I stood with my eyes locked on that spot of ground, my hands pressed to my stomach. I stood there until I lost track of time, until I could finally force air into my lungs again.

I pictured myself in a Grace Kelly movie—not one I knew, but one that hadn't been written yet. One directed by Alfred Hitchcock in which some horrible fiend was chasing Grace and she staggered against the wall in fright. Any minute, Cary Grant or Gary Cooper would swing her into his arms and shake her and say he'd come to save her, but she would wrench away. She would stand as straight as a lightning rod and lift her chin at him the same stately way I lifted mine, and she would say something sophisticated in her practiced, melodic voice.

I began to wander mindlessly, uncertain where to go. I left the cemetery and wandered the width of Lafayette Square, past rows of three-story houses, one of which had to be Miss Shaw's. I kept right on going. I didn't change direction or figure out where I was headed until I crossed Chouteau Street.

That's when I began to walk in the direction of the Ville. I felt as drawn to the Crocketts' house as shavings are drawn to a magnet. But where I'd once felt at ease roaming the Ville with Aurelia, I now felt like an interloper. On a street that had once seemed to pour its life out on me, I felt like anything I touched would dissipate into dust. I had given up my right to be here.

Yet here I was.

Aurelia's neighborhood seemed to crank to life the moment I stepped into it. Ahead of me a tabby cat with a cockeyed tail crossed the street at an angle. From an open window, I could hear a record player skipping over a song by Mamie Smith, one of those women who sang so strong, Eddie Crockett said the town musicians called them lung busters. A lone figure turned and swung a broom handle— a little boy not much bigger than Garland, who kept pitching a bottle cap caked with dirt into the air and aiming to slam it.

Still, the silence troubled me. Not silence, exactly, but the absence of the one sound that I loved above all others. The sound of

Aurelia's daddy wailing on his horn from the second-story window-sill like nobody's business.

I rounded the front of the Crocketts' flat, my heart feeling like it was going to rattle out of my chest from misery. I peered up at Eddie's window, noticing how empty and sad it looked. And while I was staring upstairs, I missed seeing him sitting right there on the front stoop.

"You gone and missed Garland's birthday party," he said, like I'd stopped by not three hours before.

That moment—seeing him there on the stoop—was the first time I understood that something doesn't disappear when you push it away. It waits for you, and eventually, when it beckons, you've got to go back to it.

Eddie Crockett wasn't holding a horn, but the fingers on his left hand kept moving just the same, rippling over invisible keys.

"They all went over to the Y to go swimming." When he spoke I felt like he shined on me, like the sun had suddenly moved out from behind a cloud.

"I'm too scared to see Aurelia," I blurted out. I hadn't known I was going to cry; I think Mr. Crockett saw it before I did.

"Baby girl," he invited me in a voice as warm as coffee and as rich as alderwood, and I went to him. He held me the way I'd always dreamed a father would hold me, safe against the front of his shirt while I clung to his collar and cried on his buttons. He held me tight with one massive fist pinned against my shoulder, rapping me with his knuckles for comfort. His empty shirt sleeve dangled at his side, ending in a thick knot.

"I'm s-sorry," I said with my teeth clenched, tears soaking his pocket, my nose starting to run. "I . . . I . . . *can't* . . ." I shook my head at him through my tears. "My sister is gone, and there isn't *anybody* . . ."

"Baby girl," he said, while I cried for myself and for Eddie Crockett's music and for Aurelia and because I didn't know if my mama or daddy ever really loved me. "I don't know what you been doing."

And Eddie Crockett, with his wounded arm, said, "Have you forgotten that there's just hurts you got to give over to the Lord, child? Because if you don't figure out how to do that, a body bigger than the whole world still won't be big enough to hold it all in."

Chapter Seventeen

$\mathcal{I}$ thought the first day of school would never get here. Now that the morning had arrived, the rubbery smell of my new book satchel filled the air as I stood on the front steps, watching the buses pull up. I waited for Aurelia, terrified that she wouldn't talk to me.

When I laid eyes on the low-slung building that morning, it seemed to have diminished in size. The grass in the schoolyard poked up in patches as iffy as fur on a mangy dog. Summer flowers that still bloomed in clumps beside the flagpole would be trampled by our horseplay within three days' time.

One new portable building had been set beside the others, its aluminum glinting bright beside the more weathered ones. A teacher stood on a chair outside her portable classroom, washing windows.

I saw the roof of the Ville bus coming as it slid behind the fence that separated our sidewalk from the long row of multiple-family dwellings behind it. I heard the engine shuddering as the bright egg-yolk-colored bus swayed stiffly around the turn. The monstrous flat face of it aimed straight at me with its grinning chrome grill, the headlamps like two colorless, knowing eyes.

The fender was about to swing up over the curb when the bus driver honked at me to get out of the way. I jumped two steps back, stumbled up over a third. For a few breathless seconds, the bus idled without opening its doors.

I was still waiting for the Ville kids to unload from the bus when Rosalyn and Cindy came from the opposite direction and shoved their way past me.

"What's the matter, Jenny?" Rosalyn said, low enough so only I could hear. "You waiting for the rest of your class to get here? Heard you're wanting to go to school in the portables this year. Heard the only friends you have go to class in those buildings."

It would have been the perfect chance to haul off and belt Rosalyn with my satchel. But the bus doors pleated open and the Ville students started hopping off. They didn't jostle me the way Rosalyn had done. Their tight-knit groups parted respectfully around me, giving me a wide berth, although they didn't make any sign of noticing I was there.

"Aurelia?" I looked everywhere for her, but she wasn't there.

The driver leaned forward and tipped his hat to me. "You waiting for Aurelia Crockett to get off this bus, you going to be standing here all day. Darnell bought himself a car, and they be arriving to school in style."

No sooner had he said that then a black rattletrap Ford pulled up behind the bus. Daddy's favorite saying about Fords came to mind: F.O.R.D. Found on Road Dead. I could see Garland's nose pressed against the glass. When the door opened and Aurelia climbed out, she looked first-rate.

She wore a pair of new Buster Brown saddle shoes and a skirt I recognized from last year, only her aunt must have sewn trim on it because it had a ribbon now that dressed it up. She wore her hair slicked down with gel and a white plastic bandeau. Aunt Maureen hadn't let her wear gel in her hair before. She wore a necklace of white beads as big around as Superman marbles.

Aurelia made a fine fashion statement, which is what everybody tried to do on the first day of school.

"Well, woo *woo*," I said, desperate to make her glance in my direction. "Don't you look nice?"

"Come on, Garland," she said. "We don't got all day for you to be scared about school. You take ahold of my hand now."

THE PENNY

I remembered that Garland's birthday had come and gone. He must be starting kindergarten in the portables with the rest of them.

When Garland saw me standing on the steps, he wrenched loose of Aurelia's hand and ran over.

"Miss Jenny," he said, lifting his palm up so I could see what was in it. "Look what I brought to the first day of school." He unclenched small, sweaty fingers and showed me the penny in his hand.

"That the one I think it is?"

"The same one I picked up the day you went to church with us," he said. "You saved yours. I saved mine, too. You remember?"

"Yep, I do. I remember lots of things."

But Garland must have caught me looking at it like I had no faith in it anymore. He tightened his grip around his penny again and shoved it inside his pocket.

"I brought it because this is my first real day of school," he insisted. "I wanted to have it with me after everything you said."

My reply sounded empty even to me. "Well, good. You hold on to it now." I raised my gaze to see Darnell behind the wheel, his arm extended across the front seat, watching us.

"You save up your box money for that car?" I asked, trying with everything I could to be friendly and erase the disapproval in his eyes.

I'd forgotten that Darnell wouldn't be coming to our school this year. I'd have no chance to redeem myself with him. After he dropped these two off, he was moving up to high school.

"Hey." He said the word sharp, meaning he wanted to talk to Aurelia and not me. "You going to be okay?"

"You get on out of here," Aurelia hollered, waving him off. "You're going to be late like the rest of us." Then: "Garland, come on." When Aurelia reached for Garland's hand again, she made a point of not meeting my eyes. She gave me plenty of space, just the same as everybody else.

"I saw your daddy," I said.

Long ago, when I'd tried to revive that redbird, I had held it in my grasp and rolled drops of water down its face, trying to make it move again. Instead it lay against my skin with its eyes clenched shut, its body dry and stiff. Aurelia's voice held the same dryness, the same stiffness, when she spoke now.

"I know. He said you came over. Seems funny you feel like you can walk into my house any time you want to, but when I want to bring news over to your place, I got no right."

"You should have called, maybe."

"See, that's what I mean. Come on, Garland. We got to go."

All this time, I'd been picturing how I'd keep Aurelia arguing and eventually I'd wear her down. I'd bring her around to my way of thinking. But what I hadn't imagined was the way it would wrench me inside, like I was falling down a well and there was nothing to stop me at the bottom, seeing Aurelia so hurt.

Once, I'd peered into a church window made to look like a dove's wing. Once, I'd thought Jesus could be more than just a doe-eyed picture I'd seen hanging in that foyer at Antioch Baptist Church on my way in. I'd seen the image of wheat in the window, a shape that pointed me to the wheat on the copper penny I held tight beneath my thumb. When I'd listened to Aurelia's preacher, I'd thought Jesus would come out swinging and throwing punches and wrestling the devil to the ground on my behalf.

But I'd given Jesus plenty of time to prove himself just the way that preacher said he'd do. As far as I could tell, Jesus had never even gotten started.

What difference did a penny make when I kept hurting every-body I loved this way?

"Go ahead." She made me so frustrated, I wanted to shout, *You ever think there might be a reason I did what I did?* But it was easier to hide behind being irate. "I sure don't care."

I saw her lay her hand against Garland's shoulder to hurry him along.

"That's right," I said louder. "You go on inside."

I saw Garland's head twist, saw his dark eyes search for my own. I narrowed my brows and glared fiercely at him. That was the last thing I needed, some little kid making me feel bad. Which doubled my aggravation, remembering how Garland had shown the penny to me in his sweaty palm. Now that I sneered at him, he scurried to his cousin's skirt in fear.

Darnell still hadn't driven away from the curb. Aurelia ignored me, but Darnell didn't. I saw him reach for his car handle. Any second he would unfold himself from behind the steering wheel of his rattletrap and come after me.

"You bothering my cousin for kicks? You don't talk to her, you hear me?"

"Aren't you supposed to be somewhere, Darnell?" I said with my fists half clenched at my sides. "You don't scare me."

"You mess with my cousin—" Darnell revved the engine on the Ford and from the way it clanked beneath the hood, it sounded like it was about to fall out. I saw him spit out the window and knew good and well what that meant. I'd seen him spit plenty when we'd arm wrestled in the Ville. He spat when he got mad. Darnell uttered the words just the same as when my elbow was planted on the porch table and he had my fingers in a vise and he thought he could slam my wrist down easy. "You're declaring a war you can't win."

"Too bad."

"You hurt her good."

"Well, maybe it's her own fault for letting herself get hurt by the breeze blowing the wrong way."

When Aurelia finally piped up behind me, her voice sounded as thin as a reed on the Blue Notes' oboe, ready to snap.

"Stop it, both of you! You're scaring Garland. He don't know what to think, the two of you talking that way."

Darnell spat again.

"Darnell," Aurelia said. "*Go on.*"

Class must have already started. Somewhere in the back of my mind, I thought I remembered hearing the bell ring. The doors to the portables had been firmly latched. Aurelia struggled with the unwieldy screen and managed to get somebody to unlock the door. She stuffed Garland inside, her backbone set straight as one of those broom handles they used to play games in the street.

"You said you were my friend," I accused, "but I guess it's plain you don't care that much about me," which made Aurelia wheel on me so fast that I got dizzy.

"You expecting me to say you're right so you can feel good about yourself? Well, you're expecting wrong."

I dropped my satchel, just stood there on the sidewalk.

"What is wrong with you, Jenny? What is *wrong with you*? One minute you're shoving us away and building brick walls around yourself so you won't get hurt. Next minute you're expecting us to be so perfect to you. There's no way we can do it."

"There is *nothing* wrong with *me*," I lied.

Aurelia went on inside then, but Darnell revved his engine again. When he did, he made such a racket that our principal finally came to investigate.

"What's going on out here?" Mr. Lancaster demanded.

I remember thinking two things when Mr. Lancaster came: (1) It was only the first day and I'd already made a mark for myself, just as sure as Aurelia had made hers with her saddle shoes and gelled hair; and (2) If Daddy got a call that I'd been out here shouting, he'd wipe the smile off my face with the back of his hand and then some. I was going to get it.

I'd lost Aurelia for good. I felt like I'd lost everything.

But Mr. Lancaster didn't notice me. He kept glaring at Darnell like a pit bull. Without taking his eyes off the ramshackle car, Mr. Lancaster snapped open his watch and held it so he could see its hands clicking slowly around in circles.

"Miss Blake, is this boy bothering you?" which struck me as odd because he'd called me by name and he knew Darnell just the same as he did me. Darnell had been one of his students last year.

I stared daggers at Darnell, but he didn't return the challenge. He just waited, looking at me. Then it must have hit him for sure because I saw him get scared. That's the minute I realized what I could do to him.

Daddy had put the meanness in me. The malice rose in me so fast I didn't see it coming. I could say one word and end it right here. I could pay Darnell back for every time he'd looked at me like I wasn't good enough to be seen in his neighborhood. I could pay him back for every time he'd glared down his nose at me, every time he'd tried to keep Aurelia from me because he thought it was my fault he couldn't try on a hat at a gentlemen's shop or buy a soft drink at a soda fountain.

He's acting out-of-place to me, I could have accused. And it wouldn't have been far from the truth. My word against his to Mr. Lancaster and I could have gotten Darnell into plenty of trouble.

He knew it, too. I saw a muscle flinch in his jaw. He just sat there in his car waiting for me to turn against him.

"You don't know a thing, Darnell," I said.

"Oh, yeah?"

"You don't know a thing about what's going on with me. The more you keep acting like you do, the dumber you seem."

"So, why don't you tell me?"

"What?"

"Why don't you tell me what's going on? If it's so important that it ruined your whole life, then why don't you tell me?"

I jammed my new satchel up beneath my arm. His daring me to speak felt especially dangerous. Daddy's words whispered their ominous threat; he had warned me, and I knew clear down to my soul that he meant it. *You breathe a word to anybody about what goes on in this house and you'll stir up trouble for the whole family.* "I wouldn't tell you anything if I *had* to, Darnell."

Yet one angry challenge from Darnell and here I was, perilously close to blurting everything out. Darnell stared me down, daring me to try to explain my deeds and my dark feelings when even *I* couldn't say where they had come from. It terrified me that he could make me even *think* of saying something.

"Miss Blake?" Mr. Lancaster persisted. When the principal grasped my shoulder this time, I recoiled, feeling Daddy's control over me, feeling encroached upon, not wanting any man to invade my space. The principal raised his brows at me in surprise.

"Miss Blake, you need to get to class. If you don't, you'll be marked tardy." I saw Darnell turn his attention to the road straight ahead. He stared at the spot where the two lanes converged into a point on the horizon, and re-curled his fingers around the steering wheel.

"It's okay," I said. "He's my friend. He isn't bothering me."

"I'm not any friend of yours." Darnell flexed his hands against the steering wheel again.

"Miss Blake, I don't think I need to remind you that this sort of behavior isn't appropriate."

The principal exhibited the clicking hands of his watch to Darnell. "You see the time on this watch? If you're not gone in three seconds flat, I'm calling the police. I will not have a kid like you hanging around, disrupting the Harris campus."

"He's going on to school." I turned to Darnell. "Aren't you?"

Aurelia's cousin arched his neck and rolled his eyes skyward, pushing against the wheel as if he wanted to push away Mr. Lancaster's words; he glowered at the dashboard like the car itself had become his enemy.

I had to bite my tongue to keep from saying, *"There's all sorts of things that aren't appropriate, Mr. Lancaster, and I can tell you exactly what they are."*

Darnell threw the Ford into gear and it sounded like it might detonate as he laid his foot on the accelerator. All that week you could tell Darnell had peeled out of there. His tires left black rubber scars beside the curb in the street, scars just as dark as the scars on my heart.

Chapter Eighteen

That afternoon after school, even though I'd been scheduled to go to work for Miss Shaw, I went to the Fox Theater by myself and saw *The Country Girl* instead. It was the first time I'd ever gone to a picture show without my sister. I huddled alone, the itchy seat giving me fits, the popcorn tasting like greasy pulp, the guilt over not showing up for work eating a painful hole in my stomach.

"How could you be so angry at someone you didn't even know?" Grace asked William Holden as I nestled deeper into my seat, my hand curled inside the popcorn bucket. Leave it to Grace Kelly to voice the precise thought that had been running through my head all day.

William told Grace, "Maybe I really wasn't. Maybe I screamed at you to keep myself at an angry distance." And I thought, *Me, too.*

I walked out of the darkness into the late-afternoon light and realized I'd been so focused on watching Grace Kelly that I *felt* like Grace. If I had caught a glimpse of myself in a reflection as I passed a window, I would have been astonished not to see the polished woman who spoke with trained, rounded vowels, and touched the stray wisp of hair at her neck whenever she considered a thought, and clasped her hands over the hollow at her throat when she had something consequential to say.

I remembered making fun of my sister as she peered at me through tortoiseshell sunglasses, imagining herself as Grace. And here I was, imagining the same. *You're not her. You'll never be her.*

Well, now I understood Jean exactly. Thinking about all things Grace Kelly made it a lot easier not to think about Aurelia or Miss Shaw or Daddy or anything else going on.

"You have the strength to trust," Miss Shaw had told me once. *"You hold on to that because it's being given to you."*

Yes, I could have answered her then if I had known. *I want to trust you.*

Mr. Witt tipped his hat at me as I stepped outside the Fox Theater box office. "Glad you've been making good use of those free tickets, Jenny," he said.

"I've been making good use of them, all right," I answered. "Can't use them up nearly so fast now that Jean isn't here."

The green, silver-lettered awning that shaded the door to Shaw Jewelers lifted and fell in the evening breeze. From where I stood, I could see the CLOSED sign Miss Shaw must have flipped inside the door when she'd finally given up on me. Every evening when Miss Shaw departed, she adjusted the chain so the sign would hang at its usual perfect angle. Now it hung sideways, as if she had slapped the card over in frustration and left in haste. When I cupped my hands around my face and peered inside the darkened shop window, I could see a folded rag and a pile of price tags and an assortment of office files she had readied for my attention. I stood on the outside looking in, my insides consumed with a gnawing sense of regret.

I knew where I had to go. I began to run.

I ran because I wanted to get away from myself, because I wanted to get away from my whole life. I ran because I wanted to escape the fear that all the pennies I'd found on the pavement were meaningless, that they didn't carry a message from someone who cared about me the way Miss Shaw said they did.

I looked up every so often, searching people's faces to find the one person I needed most. But Miss Shaw wouldn't be walking along the sidewalk anyway. If she wanted to find me, she would tie on a scarf and don tortoiseshell sunglasses and drive through the streets in her baby-blue convertible. Nobody ever saw her driving without her scarf, knotted beneath her chin.

When I heard a car approaching from behind, I slowed down, thinking for one insane moment that it might be Miss Shaw searching for me. But when it turned out to be a police cruiser instead, I hurried away from the curb and stood against the wall of Baker's Alterations and Dry Cleaning, staring at the electrical lines overhead, gasping for breath.

The sound of my sandals slapping the pavement seemed to come from far away. I swung aboard the first streetcar that intersected my path. Every seat was taken, even now that dusk had settled in. I held onto the brass rail overhead as hot air chased my hair across my eyes in tatters.

When I disembarked and neared the house, my feet slowed. My sandals seemed to weigh more with each step I took as the tar sucked at my soles. I wanted to tell Miss Shaw the truth about my life so bad that I felt like I was going to burst open, but I just couldn't trust her, or anybody else for that matter.

Miss Shaw's house, across from Lafayette Park, was encircled by a high brick wall and latched behind a formidable double iron gate. The courtyard, which once must have been laden with flowers, was now overrun with brambles and weeds. It astonished me that Miss Shaw would run a jewelry shop where everything glittered with light, yet she would live in a house like this one. Any house where Miss Shaw lived ought to be dazzling with gleaming windows—shutters thrown open, flowers overflowing their pots along the windowsills. I'd noticed Miss Shaw's cheerful blue convertible parked out in front. But the façade of this brownstone looked like a closed, empty face.

As I raised my hand to the brass knocker on the towering mahogany door, I was terrified that I shouldn't have come.

When I lifted the knocker and let it drop, its heavy echo lingered for a lengthy moment. My ears buzzed; maybe I shouldn't have come. But if I was known for anything, it was for being stubborn. I remained rooted to the spot. After an excruciatingly long time, heavy footsteps approached the door. I had no idea what to expect as the door swung open.

The woman wore the crisp uniform of a professional housekeeper, spotlessly black with a ruffled white apron, and a cap pinned over her hair. She opened the door only a crack and looked as if she wanted to keep me out.

"Yes?"

"I—I'm here to see Miss Shaw."

"I don't know—"

"Miss *Opal* Shaw," I persisted, fully expecting her to say that I had the wrong home entirely.

But hearing the name a second time seemed to clarify it to her some way. She gave a nod that told me she understood, but that it was still entirely her own prerogative whether or not she allowed me to enter.

"Is she here?"

"Miss Shaw?"

"Yes."

"And who might you be?"

I told her my name, and it surprised me to no end when she seemed to recognize it. She stepped backward and gave me entrance immediately.

"Of course, Jenny. If you'll wait here in the sitting room, I'll let her know you're here."

I sat perfectly still on the silk couch, allowing neither my feet to jostle nor my hands to fidget. Beyond my left elbow sat a crystal canister filled with butterscotch drops, but I didn't dare help myself to one. She'd put me in a small sitting area at the front of the house, where every stick of furniture faced the white marble fireplace with its ornate andirons and the adjoining bay window swathed by yards of lace.

Until this moment, I hadn't known a house existed like this anywhere in St. Louis. This was a progressive city, with its jazz music, and its blaring televisions that had recently amazed viewers with the first coast-to-coast broadcast, and its Sportsman's Park baseball team that had been sold to Anheuser-Busch. But this house, with its musty smell and its broad open archways and its mahogany newel posts, its velvet-seated chairs and its fringed rug that felt as spongy as moss when I'd set my foot upon it, seemed like it dated back to the days of Tom Sawyer. Everything inside this place seemed bound to the past.

The house, which had seemed silent at first, now whispered with sound. A floorboard complained overhead. From somewhere in the distance, I heard what sounded like a kettle clattering to the floor. I stared at an oil painting of the Soulard Historic District, bouncing the toe of my left sandal on the floor.

When Miss Shaw finally entered, she looked just as beautiful and timeless and poised as always, wearing her blue jacket buttoned at her waist and a pearl brooch upon her collar. "Oh, *Jenny*."

The white linen of her gloves felt smooth and cool against my skin when she took my face in her hands.

"Are you okay? I tried to call to find out why you didn't come to work this afternoon. Do you know how impossible it is to get through on your family's party line?"

The worst thing you can do is go into a day being afraid, I remembered she'd once told me. I stepped away from her hands, not wanting her to touch me. "I'm not coming back to the shop. I don't need your job anymore," I lied.

"Jenny, please don't—"

"Besides, if I *were* to have a job, I'd want to work for someone who everybody *likes*. Nobody likes to be with you because they're all afraid of you. Nobody knows a *thing* about you."

I heard the wind rustle the leaves outside.

"That's why I came here. I wanted to say that."

The distant barking of dogs made town seem far away. The giant house stood dignified and serene around us, waiting, as if it, too, wanted to keep Miss Shaw's secrets concealed.

"And I wanted to find out why you didn't tell me about the grave you go to. I wanted to find out why you didn't tell me the rumor was true."

Miss Shaw lowered herself to the couch.

"I *gave* you the chance to tell me. When we were riding in your car that day. But you didn't."

She clutched her throat with her glove, the way I'd seen Grace Kelly do in the movies about a hundred times.

"I said, 'They say they've seen you in a cemetery sitting on the ground beside a grave without any stone. It's crazy, isn't it, all the things people say about you?'"

As she began to tighten her earbob, I could see her hands shaking. "Everybody has stories they'd rather keep to themselves. Are you going to make up your own mind about me, or just go by what other people think? Haven't you figured out we met each other for a special reason?"

"We met each other because of the penny. But I don't care about the penny anymore."

"It's more than just a penny. It's a message. Can't you see that?"

I wanted to clap my hands over my ears. "Don't talk to me about the penny anymore," I insisted. "I'm sick of hearing about the stupid penny."

She gave up on her earbob and let it fall into her lap.

"I'm not letting go of you," she said. "Because I know I'm not supposed to."

"You sit at a grave with no marker." Childishly, I wasn't going to let her divert me from my anger, my distrust. "And no one who talks about you has any idea who's in it."

"You know the other thing everyone whispers about?" Miss Shaw asked, her eyes boring intensely into mine. "Everyone wants to know why I don't take off my gloves. They haven't asked, but they've thought about it. Haven't you heard them gossiping about that, too?"

Dumbly, I nodded.

She fumbled with the miniature buttons at her wrists. Once those had been freed, she tugged first the end of one finger then another. She loosed her right hand and then her left. Fear shot through me. "I'll have to show you," she said.

For all the stock I placed in people's hands, I never could have guessed what Miss Shaw's hands looked like. When she slipped the gloves off and laid her fingers before me, the hands Miss Shaw revealed spoke a terrible story.

"What happened?" I barely dared to ask.

For so long, I'd wanted to see her hands. Wanted to find out who she *was*.

Miss Shaw's hands were the most damaged hands I'd ever seen, yet they were also the most gentle. Where the underside of Miss Shaw's thumb met her palm, the skin was drawn so tight that it appeared translucent. Each knuckle was webbed with angry white slashes. Thick ropes of red ran the length of several of her fingers. I couldn't take my eyes off of them. I wanted to take her hands into my own and weep over them.

I remembered the first time I'd seen my hands and Miss Shaw's side-by-side in the jewelry case. Hers had appeared so refined and beautiful; mine had been so small and grimy by comparison. Now it seemed the opposite. My hand appeared stronger, more capable, than her scarred one somehow.

"My mother had a mental illness, an explosive temper. She punished me by locking me in a dark closet for things I didn't do. This happened to my hands on jelly-canning day. I broke one of her plates while I was washing dishes."

I reached to take her hand and she flinched. When Miss Shaw held her hand level so I could grasp it, I could see it was a struggle for her to let me do it.

"That's my mother in the grave, Jenny. That's how she repaid me for breaking her best china plate. She grappled me by the arms and made me plunge my hands in the boiling water."

For all these long years, I had managed to build walls around the hurt in my own life. Nothing could have prepared me for the surge of distress that hit as I realized this mysterious friend—whose kind interest in me had worn down my guard—had endured a wound so demeaning and awful herself.

"Mother boiled my hands with the canning jars. She held them down so long, I wanted to die. Not just because of how the water cooked my skin on the outside, but because of how it killed me on the inside." Miss Shaw said, "Not many people know how it feels to be so hurt on the inside that you'd rather die than live with it."

But I do. Oh, I do. I couldn't hear past the roaring in my ears. I physically ached for her, in a way I never could have grieved for myself. And yet, I *did* mourn for myself. Touching Miss Shaw's wounded hands brought me up against every crippling wound that lay inside me.

Her bare fingers lay slender and scarred and cool in my palm. I couldn't take my eyes from them, I suddenly loved them so. "Your hands are beautiful."

"Are they?"

I raised them to my face and touched their coolness to the side of my cheek. "Yes." I lifted my eyes to hers.

I began to sob uncontrollably, and Miss Shaw gathered me into her arms and held me in such a way that I felt secure for the first time I could ever remember. She let me cry for a long time until she finally asked me if I wanted to talk about anything. I opened my mouth intending to say no, but the truth started pouring from my lips and did not stop until I had shared everything with Miss Shaw about what Daddy did to Jean and me and how Mama did nothing to help us. I told her how afraid I felt every minute of my life. Miss Shaw cried with me and assured me that she understood and would help me in any way that she could.

Miss Shaw might never know how telling me the truth about her life had given me courage to tell *her* the truth, too.

I told her how I resented Mama and was ashamed that she didn't love us enough to protect us. Miss Shaw told me that she understood about feeling ashamed.

"I never wanted to mark her grave, you see. I never wanted to inscribe a name to it that said, 'My Mother.' Because to inscribe even that much on her stone meant I had to admit that the person I wanted to care about me the most was the person who made me believe the worst about myself."

I couldn't believe Miss Shaw was telling me these things. I couldn't believe it had happened in her life, too. *She's done a fine job of hiding it*, I thought.

"After a while, I wouldn't let myself care anymore. I thought I had buried my pain with her, but actually I buried it inside myself where it silently continued to hurt me. I tried to hide it just as I tried to hide the scars on my hands." Miss Shaw nodded toward her gloves on the table beside us.

I reminded her, "But you go and sit beside her. That's what everyone gossips about. You should hear what they say."

"She died soon after, while my hands were still bandaged, before I had the chance to forgive her. It took me a long time to forgive her in my heart. I go to that grave every day to remind her—and myself—that I forgive her now. That Jesus sees our big hurts and our small hurts, and offers grace to heal them all."

Her words touched a place deep inside me.

I'd wanted to trust Miss Shaw for so long, but Daddy had it so I had a hard time trusting anybody.

"Haven't you heard that God gives one of his most delightful gifts when he gives people to each other? I believe God has given us to each other." She paused. "Don't ever let someone pass off this earth without forgiving them, Jenny. Unforgiveness will hurt you every day of your life. Just see how it hurts me."

So many times in the past I'd put a clamp on my heart, refusing to let her see what was inside me. But something broke in me that day, and I finally felt free to pour forth my questions and views about many things. We talked for what seemed like hours.

"You've been hiding your hands from me and everybody else," I mentioned. "So, are you going to keep hiding them from Del Henry?"

Her maid, Doris, had brought us a pot of tea, and Miss Shaw filled the cup at my side. I said, "I sure don't think Del Henry comes into your shop to buy charms for his granddaughter."

Color rose in her cheeks. I'd never seen Miss Shaw blush before. I said, "Now that *I've* been to your house, I think you should have Del Henry over, too. I think you ought to have him over for dinner. I know he'd jump at the chance to be with you."

All the time I'd known her, I'd never seen her speechless. Because I knew what we shared, Miss Shaw meant more than anything to me now. I wanted to be there for her and save her from being alone. "I *knew* you liked Del Henry. *Anybody* could have seen through *that* plan."

"What plan? Jenny Blake, I don't know what you're talking about."

"The bricks. Nobody uses bricks in a *jewelry* store! You wanted bricks in your window because you knew Del Henry collects bricks.

You thought it would give him a reason to come into the store and see you!"

"Oh, *that*," she commented as, barehanded, she sipped her tea with great innocence. "Well, it worked, didn't it?"

"It worked."

"What more could I ask for, then?"

"There *is* another thing you *could* ask for," I hinted mysteriously.

She waited with the question in her eyes. *Yes?*

My voice went as conspiratorial as Jean's was when she told me the latest gossip she'd heard on our party line. I proceeded to tell Miss Shaw everything I'd observed while I'd worked on her watch displays. I told her how Del Henry had checked his reflection in the mirror at least a dozen times, and how he'd adjusted his new suit, and how Joe had teased him because it was from Boyd's.

"And there's something else, too. Be prepared, because one of these days, he's going to ask you to Rigazzi's for Italian."

"Well, can't he see?" she said with a little *humph* of impatience. "That's exactly what I'd like him to do!" Then, "If Delbert likes Italian, I could certainly bake some lasagna. I could fix veal parmesan. Or even spaghetti and meatballs. What do you think?"

"How am I supposed to know what you ought to fix him?" I asked her. "You think I know everything?"

"Oh, Jenny," she said, laughing. "Sometimes I think you do."

Miss Shaw wore a satisfied grin for the rest of my visit and I felt important for my part in it. When I left that evening, even though the sky was already dark and the moon was beginning to appear and I knew Daddy would let loose on me the second I stepped through the door so late in the evening, I felt like I'd stepped out into light.

Chapter Nineteen

$\mathcal{I}$ couldn't have known, when I walked along with the jostle of students the next morning, that Aurelia and I were about to start out on one of the most astonishing days of our lives. There wasn't a thing that could have warned either of us as I shoved my satchel inside my locker and slammed the door hard to make it stay shut. It was only the second day of school and I'd already committed a vast fashion mistake with my satchel. Everybody else carried their books bound by a belt.

Mrs. Huffines started us off simply enough that day with eighth-grade math. I could only guess that they were working on the same fractions, decimals, and percentages next door in the portables. Mrs. Huffines resembled a homing pigeon as she paced across the front of the room, her derriere swinging to and fro. She was right in the middle of demonstrating how to divide a four-digit decimal number by a two-digit decimal number (you first place the dividend above the division bracket, then you place the divisor beneath it. You multiply them both by ten so they're no longer decimals but whole numbers) when the sirens began to sound.

We froze in our seats, looking at each other, trying to figure out what we were supposed to do. The siren keened up the scale and then stayed there, shrieking.

"Be orderly, please," Mrs. Huffines said, her instructions suddenly very pointed. "This is an air-raid drill in case of nuclear attack," she told us in such a calm manner that we realized the teachers had been given prior warning. "The way we take action today might very well save our lives someday."

This was about the most exciting thing that had happened to us in a schoolroom since Toby Wallace did his science project on how the size of a pumpkin relates to the force needed to break it. We filed into the hallway as directed, sat in a line against the wall, and positioned our heads between our knees. Even in this pose we couldn't help conferring with each other.

"Expect they'll take us down the street to the fallout shelter?"

"It's happened! The A-bomb. They've launched it!"

With our heads positioned between our knees, it was impossible to tell who was talking. Muffled voices went up and down the line.

"I'll bet they saw something coming toward us in the sky."

"I think I saw something."

"You can't see anything. You have your head down!"

"I don't mean *now*. I mean *then*. I saw something in the sky right before the alarm."

"Well, I hope you can see the stitches in your pants right now."

"Shut up, why don't you?"

"We're goners, all right. It'll hit any minute."

After half an hour of making sure we weren't about to get wiped off the map, Mrs. Huffines herded us back to the room to pick up on decimals where we'd left off. But suddenly I smelled an odd mixture of smoke and melting plastic. Running to the window, I saw smoke churning out from under the portables' bathroom. Set loose by the bomb drill at last, Andrew Scott and Charlie Bidden must have seen the perfect opportunity to make good on their cherry-bomb-the-portable-bathroom plans.

Mrs. Connor compared notes with Mr. Lancaster. "We're going to have to bring the whole school outside until the coast is clear. I could have *told* you those weeds would ignite. At least everyone's accounted for."

"Is it cherry bombs?" I asked stupidly.

She didn't seem to hear and went right on talking in Mr. Lancaster's ear. "*Portables*. What a nuisance. I don't know whose idea this was in the first place. If these colored children had stayed where they were supposed to stay, in their *own* brick building, I can tell you for sure *that* building wouldn't ignite. Now *this* is going to be mass hysteria."

It didn't look like hysteria to me. Mrs. Connor liked to make a production out of everything. Except for the excitement over the smoldering grass that threatened to make headway in the direction of the National Bank, and Mr. Lancaster picking up the hose to spray around the portable and douse the blackened grass, the mishap didn't seem all that threatening. Mr. Lancaster rattled around inside the main building for a while, making sure nothing inside had caught fire. Until he gave us the *all clear*, we stood in the yard and sized each other up, the portable kids and those of us who went to class in the real-brick building. It was our first chance, as an entire class, to be in the yard at the same time and get a good look at each other.

"Come on, students." Mrs. Huffines clapped her hands. "Back inside. We're free to go and we're wasting time."

But nobody moved.

"Come on, students. Math is over—and we're halfway through the history period and we haven't even started on the lesson."

Maybe it was just the same as Monday nights on the *Admiral*, where everyone was so used to judging people's worth by the shade of their skin. Maybe somebody made a comment to somebody else, and that's what got everybody shinnied up. Maybe it started because somebody looked across the yard and thought of the protestors marching with their signs, yelling that different colors shouldn't mix.

One minute we were standing around wishing for a way to miss out on history period entirely, and the next, most of the white kids I knew had taken off through the weeds toward the damaged portable, their footprints smudging the burned grass. As soon as they pushed against it, one side of the schoolroom lifted. It hung in the air for the longest time before it dropped to the ground again. The portable pitched to one side like a railroad car jostling over a snag in the track. The other side lifted, smashing down to the ground with splintering wood, shattering glass.

Kids got on every side, rocking the whole building. Farther and farther it tilted as erasers took wing and wooden chairs cartwheeled out and insulation flew and a spelling book fluttered to the playground like a battered sparrow.

"Oh, of course *you're* not going to do this," Rosalyn shrieked at me as she jumped in to shove, too. "They can take their portables, all right! Send these things back where they ought to have stayed."

Somebody else shouted, "Now *this* is really rock-and-roll!"

Aurelia and her classmates huddled around the colored grammar schoolers, their eyebrows knit together in indignation, too shocked to do anything but watch. I saw it all, and the same thing came up in me then that had come up when I faced Darnell on the first day of school. The meanness that had spilled over from Daddy, that I hadn't known was in me, filled me up until there was no room for anything else.

Suddenly I wanted to rough up the portables, too. I wanted to stand beneath the rain of glass and listen to the dented tin echo as loud and hollow as a kettle drum. I wanted to be powerful. Not powerful with love, not powerful with greatness, but powerful with the ability to crush something and see it destroyed.

I felt it soul-deep, a dark authority that urged me on in a voice that sounded like Daddy's. If I went out and smashed up something myself, maybe that would fend off everything that hurt inside of me. *Because the harder I try to hurt something, the more I can keep from feeling the shame in me.*

Rosalyn's fingers were real cut up, and her knuckles oozed blood when I ran up beside her. Down the way, one of our teachers had retrieved a tire iron from his car and started prying loose the pre-fab panels the way you'd peel away a deviled-ham can. I glanced at Mr. Lancaster and Mrs. Connor to see if they'd get as mad at these grown-up teachers as they'd gotten at the cherry-bomb boys. But they stared ahead like they didn't see. I guess they figured it was out of their hands.

With my own knotted fists, I pummeled the ruined walls. I detested my hands because they resembled Daddy's. I hated my stumpy fingers because they were shaped like his. But even though I loathed the malice rising in me, the harder I hit, the better I felt. Rosalyn glanced at me with approval. I'd moved up several notches in her estimation, I could see. As the portable fell toward us, Rosalyn shielded her face with injured hands, and I shoved the wall so hard that I felt it clear to my backbone. The door flew off its hinges. It lurched onto the other side again, with loose school supplies launching through the shattered windows. Some teacher's purse must've opened up, or somebody's lunch money must have come free from its handkerchief, because right then, over my head, an arch of pennies sailed out—a spray of stars, glinting copper in the sun, like a gift, pausing in the light overhead, reminding me that Jesus saw, that he cared, that he loved me no matter what I'd done, that he loved me no matter what had happened to me. Everywhere I turned, pennies rained on me like grace. Rosalyn raised her hands to shield her face, and I raised my hands to catch pennies.

I wasn't going to let Daddy's anger turn me into a person like him. I had wanted to break things, and here I was with pennies instead. As I bent to gather them up, their divine message to me ripped the force right out from under my anger. Pennies lay everywhere at my feet, mixed with shards of glass and slivers of asbestos and tin.

I picked up as many as I could and shoved them into my pockets. Rosalyn kept right on shoving the wall away, and she took it on herself to let me know she thought I was shirking my job.

"You're so stupid, Jenny, you don't even know how to knock a portable building down."

Well, no. I didn't. It had never been high on my list of things to learn. From that moment, seeing what was going on inside me, seeing all those pennies flying overhead, Rosalyn Keys ceased to annoy me. I guess that was the moment I could first see it—how a person's words said a whole lot more about the person who said them than they did about the person they were said to.

Leave it to Aurelia to be brave enough to walk right up to me in the middle of the whole thing. I sighed deep. What could she want now, after she'd given me the cold shoulder and said, in no uncertain terms, that she didn't want a thing to do with me?

I soon found out.

"Jenny, I can't find Garland."

"What do you mean, you can't find Garland?"

"He isn't with his class."

"He has to be."

"Well, he isn't."

Garland had to be around somewhere, I knew it. With my eyes shaded, I surveyed the kindergarten class assembled in the shade of an ash tree. His teacher sat on the ground in the middle of the pack, playing finger games and reciting stories, anything to keep them from crying. The portable hung in the air again, and in that instant, it got so quiet you could hear the buzz of people talking, the elegant trill of a cardinal in a tree overhead. By the time the portable came down with its resounding crash, Aurelia had gone to check Garland's class again. When she turned to me from a distance, she shook her head.

Aurelia must have said something, because I saw the teacher stir. I heard someone shout from one group to another. Garland's teacher came running with her skirts flailing, sweat sheening her burnt-coffee-colored face, leaving her flock behind to find one little lost lamb.

The portable slipped sideways and, for one split second, I caught a glimpse inside the window. I could just make out the black silhouettes of the presidents of the United States on the tattered display. Every president from George Washington clear through to Dwight D. Eisenhower. The portrait of Abraham Lincoln, crisp as a kettle, stared into space with a grizzled beard and lips that slipped into a half-smile.

My heart knotted inside my throat. I shoved my hands into both pockets and felt the warm copper of all the pennies there. Just like the stained-glass wheat I'd spied at Aurelia's church, that side view of Abraham Lincoln was on every coin I'd just finished stuffing into my pocket.

When you live with somebody who hits you all the time, you just get used to doing things scared. I grabbed Rosalyn's arm and she tried to shake me off.

"You've got to stop rocking it, you hear me?" Maybe a few of them listened, I don't know. "You got to *stop.*"

Somebody gave the portable one last shove so hard that it pitched wildly starboard and came to a crashing rest on its side.

I just kept screaming. "You got to *stop!* You *got* to!" Then I looked around, amazed and baffled. Everybody already *had* stopped. The only person still shouting was me.

Aurelia clambered her way up the underside of the building by finding footholds in the dented panels. Mr. Lancaster shouted at us, but the climbing didn't look too hard so I scaled it, too, right behind Aurelia.

"Mrs. Connor is calling the fire department. They'll have ladders."

But as we dropped inside the gaping door onto a tangle of drywall and desks, I heard Mr. Lancaster climbing up after us.

I'd never been inside a portable before, even one that was right side up. The space seemed to stretch as long and narrow and dark as a tunnel until our eyes adjusted. Debris had gnawed through the insulation in plenty of spots. The only way to move around in here without getting cut was to test each step before taking it.

Aurelia pointed toward the rear of the classroom, with the bathroom door flapping sideways on its hinges.

"Maybe back there. Be careful, Jenny." Her beautiful brown cheeks were burnished with tears, streaked with soot. "We've got to find Garland. This whole place could cave in like a tin can."

"If he's in here, we'll find him, Aurelia."

"Girls. It's too dangerous," Mr. Lancaster shouted. "Come out and let a grown-up do this."

I don't know what Aurelia thought, but I figured that the grown-ups had already had plenty of time to make things right. Mr. Lancaster's outline loomed behind me, and he looked as big as a giant as he reached to collar me.

"I don't think he's over here," Aurelia called. "I can't see anything."

Just then I heard a small voice whimpering. There were so many loose pieces of glass and plywood, I didn't know where to step as I lurched out of Mr. Lancaster's reach.

I found Garland wedged beneath the inside wall and the sideways commode, which must have been the only object in the whole place bolted tight enough not to shift or break loose.

"Aurelia. Over here!" As I made my way toward Garland, Mr. Lancaster went into immediate rescue mode.

"Jenny Blake, get back. Let me lift him."

"Is the A-bomb gone yet?" Garland asked me. "Was it the bomb that got us?"

What we saw when we approached stopped us, all three. Garland braced his head against a snarl of pipes, completely unaware that a piece of metal window frame had impaled itself in his head. A stream of sticky black, darker than his skin, ran down the length of his neck and encrusted the collar of his little shirt.

"Is the bomb gone yet?" he repeated.

"It wasn't a bomb, Garland. It was a practice."

"But the sirens kept going and going."

"I know."

"I thought we were supposed to hide because it was a bomb."

Garland's face was so dark and dirt-smudged. Even his brows and eyelashes were caked with soot.

"Don't move him, child." Mr. Lancaster touched my shoulder. "We'll get an ambulance."

"When are you coming to my house again?" Garland asked me. "Why were you looking at me mad the other day? I got something I been wanting to show you. Got a new broomball move—bouncing it off the front step at Carter's so it curves across the street. You want to see that?"

"I'll get help," Mr. Lancaster told Aurelia. "You stay with your cousin."

Aurelia nodded, too stunned to speak.

"I want to see your broomball move," I said.

Garland reached his hand toward mine. "Would you hang onto me, Jenny?" he asked. "You want to hang onto me? Because if you do, it'll make me feel better."

Mr. Lancaster was babbling to Aurelia, distraught. "We're going to get your aunt here . . . Not going to tell her what's happened yet. . . . Not going to get her all worked up or anything."

"Of course I'll hang onto you," I said, and the rush of blood in my ears came because, after all the lies I'd told, and me chasing Aurelia away from my flat, this one small boy was the one to make those missteps fade into the background. Garland's little fingers, warm and sticky, slid against mine without hesitation. I wrapped my knuckles around his and stared at the knot we made together. If all my life had been shaped by other people's hands, then Garland helped shape my life now because he'd offered me his hand so freely.

Mr. Lancaster left to get help, and as the three of us waited alone, we listened for sirens to run their scales, coming toward us. It had started with Garland asking me to hang onto him in that damaged portable. I hung on to this truth that I found in Garland's grasp: that if you offered your hand to reassure and be of good use to someone, it went a long way toward helping you overcome how somebody else's hand had done you harm.

Another slab of drywall collapsed, crumbling apart over us like a dry biscuit.

"Watch out!" Aurelia shielded her cousin with her arms. She and I met each other's eyes, drywall dust spattering our faces. "If you hadn't been the one to make them stop, Jenny, they wouldn't have. They never would have listened to me."

I ducked away so I could look at her straight. "Maybe they would have."

"If you hadn't been right there and all of a sudden started screaming . . ."

I just kept thinking, *But I shouldn't have been right there in the first place.*

Aurelia asked, "What's gotten *into* people? Why are people so mean? I don't understand it."

I couldn't say what had gotten into them. I couldn't say what had gotten into me, either. But I kept my promise about hanging onto Garland even after Mr. Lancaster told me I had to step aside to make room for the emergency workers. I told Mr. Lancaster that I wouldn't, and I just wedged myself closer in beside Aurelia's little cousin. I wished I'd taken time to tell Garland how the pennies had come spraying out at me like hose water. He'd always been one to believe God was putting pennies in our paths to remind us about his love, ever since the day I got saved at Antioch Baptist Church. I realized God used pennies to say the same thing I'd told Garland: *I'm not letting go of you. No matter what happens.* Garland would have loved to hear that.

I kept my promise even when Mr. Lancaster pulled out his hand-kerchief and said, "Here, let's clean you up some, boy. Just wipe some of that blood off. Wouldn't do for those kids outside to get upset—"

"No." It was the first time Aurelia had spoken since we'd gotten down there. Her answer was as firm as the ground, as sharp-edged as one of those bricks Del Henry was so proud of collecting. "You can't clean that up, sir. You leave him the way he looks so everybody out there can see."

"Let's get him out," a fireman said. Then everything started whir-ring fast, vague, and distant so that it's hard to remember at all. We stuck together close, climbing up out of that portable. I didn't let go of Garland's hand until he got hoisted from the gaping hole ahead of me. I could see Aurelia's lips moving, and although she'd talked lots about praying, that was the first time I'd seen her do it out of the pew. When the schoolyard crowd got a good look at what had happened to Garland, their murmurs subsided. It got so hushed, you could almost hear the grass grow.

Only the bluebird tuned up again, proclaiming its strident, clear song from the ash tree.

Chapter Twenty

$\mathcal{A}$t home that night, my mind ran so fast that I felt like I had light-ning trapped inside my skull. But everything around me moved as slow as the water in the Mississippi. Daddy cutting his Salisbury steak one-handed, rocking his fork in a slow see-saw. Me rinsing the plates before I propped them in the drainboard, the bubbles sliding away from me in slow circles. Mama bouncing the clean laundry in its basket, asking me to help her fold the bedsheets. Our slow dance, matching corner to corner, seam to seam.

Other than leaving right in front of Daddy or making a phone call that would get me hit again, I didn't have any way to find out how Garland had fared. Our principal had sent the portable kids home early; I'd overheard him say to Mrs. Connor that he didn't know where to put them. Our class had been rounded up, returned to our room, and made to sit through Mrs. Huffines' insufferable lesson on which American colonies were involved in the First Con-tinental Congress, scripting the *Declaration of Rights and Grievances* to be sent to King George III. A lucky few of us got to escape our seats for a few minutes to have Mercurochrome smeared on various scrapes and cuts by the school nurse. Getting out of Mrs. Huffines' lecture was "a right and a grievance" I would take any time.

Normally I could walk around the flat with Daddy's finger-sized bruises on my arms and Mama never said a word. I was so used to her looking the other way that it shocked me when she noticed the red smears of antiseptic on my hands and started lecturing.

"You don't get any of that Mercurochrome dye on those bedcovers, you hear me?" She nodded her head in the direction of my hands while we were folding sheets together. "Just patched the one and bleached them all, and I don't want to see any spots anywhere."

I stopped altogether and looked at her for a minute. "I tried to wash it off, Mama," I told her, "but it wouldn't come."

"I didn't say to stop helping me." She shook her end of the sheet at me like a matador urging me to charge. The sheet sounded a *snap* in midair. "I just said you need to watch out." Then, "You could try again. Wash harder this time."

A wave of weariness broke over me. "There are some things that don't wash off, Mama." It made me so tired that she never changed.

"It seems to me you could take better care of your hands. How could you let them get all cut up like that?"

"Maybe you don't want to know how I got all cut up," I said. "Maybe you don't want to know *anything*."

"Knowing isn't what hurts the most," she said. "It's trying to do something about it."

Daddy thumped into the den then, carrying his workboots and a tin of saddle soap. "Trying to do something about what?" He dropped the polish and the boots on the floor and waited for Mama's answer.

The cat clock in the kitchen ticked off the seconds between us. The longer Mama stayed silent, the more my heart twisted tight. Mama wasn't going to respond the way I still stubbornly hoped she would. My chin dropped in disappointment. And that's the minute the phone rang.

Daddy plopped on the couch, twisted the lid off the saddle soap. He dipped his brush into the soap and daubed it across the leather upper. "They'll have to call back tomorrow at a decent hour," he said. "Why would anybody think we'd be answering the telephone this late?"

"Maybe it's Jean," Mama suggested.

"She knows we wouldn't want to be interrupted."

"But Jean's our *daughter*."

Daddy got his rag and polished his boot toe to a shine while the telephone kept up its shrill ringing. I knew who was on the line. I knew it must be Aurelia calling to tell me about Garland. And no matter what happened to me because of it, I sure wasn't going to miss talking to the Crocketts. Not this time.

When I stepped toward the phone, Daddy's shoe-polish rag froze. "What do you think you're doing?"

"I'm answering it," I said.

Mama tucked the sheet under her arm, trying to head him off. "Jenny. They'll call back, whoever it is."

I didn't say another word. Any minute now he'd be up from his seat swinging, and heaven only knew what he'd do to me with his workboot. When I reached for the receiver, Mama's hand clamped over mine. "Don't do it."

Who can say what makes a person scared to do something one day and willing to stand up and do that same thing the next? Maybe it's just frustration or disappointment. Maybe it's getting tired. But I don't think so, really. Because those are all the same things that make a person give up. I'd decided it would be a mistake to give up just yet. "This is somebody I have to talk to."

"Don't give him any more reasons to hurt you," Mama whispered. "It's your fault, you giving him so many reasons."

"I'm not giving him any reasons at all, Mama." I lifted the receiver in defiance. "It's about time you started seeing that."

The voice that came through the earpiece sounded tinny and distant, as if it came from a different world. Indeed, for me, it did. Aurelia wasn't on the line. I heard Aunt Maureen's disjointed words instead. *Got the metal out of his head . . . Keeps forgetting things . . . There's some miracles that happen and there's some that don't, child.*

THE PENNY

I stood with my feet apart, my knees bent, watching my daddy, waiting for him to manhandle me. Aunt Maureen's voice, as dark as her skin, lured my heart to a different place. *Homer Phillips Hospital . . . Sure want you with us . . . Garland says . . .*

I held onto the receiver with two hands, knowing anything I uttered ("I'll be there." "Is he okay?") would cut my time before Daddy started swinging. "I hear you," is all I said before I hit the button and opened the line again. And I *did* hear her. *We want you with us.* Daddy laid his rag aside as I dialed TA2-5065. The dial clicked through its exchange in slow motion, slower than Christmas. Daddy twisted the lid shut on the soap, set it firmly on the coffee table, and rose.

"Will you get me at my house?" I asked urgently when the call went through. "I need you to help me." And that's the last thing I uttered before Daddy tore the phone out of my hand.

When the baby-blue convertible swept up in front of our flat, Miss Shaw found me waiting on the front curb. She didn't drive off right away when I climbed into the front seat beside her. "What happened, Jenny?"

She leaned forward to get a better look at me. My shoulder was throbbing where Daddy had punched me, but if she was judging by my face, Miss Shaw couldn't tell a thing.

"Nothing happened," I lied. "Can you just drive me somewhere?"

Miss Shaw shifted into first and we edged forward. "Somewhere?" she asked. "Anywhere?"

The white leather seat felt cool on my backside. The last time we'd driven together like this, we'd been racing up the road, Miss Shaw in her sunglasses with her hair battened down by her headscarf, and me with my curls flying in so many directions I might have been mistaken for a brush bush. Last time I'd been in a tizzy with the thought of riding in a Grace Kelly convertible and making Jean jealous.

It was no use, fighting down the sudden longing I felt for my sister as I sat in Miss Shaw's car again. I wanted Jean with us so bad that I thought my insides would bust open. I wanted to stand up and cheer for her, I was so proud of my sister for getting away.

"Drive me to Homer Phillips Hospital?"

I expected Miss Shaw to put on the brakes, steer toward the curb and start asking all sorts of questions. But once again she surprised me. She didn't make any argument about driving me to the colored hospital. We drove in flashes of chrome as the streetlights flickered on and the last tendrils of daylight disappeared below the horizon. I'd thought she'd drop me off at the front walkway, but instead, we crept along the rows of cars, looking for a parking place.

"You don't have to come in. I can find my own way home," I told her. "I'll bet someone would give me a ride back or something."

"I won't let you find your own way anywhere," she said. "Do you think I'd let you go through this by yourself? Besides, do you think they'll let you past the nurse's station without a grown-up to escort you?"

She steered the sleek convertible into a narrow parking space, punched a button with her gloved finger, and watched in the mirror as the white top curled over us like a cresting wave. "Did you think I wouldn't want to come in with you?"

I shrugged.

"Do you mind if I do?"

I told Miss Shaw, "I figured you had other things to do. I don't want to be trouble."

"Well," she said, "what would those other things be? What would be more important than helping you?"

When we walked inside, the admittance nurse wore a cap fastened to her head with at least six bobby pins that I could count. She scribbled on a chart in sharp scratches even as she glanced our way. Then she tapped her pen. I could tell she expected Miss Shaw to ask the questions. I guess maybe I did, too, but then I realized that, although Miss Shaw had probably guessed, I'd never told her who we were coming to visit.

I did a double-take when I saw what held Miss Shaw's attention. I'd certainly never seen her do something like this in public before. I watched, disbelieving, my mind commending her with each finger she tugged loose.

Miss Shaw acted like nothing out of the ordinary had happened when she finished taking off her gloves. She simply stood there and held both of her gloves in a bunch beneath the handle of her pocketbook. She nodded for me to get ahold of my amazement and speak for the both of us.

"We're looking for Garland. Garland Crockett," I said.

Chapter Twenty-One

When we neared Garland's room, I turned to Miss Shaw to see if she'd come inside with me, but she was already nixing the idea.

"You go on," she said, giving me a fresh dose of encouragement that she must have known I needed. "I'll wait right here."

Still, I hesitated.

"Go on, Jenny Blake. This is a time for family."

"But I'm not—"

"Not what?" she inquired. "Not family? Maureen called you, didn't she?" I'd shared parts of Garland's story with her on our way up the elevator and along the unending hallways. Now that we'd found the right hospital wing, Miss Shaw hung back and inclined her head briefly, which meant *keep on going.* "Why don't you step inside there and find out?"

"You sure?"

She shot me a bright smile that made her more beautiful than I'd ever seen her. "I'll be right here." She slapped the seat of a plastic couch beside the wall. "Right *here.*"

My lone footsteps resounded to the end of the corridor and back, although I tried to keep my loafers silent. I read the names posted beside each doorway, trying to remember where the nurse told me Garland would be.

The hushed voices of the members of Antioch Baptist Church created a warm hum in the quiet hospital. As I rounded a corner and ran into the full gathering, I felt unworthy to come closer. Sure, they'd let me step inside their church with Aurelia and listen to the message about the Holy Ghost and receive Jesus, but this was a whole different, personal, *exclusive* matter. Some folks sat against the wall staring at nothing. Others chatted just the same as if they'd been at a Sunday picnic. Most were teary, dabbing at their eyes with wadded Kleenex.

Two ladies hung onto each other and prayed. The men gathered in their own tight group, their weight shifting from one hip to the other when they got uncomfortable, their conversation coming and going like a string of rainstorms, words pouring down, letting up when there was nothing left to say. Somebody was handing out egg-salad sandwiches wrapped in wax paper. It seemed like, no matter what else went on in the world, there was always somebody ready to eat.

Now that I knew so much about Miss Shaw, I understood that there were two sorts of living: one where you ran away from things that hurt too much to look at, and one where you looked at those hurtful things and kept right on going forward anyway. God's willing to show you your own heart if you want to see it. God's willing to take hold of what's there and fix you up when you're ready. Every trek starts with putting one foot in front of the other, just one stride at a time. The moment I took my first step toward those strangers, that's when I found the first familiar person in the crowd.

He stood square-shouldered, and his eyes, the clear-shine color of maple syrup, drew me like a beacon. I recognized him by his hair parted on the side and his sizeable nose and the curls overlapping his collar and the way he held his hand toward me. He wasn't wearing his satin stole or his robe, but he stood out just the same. He was the one who'd first started telling me Jesus stories. Reverend Monroe.

"Garland's been asking for you, girl. Maureen said you'd come if you were able to."

I waited for him to say something like, *That's why we want you around here. She told me what you done. She told me you made them stop all that rocking.*

193

I was all ready to answer, *But I didn't stop it. And even if I did, I didn't stop it soon enough. You should've seen me shoving and pushing the portable alongside the rest of them.*

But Reverend Monroe mentioned nothing about my presence being wanted because of something I had done. I waited for it, but it never came.

Finally I asked, "Is he in there?"

"Yes." Reverend Monroe gave me a nod. "You go right on in." Then, "We're mighty glad to see you, Jenny—mighty glad. My, but the Crocketts love you, child."

People stepped aside and left me a path to the door. As I went forward, I couldn't help overhearing the whispers: *Haven't told the boy how bad it is in his head. . . . Lord, have mercy. . . . He's just this side of death. They think he'll pass before morning.*

I smelled Aunt Maureen's sweet hair gel before I saw her. Next thing I knew, she'd enveloped me in her arms, and Darnell straightened up where he'd been leaning against the wall and Eddie stood near the bed with his empty shirtsleeve tucked into his pocket. Looking at Eddie's empty shirtsleeve, I thought how it didn't seem fair, some people didn't do anything to deserve difficulties and they raked in more trouble than they could bear.

"You find yourself a place with us," Eddie directed. "Get over there close to Garland so he can see you." It swept me up in such a feeling of *belonging,* their welcoming me to suffer this with them. Looking at the glad reception on their faces, I began to understand love.

Garland sat cross-legged in the center of the bed. He wouldn't lean against the pillows even when you told him to. The doctor had wound white gauze around Garland's head, so thick it looked like a turban. On top of that, someone had taped an ice pack to the side of his head. His skin was dark chocolate against all that white gauze and bed linen. His hand against his knee was only about as big around as a dogwood leaf. Garland took one look at me and said, "You didn't tell me there was a big spear sticking out of my head."

"Nope."

"Aurelia didn't tell me, either."

I told him no, she sure didn't.

Garland said, "You didn't have to worry. You were holding my hand. I wasn't scared."

When the nurse came in to check something with Aunt Maureen and Eddie, Garland spoke under his breath so nobody but me could hear.

"Everybody's trying to keep me from knowing it, but I do. Something in my head got rattled."

"You just don't listen to what they say."

"They don't think I got it figured out," he said in a whisper. "They don't think I know what's going on."

Later on, someone would tell me that the metal windowsill didn't have much to do with Garland's problem. The wound bled plenty when the doctor pulled out the lance, but the metal had only nicked an outer layer of bone from Garland's skull. He didn't have a concussion, either, which was a miracle after all that shaking around. It was a blood vessel that had burst, but no matter how much ice they packed on his head, it wouldn't clot up. A boy's brain can only function so long, being flooded with blood like that.

"Aurelia's scared," he told me. "She's scared of losing you. You got to make sure that doesn't happen."

I glanced across at Aurelia. Aunt Maureen and Eddie Crockett and Darnell were putting up a much better front than she was. Of all the Crocketts, Aurelia looked the most wrung-out and afraid. She kept turning away so Garland wouldn't see her crying.

When Garland winced sharp and threw up, Aunt Maureen held up a pan he could get sick into.

"Promise me Aurelia won't lose you," he said, grabbing on to my hand again while Aunt Maureen wiped his face with a towel.

"You just get better." I told him I'd promise him anything.

Miss Shaw once told me that God still works miracles today the same way we read about in the Bible. I lived in a house where I longed for the miracle of Daddy's never coming to my bedroom. But I had not seen any of the miracles Reverend Monroe had talked about yet. That night at the hospital, while Garland drifted in and out and I fought to keep my eyes open, Miss Shaw came to find me and insisted I stretch out so I could rest. ("I don't need to rest," I argued. "I can sleep the rest of the week. I need to be with Garland.") She told me she'd phone my parents and tell them where we were so they wouldn't worry.

I remembered the shredded cord, the telephone's clattering face-plate. "I don't think we have a phone," I told her.

But Miss Shaw managed it. After asking the names of the families in our flat, she got the Shipleys to relay the message.

She claimed a corner of the couch in a hallway waiting area and let me get comfortable in her lap. I drifted in and out, expecting any minute to see Daddy burst through the doors that had a sign reading QUIET PLEASE. Expecting him to grab me up by the collarbone, shaking me and shouting, "What do you think you're doing, trying to get away from me? What do you think you're doing, trying to get away from me, just like your sister did? You think I'd let that happen again?"

But as the night wore on, I drifted to the gentle melody of someone singing outside Garland's door, the wordless tune of some hymn I didn't know but would never forget. At one point in the night, I awoke to find Miss Shaw sitting over me, her bare fingers stroking my hair, her eyes seeing beyond the window behind the nurse's station. Who knew what she could be thinking of? I woke later to find her chin planted forward and her eyes closed, her snores as soft as cotton, but snores just the same. A strand of hair had escaped from her salon coiffure and fell limply beside her jaw.

Her hand lay beside my cheek, and I examined it, the scars from her burns stretching red and fiery and tight along her fingerbones, as if the heat had caused her skin to shrink. I did not stop to think; I was too sleepy. I only remember pulling her hand to me, floating off again, her cool, rough touch a pillow beneath my ear.

I moseyed in and out of dreams. As I unfolded my legs and dimly noticed the ache in my hip, I realized what the wakeful hours of the night could best be used for. I prayed as hard for Garland to live as I had ever prayed for Daddy to stop hitting me. I prayed for Jesus to touch Garland's head and make the broken pieces join up. I'd jerk awake and realize that sleep had made me abandon my post, and I'd start to have it out with Jesus about Garland all over again.

You have no right, a dark voice warned me. *What makes you think your praying makes a difference when there are thirty others down the hall who'd be better at it than you are? What makes you think God will listen when your own life's so dirtied up that you haven't found your way out yet?*

I shoved that voice aside and kept right on going.

The next thing I knew, Eddie Crockett jiggled my shoulder. I lifted my head to see Miss Shaw doing her best to smooth down her disheveled hairdo.

"Jenny," Eddie whispered. "Sweet Jenny, you better come around."

It was still dark outside the hospital window, too early for anything good. At first, I felt guilty because I'd been carried away from my prayer duty by sleep. I shot up fast and asked, "Was it . . . ? Did he . . . ?" Then, "Where's Garland?"

"Garland's right here," Eddie said carefully, as if merely looking at Garland might give me a fright. And he *was* there. He was sitting in a wheelchair in his pajamas with his head unwrapped and his favorite blanket balled inside his arms. A nurse rolled Garland in the chair. Aunt Maureen toted her travel case like they were all planning on going somewhere.

I scrubbed my eyes. "What?"

"They're all gone," he said. "Reverend Monroe said to tell you it would please him no end if he had a chance to see you next Sunday at church."

"All those people left? Why did they go? I don't—"

Aunt Maureen propped her bag beside me. Darnell spoke with slow emphasis, obviously impatient.

"We're . . . going . . . home."

Eddie said, "They don't know what made his head stop bleeding. They don't know why Garland's brain absorbed all the blood on its own. But it did. All they know is there's no reason for our Garland to be taking up space in a hospital bed anymore."

"Jenny." Aurelia's words finally made the truth sink in. "The doctors don't understand it, either. But he's going to be okay."

He's going to be okay.

I hadn't realized I had a crushing weight in my chest until it broke free and lifted. Relief washed over me. The thought of something being okay for a change, the thought of something being *miraculous*, being *good*, left me feeling dizzy. And it was *Garland*. I had to remind myself over and over again that it was true.

Garland's going to be okay.

After we all hugged each other good-bye and Miss Shaw and I headed out to climb into the convertible again, morning was just starting to tinge the St. Louis sky with a first hint of radiance. I kept whispering over and over to Jesus, *Thank you for Garland. Thank you. Thank you.* In every tree, the sparrows were setting out to sing the world awake.

"I'll get you home," Miss Shaw said, "but maybe you shouldn't try to sit through a school day. You must be exhausted. I don't see how you could possibly make it through."

I knew she was trying to be nice, but it didn't make any difference. I'd have to get through the day in the way Daddy insisted, no matter what the night before had held. I glanced at Miss Shaw, praying that she'd never know how Daddy would punish me in spite of the phone calls she'd made and the messages she'd gotten the neighbors to deliver.

My mind searched for a change of subject. I couldn't help myself. "You were snoring," I said.

"Me? Snoring?" She shook her head at me like I was crazy and touched her chest in feigned horror. "I don't snore."

She had donned her gloves again, and her elegant little hat, which I guess she always wore when she ventured out into the fashion realm.

"I'm too much of a lady to snore."

I laughed. "Don't worry." I gave her a slight hug of appreciation. "Some things I'll never tell."

You'd think by now I could turn off my ears and not listen to the things Daddy said about me. But of all the men alive on earth, he was the one who had given me life. Of all the words flung toward my heart, his were the ones I had taken for truth from the beginning.

When the police came and set the portable school building aright before the movers hauled it away, the outside looked almost untouched except for the few panels of corrugated metal that had been pried loose. Only a few wrinkles remained on the outside to show that the place had been in danger of collapsing in on itself. The damage was mostly on the inside, sort of like me.

Please God, I prayed. *If you could hear me praying about Garland, you've got to hear me about Daddy, too. Please God. Don't make me have to hear the things he says about me anymore.*

But Daddy kept right on telling me I'd amount to no good, he kept telling me I was dense, that I kept sticking my nose in where I wasn't wanted, the whole time the members of Antioch Baptist Church kept stopping by and telling him what a fine daughter he had. If God had a sense of humor, this was absolute proof of it: Daddy accepting thanks and blessings from the Crocketts. Aunt Maureen brought us over a ham and homemade biscuits. T. Bone Finney brought Mama and Daddy tickets to the Blue Notes' show over in Westlake Park. Darnell dropped off a box of pullet hens which Daddy promptly added a FOR SALE sign to and left out in the front yard for the neighbors to disperse.

Garland missed three days of school—not because the doctor could find anything wrong with him, but because Aunt Maureen wouldn't let him out of her sight. Mr. Lancaster, out of sheer lack of space in his remaining prefabricated classrooms, combined the portable second-grade class with the portable third-grade class. On the fourth day, when Garland returned, Aunt Maureen marched up the school steps with the same dogged cadence as a soldier, holding Garland's hand, ostrich feathers trembling atop her purple hat, emphasizing the importance of her mission. I'd have given my eyeteeth to have been able to slip inside the principal's office and listen as she started with her first question, pointed and solemn: "Would my son have ended up in harm's way on your campus, Mr. Lancaster, had he not been a colored child?"

Mr. Lancaster's face turned almost the same hue as Aunt Maureen's Sunday hat. He looked incensed that she would dare pose such a question at all. "Your child is attending an integrated school, Mrs. Crockett. I don't think you can ask for any more than that."

THE PENNY

"Yes," Aunt Maureen insisted. "I *can* ask. I will continue to do so. You are responsible for *all* of your students, Mr. Lancaster, not just half of them."

In spite of Mr. Lancaster's indifference, or perhaps because of it, our days at Harris School went by uneventfully. Almost before we noticed it, autumn had begun dwindling toward an early winter. A cold snap had sent everyone scurrying to their cars for heavy jackets during the Friday-night football game. A crisp pair of cement mixers moved in during science period one morning, their revolving drums making such a racket that Mrs. Huffines had to shut the windows and shout to be heard as she described the reproduction practices of amoebas. She finally gave up and assigned us protozoan crossword puzzles, while the trucks clambered and workmen hammered wooden forms together outside.

The end result, by the conclusion of the day, was nine perfect concrete slabs poured at various angles. By the time the slabs had dried several days later, a derrick crane moved in, and we watched while each portable was wrapped in a web of chains and hoisted from its grass-bound lair to be set firmly in place on a concrete foundation. I didn't see how this helped much, though, making the portables permanent when everybody who'd protested by carrying signs had wanted them moved out altogether, not cemented down.

I guessed there were different ways of fixing things.

When an editorial appeared on page two in the *Post-Dispatch* discussing the color line at Harris School and the one girl who had overlooked the social order, Daddy charged me with humiliating not only our family but the entire neighborhood as well. Every time he glowered across the room at me, his mouth formed a grim line. I kept waiting for him to thrash out and send me sprawling with broken ribs or a black eye, but he held back.

He left to install a chain link fence around an empty lot and returned that night with heavy footfalls, telling Mama how Tom

Leeper had shamed him good in front of the fence crew when he told everybody how I'd gone to the hospital to visit a colored boy. "Doesn't your girl know she's better off staying with her own kind?" Daddy mimicked. "Doesn't she know it's how we keep the peace, making sure everybody stays apart?"

"You looked like a fool." If Daddy said it once, he said it a hundred times. "Why did you have to go and make a spectacle of yourself?"

I wanted to make a spectacle of myself. I wanted to do something right for a change.

"You couldn't do anything right if you tried, Jenny."

Let me tell you, when a voice just keeps needling at you, it can have the same effect as a steady drip of water wearing a rock into sand.

"You're worthless."

"You'll never amount to anything."

"You've made us into the laughingstock."

The more a father tells you he's ashamed of you, the more you start to believe it.

But God had a way of making sure I heard another voice, no matter how Daddy worked to degrade me. As I carried my lunch tray toward a vacant table that Wednesday, Mrs. Henderson—the teacher from across the hall—laid a penny on my tray.

"It matters, Jenny," Mrs. Henderson said. "I want you to know how proud I am of you, standing up for what you believed the way you did."

I stared at the penny Mrs. Henderson put on my tray. How could she know that pennies meant something special to me? I remembered the times I had given pennies away to other people, thinking how I'd wanted to help them because of what God had done for me. I guessed maybe somebody had told Mrs. Henderson about it. *If somebody told her about it,* I thought, *maybe it did make a difference.*

I jostled past a crowd of kids and, as if in answer to that thought, another penny appeared on my tray. Then another. And another.

"What are you doing?" I said to all of them. "Why does everybody keep giving me pennies?"

"You're something, you know," said Tyler Jackson, one of my classmates.

"You did something really hard," Connie Martin agreed.

"None of the grown-ups would do it," Dennis Smith said.

The lunchroom lady who wiped tables clean dropped three or four pennies on the table beside my elbow. Mrs. Tate set a few pennies down and said, "There's those of us who think you did the right thing, young lady."

Then Cindy Walker set a penny down in front of me without saying a word. Pruett Jones gave me a penny and said, "You gave me one of these and it made my head not hurt quite so much because I knew you cared about it."

Mrs. Dahlberg said, "I sure needed cheering up that day at the grocery store. I'd just put my best friend on a bus and I knew I wouldn't see her for months. You made me smile, putting that penny where you knew I would find it." She dropped a whole fistful of pennies on my tray.

"Remember the day you gave me a penny because I made a bad grade on my math test?" Cheryl Witsitt asked. "Giving me that penny was such a small gesture," she said, "but it gave me so much hope."

Hope welled inside my heart, too. My small acts of kindness had not only made *me* feel better, they had made a difference with other people. That's what everybody was telling me. They *had*. People I didn't even know went to fishing in their pockets. Everywhere I went, people started walking up and handing pennies to me. Pennies poured toward me from every direction. From everywhere I turned. From people I barely knew.

In spite of Daddy's jeering, I began to rejoice, too. I saw that no matter how he tried to beat me down, there could be a different answer. Reaching out to hurting people even in small ways helps to heal our own hurts. I heard the message of the pennies louder than I heard my father's scoffs. His actions worked to steal my hope, but God kept giving it back to me.

I felt satisfied and grateful, and rich beyond all measure.

Chapter Twenty-Two

$\mathscr{I}$t can be catching, believing in miracles. I believe I saw a miracle the night Miss Shaw let me sleep against her bare hand. I believe I saw a miracle the morning Eddie Crockett jostled me awake at the hospital.

I kept an eye on my wristwatch that next Monday, waiting for it to be time for the Ville kids to be out for recess. When the clock read 10:45, I told Mrs. Huffines, "I can't wait; I have to go." She scribbled a hall pass for the girls' room. Instead of going to the girls' room, though, I slipped out the front door and found Aurelia perched on the steps with Garland. I watched over her shoulder while her dark fingers folded a slip of paper into the shape of a heron.

Aurelia's hands, slender and nimble, reminded me of a sculptor's hands. Here was a girl willing to push and poke and remodel things until she got them to her liking. Maybe she'd never be able to get me to where she liked me all that much. But I couldn't imagine the ache of living without her anymore, without her pushing and prodding me.

She presented the finished origami bird to Garland and he held it in the cup of his palm, surveying it.

"Aurelia," I said. "I want us to be friends."

She didn't look up. "Well, you sure got a fine way of showing it."

As she eyed the paper creature in her cousin's hand, Aurelia asked, "Are you ever going to tell me why you were standing there shoving Garland's classroom back and forth right alongside Rosalyn?"

Maybe I ought to have pretended I didn't know what she meant.

"Are you ever going to tell me why you didn't want me at your house when I came over?"

I told her I had my reasons, but they didn't have anything to do with her.

She told me no matter what my reasons were, I still had to answer for them.

"Are you ashamed of me?" she asked. "Are you ashamed of being my friend?"

No, I'm not ashamed of you. I've never been ashamed of you. But you'd have every right to be ashamed of me if you knew what I was hiding inside. "What do you think, Aurelia?" I asked sarcastically.

But she had me. "I think you're the only one around here trying to keep people from seeing who you really are. You're the only person around who thinks you aren't worth much."

When she accused me of that, I knew she was right. My heart pounded. I knew the time had come to explain to her why I saw myself that way. I waited until Garland took the tiny bird she'd folded and ran out onto the playground with it. That's when I said at last, my voice shaking with fear that this would make her pull away from me forever, "Daddy does things to Jean and me, Aurelia. Daddy does things to us that a father shouldn't do to his daughters. That day when you came, I was scared he would do something to you."

Aurelia stared at the step and clasped her hands around her knees. I could see she was as shocked by my admission as I had been when Miss Shaw explained to me about her hands.

"That's why you wouldn't let me come inside?"

I gripped her arm. "That penny I showed you? That day at church? When I found that penny, I think God spoke to my heart that my life could change."

"That's why you wouldn't put it in the offering plate."

I stared off at the trees and nodded.

"You were trying to protect me from your daddy?"

I nodded again, then glanced sideways at her to see her reaction. I saw my face reflected in Aurelia's sympathetic tears, and I saw the truth, too. Aurelia didn't intend to pull away from me.

"I can't even begin to imagine what that would feel like, Jenny."

I could scarcely speak past the knot in my throat. "It's been hard."

I guess that's all it took to get us on even terms again—letting her upbraid me about it, telling the truth about Daddy, talking about the penny. After that, after classes had been released every day, Aurelia started sidling up to me with the advice and secrets she wanted to share while she waited for Darnell to pick her up.

She told me that Darnell thought one of the girls in his class at Sumner High School was real handsome and did some fine talking. She told me how Eddie Crockett said he caught himself running scales with fingers he didn't have anymore. She told me Mr. George at the barbershop had offered Eddie a job because he thought he would make a first-rate chin scraper with his one arm.

I taught Aurelia how to make a Grace Kelly chignon in her hair, but no matter how many bobby pins I used, it didn't stay more than five minutes before it started poking out in every direction like a chimney brush.

She showed me how to use Aunt Maureen's Finishing Touches gel before I put rollers in my hair, which was finally starting to grow a little, and my curls came out as tight and tamed as snail shells.

Our friendship cemented for good in November when Mr. Lancaster decided he would prove once and for all to the St. Louis Board of Education that Harris School was taking the call to integrate seriously. Mr. Lancaster recruited students from the Ville to perform our annual presentation of the first Thanksgiving. Garland badgered us for weeks, trying to come up with an authentic costume because he didn't want to be just any Indian—he wanted to be from the Pontiac tribe.

"We *cannot* do a children's production with a grown man in the middle of everything," the teachers lamented when Mr. Lancaster got last-minute nerves and decided he needed to monitor the program from on stage in case anything got out of hand.

"Oh, don't mind me," he said. "I'll take the part of Plymouth Rock and squat in the corner with paper over my head. No one will even know I'm there."

Aurelia and I scraped what we could together and paid Garland a whole quarter to deviate from the script and talk real loud about how much turkey he'd eaten and how he weighed about a thousand pounds, and then go sit down on top of Plymouth Rock. That got so many cheers from the audience when it happened that Mr. Lancaster never dared to complain. And when the principal gave Aunt Maureen a wary tip of his hat across the room, Aurelia and I could hardly contain ourselves anymore.

We felt so full of victory that we even worked up the gumption to ask her what riot act she'd read Mr. Lancaster when she'd visited his office that day.

"I didn't read him any riot act," she told us. "I came to tell him I had forgiveness in my heart. That's what I figured the good Lord wanted from me. Our Lord said, 'Forgive them, Father, because they know not what they do to me.' He was talking about forgiving all his children—that's what I told Mr. Lancaster."

Let me tell you, Aunt Maureen could preach sometimes. Aurelia and I just rolled our eyes.

"I'll bet his jaw hit the floor," I commented with self-satisfaction as we walked home from the Thanksgiving presentation. Garland had let me wear his paper-sack vest on which Darnell had inscribed Pontiac symbols, even though it was way too small for me.

Aunt Maureen said, "His jaw hit the floor when I told him that whatever treatment he thought the coloreds deserved, it wasn't okay with me anymore. I told him it wasn't okay with me that he treated half his school like second-class citizens."

"Sister." Eddie Crockett had been rambling along beside us. He stopped dead in his tracks and looked her over. "Maybe it's too much, you talking like that."

"It isn't, Eddie." With certainty, she said, "Somebody's got to talk about it, don't they?"

It was so cold, I could see Eddie Crockett's breath in the air. I could tell he felt the need to herd his sister along toward their car, concerned her zeal might ignite another discussion with the principal.

"Maureen, why don't you climb on in the car and we'll go home?"

"Maybe you don't think it's right for me to be human, Eddie, feelings and all, but God does. Too many people in the world believe we ought not to say what we think. If I'm hurting about something, Jesus loves me enough to want me to talk about it. I have to take stock that Jesus loves me just the way I am."

Aunt Maureen always said the best things. When I heard her get excited like that, her words made ME look inside myself, way past any hurt I'd been able to hide behind before. I thought about the day I'd finally worked up the guts to tell Aurelia about what Daddy did to us. I liked thinking how Jesus cared about me and didn't want me to cover up my feelings. Thinking about it that way gave me a new, gentle sense of peace.

Miss Shaw asked if I'd be willing to help some at the shop in December since gift-wrapping kept her busy that time of year. I knew why she wanted me—I knew she'd seen me tie beautiful gift-bows and miter-smooth corners. I couldn't help feeling prideful at her request. That was the first talent I was able to see in myself: I was good at wrapping.

I told her Saturdays would be perfect.

The first Saturday after Thanksgiving, Del Henry stopped by with a jar of jam from his neighbor's pantry and a book about how the world's first brick arch was discovered in the ruins of Babylonia. He wore his best Boyd's suit, a summer suit although winter had beset us. He also sported a fedora, which he lifted and set down so many times, it might've been attached to his head with a hinge.

When Miss Shaw asked him if he wanted to buy another charm for his granddaughter's bracelet, he took off on a different tack, a strange story about a friend of his who had come in third place at the St. Louis County Fair for being fastest at dicing six cabbages.

"This is a lovely jam, Delbert." Miss Shaw took it from him with her gloved hands. "Strawberry, isn't it?"

Glue must've clogged his tongue again.

"It's good of you to observe the beginning of gift-giving season like this."

"Oh, I wasn't observing any season," he rushed to clarify.

You're observing hunting season, I wanted to comment as I polished the counter mirror where he had once examined his hat on his head at least eighteen times. *Hunting a companion. And I sure wish you'd get to it.*

I couldn't believe the progress when Del noted, "Miss Opal, I just thought strawberry jam would be a good reason to stop by."

"And such a nice book. It definitely looks intriguing."

"Yes . . . well . . ." He cleared his throat and handed the book over.

Miss Shaw pressed her white glove demurely against her blouse buttons. "Thank you for both gifts, Delbert. I'll read the book. And the jam is certainly a lovely gesture."

"My neighbor will have honey jars available in spring."

I about flipped. *Spring? So much for progress*, I thought.

This called for desperate measures.

When Miss Shaw left to get the mail that next Saturday, I about gnawed the end off the eraser before I figured out exactly what I ought to write on the Shaw Jewelers letterhead.

I kept thinking how Del Henry was a brickman.

"Dear Delbert," I wrote in careful square letters. "I would like to go on a date with you. I would go to dinner with you if you'd ever ask me. Just in case you ever get brave enough to take me to Rigazzi's, I have to tell you that I've never been to eat in the Italian neighborhood before. I like spaghetti *very much*." (Well, I didn't know if Miss Shaw liked spaghetti or not, but when you were as involved as I was by that time, you couldn't write a letter without putting a part of yourself in it. I *loved* spaghetti.) "I would go with you to dinner if you would just *ask*."

I underlined the word *ask* three times.

Everything was starting to get that falling-into-place feeling.

I dropped the note off in the mail that day. And by the following Saturday, I had the answer.

When Del Henry walked in that time, I couldn't help noticing he had purchased a new, more appropriate all-weather suit. I looked on, admiring his tenacity, watching him straighten his tie in the reflection of the silver tea set display. Just when I expected him to ask after the shop's proprietor, he strolled directly toward me.

"Well, my, my, but what is this, Jenny? I certainly do know your handwriting." I stared at the familiar note that he held extended in his hand.

"I didn't—" I shook my head. I wasn't about to say "I didn't write it." But I couldn't exactly say "I didn't intend for you to know it was me," either.

At the precise moment I needed her most, Miss Shaw emerged from the workroom where she'd been tightening clasps onto chains.

"Delbert?"

He yanked the letter out of his pocket and presented it to her soundlessly, color climbing his ears. "I hoped you'd written this," he said simply. "But I doubt that you did."

The blood pounded in my ears. I waited for Miss Shaw to turn on me and tell me I had committed a terrible mistake. But I should've known better.

"No, Delbert. I didn't write it. But I *would* have if I'd *thought* of it."

When Del Henry saw her smiling at him, his grin grew so broad it about pushed his ears off his face. "You would have?"

"Absolutely," she agreed. "Since my young employee has written you a letter about how she loves spaghetti and would like to go to Rigazzi's for Italian, and since she is only fourteen years old and I believe that fourteen is much too young for a date, why don't I consider going along and the three of us could make it a party?"

So that Saturday afternoon we closed up the jewelry shop and went out with Delbert. We all devoured huge nests of spaghetti and then headed out to the brickyard.

"Did you know there are caves dug out everywhere beneath this city?" Del asked us. "They've been digging for red brick clay for so long, we're living on a piece of land more full of holes than a honeycomb."

Just as dusk began to fall that evening, Miss Shaw stopped beneath one of the brick arches Del Henry had been so knowledgeable about, and came up with an idea. "Delbert," she asked him, "has anyone ever designed such a thing as an arched headstone?"

"Oh, yes!" And although I knew exactly what Miss Shaw must be getting at, Del Henry didn't, so he went off on the French headstones that had been designed in the seventeenth century by the esteemed brickmaker Claude Mousset.

"My mother is buried in the Lafayette Park Cemetery, but her plot has no marker," Miss Shaw said, with no more emotion than she might have said, *Fill it up with regular, please.* "I believe you're the right person to do this, Delbert. Would you be willing to design a small marker for her?"

Del stopped in his tracks. "You would trust me with that?"

"There are a great many things I would trust you with," she said.

That was the moment Miss Shaw began to remove her gloves in front of Del Henry. She unfastened the tiny buttons at her wrists. She tugged off each of the fingers.

Del Henry examined her scars for a moment. It must have terrified her, how hard he looked at her hands.

Then I saw him reach for her. They walked along hand in hand, swinging their arms all the way back to the car.

Chapter Twenty-Three

*I*t seemed impossible that we could have ever complained about the heat by the time Christmas rolled around. The radiator in the living room woke us clanking and rattling, trying to keep up with the winter cold. Whenever the door swung open downstairs, a blast of nippy air deluged our upstairs landing. Gone were the days of streetcar rides to Miss Shaw's with heat shimmering along the sidewalks. Nowadays, when you stood in line for the box office at the Fox Theater, you stamped your feet to keep warm. You rubbed your hands together and huddled tighter inside your neck scarf. I could barely remember barefoot races across a street as hot as a stovetop, or a penny that lay in my palm as warm as if it had just been minted by the sun.

The style in Christmas trees tended toward the flashy and space-aged that year. In the broad front window of Sonnenfield's, a silver-metal tree reflected red, green and blue as a spotlight twirled on the floor beneath it. A bank of television consoles, their antennas jutting like rabbit ears, broadcast the same image on a dozen different screens.

Painted letters on the glass hawked the appliances as "the perfect big-ticket gift for the perfect family holiday." Our family already had one. I stared at the letters a long time, dreaming I had enough money to buy a television set for the Crocketts.

As for me, I didn't need a thing. I had the best present I could ever hope for. Daddy had informed me in a magisterial voice that Jean was coming home. Her secretarial school had disgorged its students the day before, and Jean waited for hours after the building was locked and the heat was turned down before she gave up and admitted she had nowhere to go but home. Laden with her overweight typewriter case and not much else, she'd tottered to a corner phone booth and called Daddy with her Greyhound Bus schedule. He told us all this with a know-it-all smile, like he'd just won the King Solomon Award for Brilliance for figuring out how things would turn out in the end.

When Mama heard the news, she looked afraid to move. At first I thought she didn't hear. One of her favorite Christmas ornaments had come from Woolworth's, a purple ball so big around, with glass so thin that Mama breathed a sigh of relief every time Daddy brought the decorations down and she found it still in one piece. After Daddy told us that Jean called, Mama stared at our purple ball for the longest time, touching the upraised, iced letters that read *Silent Night, Holy Night*, turning the ball in her hand.

My sister was coming home for Christmas.

Just as I turned from the TVs in the shop window, intending to head up the sidewalk and finish my meager shopping, something made me turn back. I recognized the man's face on the screen, although at first, I had trouble placing him.

Only one or two sets had the sound turned up. Window glass muffled what the reporters were saying, but if I stood close, I could hear. A swarm of microphones danced before his mouth, their call letters all but obliterating his face. Newsmen aimed questions at him the same way they'd throw darts in an arcade.

"Is it true that you have announced to your countrymen that you're ready to be married?"

"No comment," he said.

"Is it true you've been corresponding with Grace Kelly since you met at the *Paris Match* photo shoot in Monaco? When she led the U.S. delegation at Cannes?"

"No comment," he said.

Prince Rainier of Monaco.

"If you've come to find a bride and it isn't Grace, what sort of woman would you be looking for?"

"I'm sorry." A gentleman escort stepped in front of the microphones, propelling the prince to one side. "His Royal Highness will answer no more questions at this time." Which seemed to give the news hounds permission to lob queries at him double-time, as he tried to duck away.

"If you've never traveled to America before, then why now?"

"If this is only a regular holiday, why would you travel with a priest and a doctor?"

"If you are coming to America to sight-see, then why are you only going to Philadelphia?"

Just what we need, I thought to myself. *Jean is finally coming home, and she'll hear about this, and I'll have to listen to Grace Kelly stories all over again. She'll go bats and I won't be able to stand it.*

I didn't care how much Jean went on about Grace Kelly, though, not really, I admitted to myself, because I was so excited that my sister and I would be together. Not until I grew much older would it strike me that my enthusiasm over Jean's return could've been seen as selfish. While I was rejoicing because I wouldn't be alone with Daddy anymore, my sister was facing the fact that she didn't have any safe place to go.

Certain fragrances, certain songs, never fail to bring back the day she returned to me. I see it as if I'm opening a book and flipping through each page, seeing every detail. The naked branches of the maple tree that reached out over the street like gnarled fingers. The low rise of clouds moving through our neighborhood in a cresting wave. Daddy commenting as he stood on the landing that we might get snow. The musty smell of our flat mixed with the scent of pine boughs from the Christmas tree inside. I can still see the smugness in Daddy's eyes as he headed out to the car to go get Jean. My sister coming home, even for a few weeks, meant he'd be in charge of her, and that thrilled him. The minute she set one foot in the door, he'd have control of her again.

Mama and I waited at the top of the landing until we heard the car pull up at the curb. Mama flew down the stairs to meet them, running like a girl the same age as me. We made it down to the yard before Daddy cut the engine.

The passenger door shot open, and in those first few precious seconds, Jean leapt upon us, hugging us and laughing. A good number of neighbors braved the chilly air to poke out their heads and find out what all the ruckus was about. Mr. Patterson stepped out on the little hillock that was our yard to wish us a merry Christmas, and Mrs. Shipley brought her baby out so Jean could see it toddle around the stiff, dead grass.

Mrs. Patterson had taken it upon herself to hang a wreath on our communal front door, with bouquets of pinecones and tiny red berries and gold plastic letters that read SEASON'S GREETINGS. Jean stepped back from the breathtaking squeeze she gave me, eyed me from the top of my head to the tips of my toes, and said something remarkably adult-like.

"Who'd have thought you'd grow so much while I was gone? You've shot up like a weed."

It wasn't like I had anything to do with that. What did a person say? *Thank you?* "Well, I've been trying." Then I remembered she must've just celebrated her eighteenth birthday. She'd done it without us. She'd done it alone.

For those minutes, as we fought over who was going to lug Jean's typewriter case upstairs and who was going to get her suitcase and who got to tote her blue-and-white cosmetic case to her room, you would have thought we were welcoming Grace Kelly herself into our upstairs flat. Mama had cooked Jean's favorite custard, and she'd bought Red Hots to put inside baked apples for dessert on Christmas Day.

Once Jean's luggage had been set in her room, it seemed like she'd never been gone. At first my sister prowled the kitchen in her sullen, stealthy way, like a tiger prowling the perimeter of its cage. In the days leading up to her arrival, I had pictured those first hugs in the yard and the suitcases banging against the wall as we carried them up the stairwell smiling at each other. I had not imagined how our house would feel after time had passed and we all fell silent and tense again.

Mama chirruped like a squirrel every time Jean stalked into the kitchen, jabbering desperately about topics she thought Jean might be interested in.

"Did you know the Stinnetts sold an old hobby horse at their yard sale?"

"I read in the social section of the *Post-Dispatch* how popular it is for the Forest Park people to have hobo parties. Everyone drives to a different house for a different dinner course."

"Did you know Donna Johnson has gotten herself entered in the Miss Missouri contest? How she did that, I do not know."

Jean stared at Mama like she was jabbering in a different language, and left the kitchen.

Seeing Jean's discomfort left me feeling awkward and shy. Maybe I didn't know this person who'd returned to my house anymore. I followed her to her room where she began rummaging through her suitcase.

"Did you hear about it on the television news?" I asked, realizing this might bridge the distance between us.

"What?"

"Prince Rainier."

"I *did* hear it." She brightened. "He's spending Christmas in Philadelphia."

I couldn't believe it myself. For the first time in my life, I was *trying* to make Jean talk about Grace Kelly. Always before, when she brought it up, I wanted to stuff a mop in her mouth.

"What do you think it means?" I asked innocently.

"I think he's sweet on her."

"Do you think he'll propose?" I asked.

"I sure think it's possible," she said.

My sister began to pace again—from the bed to the dresser that I thought she'd never use again to the window where she could see into the street, the bedraggled flats decorated half-heartedly for Christmas. The third time she reached the window, she started drumming her fingers on the sill. She stopped abruptly when we heard the sound of singing in the street below. Christmas carolers.

If those singers had come this far south in our neighborhood, they hadn't just set out on a social occasion. Residents along Wyoming Street weren't the sort to invite strangers inside for hot chocolate or fudge or candy canes. The carolers would be lucky if they could entice anyone to come into the stairwell and open the main front door. But someone from downstairs, either the Pattersons or the Shipleys, must have taken pity on them because, next thing we knew, the words lofted up the stairs just as robust as the December evening air.

Jean returned to her dresser and started moving her bottles of perfume and face cleaner and box of talcum powder around. Finally she blurted out, "I didn't come back here for help. I just didn't have any other place to go."

The words that wafted up to us from downstairs were the same as the ones on Mama's precious glass ornament from Woolworth's. *Silent Night.* Outside, as cars drove past, the road crackled from the cold.

"What's it like, getting away?" I asked.

My sister jerked her head up in surprise. "Getting away from what?"

"You know. Getting away from Daddy. Being on your own. Having friends come see you without worrying. Getting to *know* everyone. Getting to make up your own mind about things."

"Oh. Oh, yes. It's fine. Really fine." Her answer came much too quickly.

"Well, I've gotten to know plenty." I launched into a long diatribe about Miss Shaw and how she'd finally let out all her secrets, and about the portables and saving Garland and everything that had happened with Aurelia.

"The only thing I'm getting to know is how to type f j f j f j f j with a blindfold tied on my eyes." Jean's voice held a sense of irony that I didn't understand. "Then, after that, we added the d's and the k's." She paused. "It's not as easy getting to know the other girls as you'd think it'd be."

"Why not?"

She used the tip of one fingernail, much longer and more glamorous than it had ever been before she left us, to worry the cuticle on her thumb. The tips of her nails were so clean, I knew she'd used Nail White. It seemed like an eternity before she would answer. "Oh, I don't know. They talk about things I don't care about much. Going on vacations with friends. Their mamas giving them advice about boys. How their daddies used to take them to the country club and catch them in their arms when they jumped in swimming. If Daddy tried to catch me when I was swimming, I'd go the other way. See—just . . . *things*. Things it's impossible for me to talk about." Then, "I don't think they like me very much."

I waited, my heart scrunching into a fist of longing, just waiting for her to acknowledge that it was nice for her and me to be together. When my sister finally lost interest in her thumbnail, she glanced up at me like she didn't much care for what she saw.

"Aren't you even glad to see me?" I asked.

"Yes." She said as if she found it extremely regrettable, "I am very glad to see you."

"Well." I stood straighter. "That's something."

"There's no way out, really, is there?"

"No way out of what?" I asked.

"This house. What Daddy does to us," she said. "You can't run away from it. It follows you every place you go."

Chapter Twenty-Four

When you grow up in a family like mine, you learn early what *not* to expect during Christmastime. You don't expect dolls wearing ruffled dresses and real jewelry. You don't expect any glittering fineries from Sonnenfield's window. You don't expect those television family moments where the daddy puts the star on top of the tree and the mama hugs him, admiring him for his general prowess while the sisters wait expectantly, knowing that this night-of-all-nights will bring only good things.

Our Christmas morning celebration the next day would be as short-lived as my reveling when Jean had stepped from the Packard automobile, followed by an isolated, simple dinner with turkey and Mama's peeled apples, which baked up astonishingly red because she put Red Hot candies in them. After that, Daddy would make his sullen retreat to the front stoop for his next beer and cigarette, his resentful insistence that this celebration-nonsense ought not last any longer than it had to.

I ached to get to Antioch Baptist Church for the Christmas Eve service Aurelia had told me about, where Christmas songs sung gospel-style came out richer and sweeter than Brer Rabbit Molasses and the velvet glow caught from one worshiper's candle to another until everybody's faces shone with a soft glimmering light that made even the most unsightly beautiful. Reverend Monroe would stand in the pulpit in front of everyone, a man I knew to be soft-spoken and gentle, a man I knew held me in high esteem, and he would bellow with the muscle of the Lord: "Even if God should send suffering and loss, I will still rejoice in my Savior! Though the fig tree does not bud and there are no grapes on the vines, though the olive crop fails and the fields produce no food, though there are no sheep in the pen and no cattle in the stalls, yet I will rejoice in the LORD! I will be joyful in God my Savior!"

I'd come up with a plan and was so sure of it, I'd even brought it up with Miss Shaw when I'd worked at the shop last Saturday. Although she usually attended Christmas Eve service at the community church that stood catty-corner to the cemetery, she said, "I can't think of a way I'd rather observe Christmas, Jenny, I really can't. And I hope you won't mind if I ask Delbert Henry to join us?"

I was so sure of my plan that after I dressed in my best skirt and velvet shoes, I knocked on Jean's door. She asked, "Where are you going all dressed up?"

"If you hurry, you can come with me." I had every intention of bringing my sister along and introducing her to everyone I'd been jabbering about.

Jean scratched her leg, and I could tell she wasn't too keen on wearing itchy stockings that day.

"I don't know."

"It won't be so bad, Jean. Just don't wear clothes that make you scratch. Don't wear the skirt with the net petticoat. Once you hear what the preacher talks about, you'll forget all about how your dress feels. Besides, there'll be *candles*. There'll be a baby up front, the Trouppes' baby, Aurelia says, sleeping on a bed of real hay."

I think I had her convinced right after I finished the part about the candles. Jean shrugged into her slip, situated her skirt properly, and buttoned it around her waist. She tugged a black turtleneck sweater over her head and slipped her arms into raglan sleeves. As she reached up to fasten her pearls at her neck and brush her hair, I thought she looked about ten years older than she'd looked fifteen minutes ago. She brushed her hair to a fine sheen that mine never would have achieved, even if it *did* have any length to it.

The tart smell of apples filled our flat. Mama stood at the kitchen counter, peeling more apples with a paring knife.

I had my money stashed safely inside my velvet purse for the streetcar. "We're headed out for a few minutes," I said.

"Don't be long," she tossed back. "You girls stay out of trouble." Then, as if one might have something to do with the other, "Don't let your father catch you." Just as our feet started clattering down the stairwell, Daddy stepped inside the downstairs door in front of us.

"Where do you two think you're going?"

I caught Jean's arm and wouldn't let her go farther.

"It's Christmas, Daddy. We want to go to church."

"With your mama slaving away, trying to get ready for tomorrow? I don't think so."

It had been a long time since he'd worried about Mama slaving over anything. "She told us we could go out," I challenged him.

Jean backed up another step in spite of me holding her arm.

"It's okay, Jenny," she said. "We don't have to do it."

"You can't stop us," I said to him while I still had the courage.

That's when he cursed and shouted,

"You just *think* I can't." He'd backed Jean all the way to the landing, but I held my ground two steps in front of her. Daddy made his stand in front of me with his arms crossed, his biceps flexing as big as two hams.

"Who wants to be first?" he asked, suddenly swinging his arms back and forth as if he were a football linebacker. "I said, *Who wants to be first? Who wants me to take them down?*"

Daddy could have tossed me down the steps just as easy as he could have tossed a sack of cotton. Still, if it had just been me, I would have fought for it. But I was thinking of Jean. I was thinking of keeping things tranquil in our house until she could get away again. I was thinking of the pew that wouldn't be full, of the heads that would keep turning and looking for us, as I yielded and backed up the stairs myself. Only later did I realize I'd been the sister standing in the most precarious position.

The next morning, we each unwrapped a new pair of stockings and a new toothbrush and a bottle of Prince Matchabelli cologne that Mama had bought for us. She had signed Daddy's name to the tags, too, and we thanked them both with polite but careful smiles. As for me, I was glad to have new stockings. Mine had a run in them, from the ankle bone all the way up. I'd been relegated to bobby socks until my next paycheck came.

Jean must have saved up good from her summer baby-sitting, because when I tore open the little box from her, I found a pair of pearl earrings.

"They'll hurt your ears," she whispered when I hugged her. "I have a pair like them. But they shine real pretty."

Stashed in a glass vase upstairs was the bright purple flower Aurelia had made me out of sheets of crepe paper. Out of all of us, Aurelia had been the one most excited about Christmas. She'd escorted me into her room days ago and whispered in low tones and carefully opened sacks to show me what she planned to give everyone.

She'd made all her best friends flowers, and she'd bought a new magnifying glass for Darnell. She'd bought a toy spaceship for Garland and a set of spatulas for Aunt Maureen.

Of all the things she'd purchased, though, she was most excited about what she'd gotten her daddy. She'd gone to Chesworth's Music and bought Eddie Crockett sheet music, a vast assortment of it.

I knew he couldn't play that without the aid of Mr. Lamoretti. Never mind his arm. "You must be crazy giving him that," I said, hands planted on my hips.

"He likes to have it setting around the house, Jenny," she assured me. "He wants T. Bone and Curtis and Chick to see it everywhere they go when they roam around here."

I shook my head.

"He likes to think about what he's going to do someday. It's more for his spirit than anything." As if that explained it all. And the more I thought about it, it did. It was just like Eddie Crockett. He liked to show everybody he was going to live his life whole even if a part of it had gotten broken.

I waited until last to give out my presents. I had spent hours at Miss Shaw's because she'd insisted I use the shop's wrapping paper for each of the small dimestore gifts I'd bought my family. When I pulled my packages out, we didn't have anything left under the tree.

"Here, Mama." I handed hers over and watched while she unwrapped a box of soaps. I'd known she'd "ooh" and "ah" over the Yardley Lilac fragrance. They smelled like the lilacs she snipped from our neighbor's yard and snuck into the house every June. ("You want to steal the lilacs off your neighbor's tree," she'd say each year as she flitted upstairs still wearing her nylon bathrobe, clutching armfuls of blooms she'd cut with the kitchen scissors, "the best way to do it is in your nightgown. That way, nobody ever gets brave enough to stop you.")

Next Jean unwrapped the eyelash curler I'd bought her from Woolworth's, exactly like the one Miss Shaw had given me clear directions on how to employ. Jean was the one who could use eyelash-curler lessons now. I fully intended to take her through every step and send her back to secretarial school in total awe of me because I'd taught her to have the fashionable wide-eyed look.

When I handed Daddy his small box, I couldn't keep my hand from shaking. I held my breath while he sliced the tape with his pocketknife and smoothed out each crease with his thumb. He lifted the lid off the box and frowned. My heart pounded like drumfire in my chest.

Daddy picked it up. "What's this—a penny? This is all you gave me for Christmas?"

I questioned the decision again in my head: *Lord, did I really hear you right? Isn't this what you wanted me to do?*

"Last summer I found a penny like this one, Daddy. And God used it to remind me how he wanted to change my life." Then to my total surprise, out of my mouth came, "Maybe you don't understand what you've been doing to us, Daddy." I took a deep breath, mustering all my courage. "But without God intervening, my life would have been ruined."

He went on talking as if he didn't even hear me. "You have a job, for Pete's sake," he said. "You could have gotten me a new cigarette lighter. Now *that*, I needed."

It made me cringe, but I touched his hand.

"No, Daddy." My voice came out just as strong and firm as I could make it. "*This* is what you need."

I told him the penny was important because it represented God's truth.

"It started something new in me, Daddy. I'm hoping it might get you started on the same road." I looked down at my shoes. "You probably hurt Jean and me, Daddy, because somebody hurt you. I'm giving you this penny in hopes that you'll let God change you, too."

Daddy looked at me like what I'd just said had blown a hole in his gut. The air in the room was thick with fear and anticipation. He set the penny in its small box beneath the tree, barely touching it, like it might burn him.

The penny sat there in its box until Mama took the tree down and folded up the quilted tree skirt. The penny sat there until the day the Grace Kelly stories started on television again.

From the minute Grace Kelly announced her engagement to Prince Rainier III, my sister acted like she'd personally been invited into a world of royalty. The announcement came in a special NBC news report right after the week's presentation of *The Philco Television Playhouse*. Jean watched the story unfold on television that week, mesmerized, unable to turn away.

"There is nothing impetuous about this proposal," Rainier repeated a dozen times into as many microphones as news correspondents hounded him for the story. "I think we are both ready for marriage."

When the reporters grilled Grace Kelly's mother for her part of the story, she beamed at the cameras.

"I knew then and there that his intentions were not just those of a smitten young man." Mrs. Kelly spoke of her daughter with such pride that it made me want to cry. "There was purpose in every word and movement."

"I am swept away," Grace announced in her practiced diction, as camera bulbs exploded in her face and she never batted an eyelid. "I have been in love before, but never like this."

"Can you *imagine?*" Jean breathed. "Marrying a real *prince?*"

"It's hard to picture," I admitted. "Living in a castle. Having everything done up just the way you like it. . . ."

Most nights while Jean was home from Lowman's Secretarial School, she and I slept in the same bed. Most nights I'd give a light tap on her door, tactfully offering her a chance not to hear me. But she always heard me; she always guessed I might be coming. She left the door open a crack so I could push it open. And we'd lay side-by-side in amiable silence, our chests rising and falling to the same tempo, our pillows bunched up beneath our ears, our legs ending up tangled by morning. If either of us got up and leaned over the windowsill, we could see Daddy below on the stoop, in one of his regular foul moods, the tip of his Lucky Strike glowing red every time he took a draw on it. The air on those few nights seemed clear as watch-face glass with my sister at my side, quiet and intensified. Even from the bed I could almost hear Daddy sucking on his cigarette, releasing it with a *pop*. Since Christmas, Daddy's mood had grown more sullen. I kept waiting for a response from him about what I'd given him as a gift, but none came.

Sometimes Jean would say, "I hate to go leaving you again."

And I'd say, "I saw Billy Manning dust-bombing streetcars. He's a real pest."

She'd ask, "You going to be all right, Jenny?"

I'd whisper, "I think so. Yeah, I'm going to be okay."

That night, because Grace Kelly had announced her engagement to a prince, I happened to think of a page from an issue of *Movie Reel* I'd brought home from Miss Shaw's and saved for Jean.

"It's a real good story," I told her. "All about Grace's parents being unhappy with her dating Oleg Cassini. I thought you'd like to read it, but maybe you wouldn't. None of it matters anymore."

"Oh, go get it," she said, bopping my shoulder. "I want to read it. I really *do*."

On hands and knees, I dug through my clothes until I found the bottom of the drawer. Just as my hand found the slick, thin pages, I froze. My stomach wrenched.

Daddy's footsteps moved toward me in the hallway. The floor creaked. I heard him take another step, measuring his weight by degrees.

I felt like I would be sick.

Help me, please, Jesus. Don't let it happen again.

The footsteps stopped outside my door. I rocked back on my heels. And waited.

I heard Daddy's breathing on the opposite side of the door. I dared to rise, but when I did, the floor groaned.

Daddy's stealth could mean only one thing. He'd gotten more cautious with Jean home. He waited to make certain no one heard anything.

Silently, I pressed my hands to the door. As if I stood any chance at all of holding it shut against him. I held my breath as the door-knob turned.

That's the minute I figured something out. While I was wondering whether my prayers made any difference at all, God must have been working on Daddy's heart even though I couldn't see it.

That was the moment the door should have inched open.

Only it didn't.

When Daddy's steps moved on, I felt the blood drain from my head. I almost fainted with relief. Until the footsteps stopped again. Outside Jean's room.

I panicked. I shouldn't have left her. What had I been thinking?

I hadn't decided what I was going to do yet. But I was onto him. Nothing Daddy could do or say could make me live in fear anymore. I listened to the One who loved me unconditionally and assured me he had a good plan for my life. The one who had been putting pennies in my path all along. I listened to Jesus saying, *You watch out for those little reminders of me right in front of your face, and I'll be the one to take care of all the big things. Always remember, I'm a step ahead of you, putting pennies in your path with my love, every place you end up walking.*

Mama's voice murmured something in the hallway. At first, I thought she'd finally come to stop him. But her voice came from too far away.

I cracked my door. Down the hall, Jean's door stood ajar. I hadn't latched it firmly behind me.

My parents' words swept over me in waves of warning. I didn't understand their meaning, but I knew the tone. Mama sounded frightened in a way I'd never heard her before.

"Now that we . . . But things have gotten . . . You said yourself . . ." And then Daddy hit her.

Jesus had been a step ahead of me all along, putting pennies in my path, and I knew which direction he intended me to walk now. I didn't know what I'd do when I got there. I don't even remember how I made it up the hall.

THE PENNY

I entered my parents' bedroom and stood in the narrow space between the chest of drawers and the bedside table. I must have been only a shadow to them, a silhouette cast aside as the light from the headlights of a car moved along the street.

"Jenny?" Mama's voice quavered hard. "Is that you?"

"Get on out of here," Daddy said. "You got no place in here."

I didn't budge. Sometimes confronting somebody is the only way to overcome fear. That night I realized God doesn't always make something go away because we pray. When we pray, he often gives us the strength to stand up to it.

I'd never been so scared in all my life. But I stood rooted. I heard a rustle of nightgown beside me and knew Jean had come, too. Her fingers reached for mine. I took them and squeezed.

Daddy advanced on us from where he'd been hanging on to Mama. "What are you two *asking for*? Get on out of here."

Thank heaven for a dark so thick that he couldn't see my knees shaking. Thank heaven I was done watching Mama handle our hurts by turning a deaf ear and blinding her eyes. Thank heaven Jean was standing beside me as a way of agreeing that it was time for the abuse to stop.

Somebody just needed to stand up, and that's what I was doing.

Daddy's voice dropped an octave. It rumbled low, ready to explode.

"You know what I'm capable of, don't you? If you two don't stop this, I'll beat you senseless."

Something new had taken me over. A determination I had never felt before and a fresh strength in my mind. Mama might have let Daddy hurt us—but I was not going to put up with it any longer. I wasn't going to let him hurt Mama or Jean or me anymore.

The angrier Daddy got, the more brutal his words became. But they were only words without life, not like the ones surging forth like heart-music in my head, not like the words that had, at last, chased away my emptiness.

Fear not, for I am with you.

Jean's hand held me in place.

The longer we took to respond, the more power drained out of Daddy's cruel words.

A light came on in the Pattersons' flat below, and our dark outlines changed direction on the wall.

I was finished holding my tongue. I spoke only once, and I knew it would be enough.

"Mama."

In the splay of light, I saw terror flicker in her eyes as I called her. It must have scared her to death to understand how much we needed her. I saw the glimmer of guilt when she realized that, for years, she'd lacked the courage to do what my sister and I were doing now.

Daddy grabbed Mama when she angled herself away from him.

"No." She rose. "It's over. I won't stand for it anymore."

Daddy couldn't win against the three of us. Maybe one alone, but not all of us together.

With his fingers, he ransacked his hair.

It's not your fault what he did to you. Maybe that assurance should have come from my mama. Maybe someday it would. But for now, I heard it from a stronger place, a soul place I knew I could depend on.

Mama bundled us in her arms. Jean sobbed.

"I'm so sorry," Mama whispered to us. "I'm so sorry."

"We have to start somewhere, Mama." My words were strong. Firm. Sure.

Chapter Twenty-Five

Since the streetcar line into downtown had been shut down and abandoned that winter, I had to ride a new city bus across town to view the Grace Kelly wedding newsreel that April. Me and Jean were both amazed how quickly the months had passed that winter, since I had stood up to Daddy and our lives had changed and my sister had gone back to Lowman's Secretarial School. Jean saved up and rode a bus three hours from her school so we could see the Grace Kelly newsreel together. I'd never set foot on a city bus before, but the Hodiamont schedule told me what time to wait on the corner until it came, choking out rancid grey smoke as it growled toward me. The bus smelled like warm plastic and fresh leather and glue when I boarded. Its seats were so smooth, I slid into the lady next to me every time we swung a corner. I could tell that when summer came, the bus wasn't going to be nearly as good as the streetcar for cooling off.

Jean waited for me beside the theater doors, her hat brim pulled low, my movie ticket already in hand. When we settled into the chairs at the theater that day, when my sister sighed in expectation, the feeling of rightness, of us beginning anew in different territory, rose right up and surprised me. I passed the popcorn to Jean. With all this sudden pleasure expanding in my stomach, there wasn't room for much else.

Just then, the curtains drew apart. The theater darkened. A roaring lion filled the screen, and an anchorman's resplendent voice announced we'd be viewing *A Wedding in Monaco*, the up-to-the-minute Metro-Goldwyn-Mayer newsreel about Her Serene Highness Princess Grace. Images flickered on screen, Jean squeezed my arm tighter, and suddenly, as we saw the deck of the *U.S.S. Constitution*, each of us might have been sailing across the ocean into Monaco Harbor to meet our princes, too.

Even though the reel was in black and white, I saw everything in vivid shades, and if you asked me years later, even then, I could still describe the colors of the water and the ship-captain's jacket and the flags draped from the masts of the yacht.

Grace fielded reporters' questions in the film with style and passion that left me breathless.

"Yes, I'm sad to be leaving home, but I'm thinking about being married, I'm happy about being married. Most every girl thinks about being married at times like this."

". . . Upon marrying His Highness, I will have dual citizenship."

". . . Yes, if we were to have children, the same would hold for them as well."

It would take two ceremonies, the newsreel touted, *to unite Grace and her prince in royal matrimony. In a ceremony broadcast to all of Europe, eighty carefully selected members of immediate family and friends were allowed in the throne room of the Palace of Monaco to witness the civil ceremony. During the forty-minute service, Grace wore a pale pink taffeta suit and white kid gloves, the couple exchanged vows in French, the national language of Monaco, and Grace listened to the recitation of her new 142 official titles, counterpoints of Rainier's own.*

I conveniently forgot to "tsk tsk" Jean about placing more stock in somebody else's life than she did in her own. I understood why my sister did it. I listened to every detail about the regal ivory gown, which had been created under top-secret conditions. I imagined myself in the fitted bodice of Brussels lace, my prayer book and shoes glistening with seed pearls. I pictured how I'd hold my head high in the Juliet headpiece with the tiny row of orange blossoms, and the round veil made from some ninety yards of tulle and a constellation of pearls, specially designed so the vast audience could see the bride's face.

Finally, because of Miss Shaw and Aurelia, I was beginning to understand the truth. The one prince who cared for me more than his own life wanted to take me by the hand and make me whole.

Jean and I sat in the audience together long after the orchestra music swelled and the credits ran and the curtains drew together. We knew that from now on, when we saw Grace Kelly, we would watch her in a different way. Both of us had our own lives to begin living now.

Something had ended. Something had begun. My sister looked at me and smiled as the theater lights blinked on. She took my hand and, together, we squinted, our eyes adjusting to the light as we made our way out into the golden sun.

Even though everyone kept asking me whether Miss Shaw had her hair styled at Rogier's Salon (which is where Debbie Reynolds had gotten hers done on the way through town), or whether she'd purchased her latest pocketbook on the third floor of Sonnenfield's, or whether she used thirty-weight oil in her convertible to keep it running so smoothly, I noticed with pleasure how the neighbors had started asking her questions directly, too.

After I stood up to Daddy that night, Mama had finally stopped looking the other way when Daddy's anger flared. Sure, her voice quavered when she said the next morning, "I am not going to let you hurt the girls anymore," but it was enough to make Daddy pause and scrutinize her anew.

It had been Mama who looked up Miss Shaw's phone number in the book. It had been Mama who reached out to my new friend that next day, not in search of charity, but in hopes of getting some sensible advice. If Daddy was willing to change, eventually there might be a chance of putting our family back together.

But Miss Shaw must have been the one to help Mama get her nerve up and move us out of that place until Daddy got some help.

Miss Shaw must've said, "I have a big, old house. There certainly would be enough room for you to stay for a while until you could get on your feet," because before I knew anything else, the two of them had decided. Miss Shaw arrived at the front curb in her baby-blue Cadillac, and we loaded a few meager bags into the trunk when Daddy wasn't home. She drove us to her place before another night passed. And ever since we moved into the big house with Miss Shaw for those few months, people got even more curious about getting to know our benefactor from the inside, too.

One rainy day, I caught Miss Shaw climbing from the front seat of her car, and she wasn't holding up an umbrella to keep her hairdo dry. She wasn't holding an edition of the *Post-Dispatch* over her head to keep it from getting mussed, either. Instead, she'd tied on one of those cellophane, polka-dotted rain bonnets, the sort that unfolds from a plastic pouch that reads ROYAL MUTUAL INSURANCE, SAFETY FOR A RAINY DAY and is given away free at home shows. Miss Shaw had trussed up her hair in that thing the same way a chef would truss up a Christmas goose.

When she stepped inside the door, she untied the bonnet and shook it dry.

So *that* was how Miss Shaw never got wet hair on a rainy day. She folded it back inside its tiny pouch and tucked it inside her pocketbook where no one could see it. Now I knew. There wasn't magic to her life after all—just practicality and smarts.

And faith. A whole big dose of faith, which she'd shown me how to hang onto. I liked to think that I helped her hang onto hers a little better, too.

Mama loved Miss Shaw's garden because it grew plenty of lilacs. She loved to snip the bushes and make up bouquets of them. Some, Mama placed in vases around Miss Shaw's house. Others, she tied with ribbons for Miss Shaw to take to the cemetery.

THE PENNY

Sometimes Miss Shaw told me she would like me to go with her. I would kneel beside her at the grave, which didn't seem so dry and deserted anymore. Del Henry had edged it with solid, red bricks. At the head of the grave, the stone he'd made read: ALICE SHAW. MY MOTHER.

Now that Miss Shaw had marked her mother's grave and had started letting people see her hands (maybe one day soon Del Henry would slide a diamond on her finger!), lots of people said the mystery of Miss Shaw wasn't such a mystery anymore.

Mixing people from two St. Louis neighborhoods, no matter what color, was like stirring water and oil. Like the instance with the portable building at Harris School, everybody would get riled up for a while. But things would get back to normal again after that, and nobody let it affect everyday life much. People stuck to their own neighborhoods because it was the only way of life they knew; it had been that way for as long as anyone could remember.

I heard Aunt Maureen tell Darnell once that she didn't like how residents of the Ville weren't allowed to work downtown unless they were pushing brooms or running elevators. I was glad Aunt Maureen couldn't be satisfied with coloreds not being equal.

You could live your life in the Crocketts' neighborhood without ever leaving those few streets; the Ville had its own restaurants, movies, shops, and schools. There were plenty of good jobs to be had, the same as Wellston or O'Fallon Park, the same as Webster or Kirkwood. But at Katz Drug they started letting Aurelia and Garland come in once a week and sit at the soda fountain, the purpose of which, the article in the *Post-Register* said, was to "give store officials the opportunity to observe customer and employee reactions." On May 7 and May 14, Maureen Crockett and Wanda Simpson were served without incident. On May 22, though, Margaret Dagen and Marion O'Fallon were ignored and then later sent away without service.

That May was when Eddie Crockett learned to play his trumpet with one hand. That was Eddie Crockett for you; he went and figured out how to do what he loved. The preacher at Antioch Baptist Church was just getting ready to start up and the music was wafting to the rafters and I was staring at the window shaped like a dove, remembering when I had looked through there to find Aurelia and how that glass dove had started it all, the day after I found the penny. All of a sudden, somebody started talking about there being special music today and everybody started clapping, but nobody walked up to the pulpit. Nobody came until everybody took their seats and the hand-fans stopped moving. Then there came Eddie, carrying his trumpet in one hand.

Eddie Crockett played "In the Garden," and he played "His Eye Is on the Sparrow," and to join those two together, he played something that sounded more like Duke Ellington's "Rockin' in Rhythm" than anything else. He started out slow. But when everybody jumped up out of their seats and lifted their hands, started singing or just smiling wide, I tell you, the trumpet man's fingers started moving faster. You got the feeling watching that gleam in Eddie Crockett's eye that he'd be working the instrument until he was satisfied, until he got his fingers trilling double time.

I listened to his sound and thought about his lessons with Mr. Lamoretti and how I'd seen the dancers on the *Admiral* rooting for the Six Blue Notes and Eddie Crockett while he played. I listened and saw how, in music, there wasn't a hard-and-fast color line. I saw how music could be a real good thing for our town.

As Eddie Crockett played his trumpet, his round, warm notes sent a message to all of us. The notes sang out that with God's help a person like me could survive a broken life and come out whole.

Epilogue

$\mathcal{A}$ long time has passed since the day I picked up the penny in the middle of Grand Avenue and the Pevely milk truck swerved to avoid me and Bennett Mahaffey went diving for his LP, which got me the job working for Miss Opal Shaw. In my mind's eye, I still see Miss Shaw, but I don't picture her in the dark workroom, holding stones beneath the light, counting facets. I picture her as I saw her that day when she talked to Del at the edge of her display case, her face soft as it turned toward the light. In that light, it wasn't gemstones that glittered; it was facets of her character I saw.

Miss Shaw isn't at the jewelry store anymore, but we stay in touch, and I am sure we always will. Del Henry's son runs the shop now. After Miss Shaw and Del got married, they went on a trip down the Mississippi on a riverboat. She told me she woke with expectancy every morning, met by long-legged birds on the far wooded banks, mists rising where cool morning touched the warmth of the river, the pewter water buoying them south to the sea.

My sister, Jean, and I did nothing but grow closer after she graduated from secretarial school. We shared family memories, bound together by both good and bad. We found strength when we accepted what had happened in our lives and saw that the days would be new, that we could help others, that we could go forward in expectancy and laughter.

How excited I was when Jean and Billy finally went on a real grown-up date! But that ended soon after when a gentleman walked into the Chicago office where Jean was typing a memo one morning.

He'd come to keep an appointment with her boss, but he canceled that and took my sister out to lunch instead.

Just a few months after that first lunch, Fred took her hand and told her he'd been praying to find a wife who needed him and he believed she might be the one. It terrified her. Jean kept telling him she didn't need *anybody*, until he finally hired a painter to hoist himself up on scaffolding ropes and paint JEAN, YOU ARE THE ONE FOR ME on every window of the high-rise insurance-company building. Everyone in her office was furious because they couldn't see out. They told her if she didn't give poor Fred a chance, they'd start deducting the cost of window-washing from her paychecks.

When I was the maid of honor at Fred and Jean's wedding, I cried buckets, not because I'd lost my sister, but because we'd had to fight so hard to find each other.

As I grew up, my wirey hair got longer and settled down. I lost the pudgy look I had as a young girl. As for romance, I am dating a wonderful man and waiting to see if God has permanent plans for us.

The seeds Jesus planted in my heart first began to grow because Miss Shaw didn't give up on me. The more her kindness nurtured me, the more the decent parts of me flourished. I wanted to give hope away to people the same way I'd given away pennies. I'd found out there could be plenty to hope for, with the heavenly Father by my side. I never gave away that first penny I found, but I gave away a lot of others.

Sharing hope with other people when they were hurting, sad, or lonely made a big difference in how I felt about myself, too. God did such an amazing work inside of me, I never stopped wanting to share it. There had been days I'd gotten plenty discouraged, thinking that my small acts of kindness didn't make any difference.

Until that one particular day when everybody started giving pennies back to me and letting me know that some of my smallest gestures had helped them have hope.

There had been so many times I'd wanted to give up, but I'm glad I didn't. Now I can see the good that has come from taking care of little things.

I helped Darnell with his lessons so he could get into Washington University. I started baby-sitting Mrs. Shipley's boy. I worked for Miss Shaw off-and-on all the way through high school. And when I told her I wished we could find a way to help other girls like us, she took me straightaway to talk to Mrs. Huffines—who had become principal at my old haunt, Harris Elementary—to invite girls to come to Miss Shaw's for warm chatter and ice-cream sodas. I learned how a person could take what had been meant for bad in the world and turn it into something meant for good. I could help other people by listening to them, and by telling my story.

When I saw it was not God's choice that Daddy still controlled my life, I realized it didn't have to be my choice, either. I did not have to hang on to the wrongs my daddy had done me. It might take some time, but as long as I was willing to search God's Word and trust where he was leading me, the day would come when I would be healed from all the pain of my past.

Miss Shaw had once said, "Don't ever let someone pass off this earth without forgiving them, Jenny. Unforgiveness will hurt you every day of your life."

I knew I couldn't ever forgive Daddy on my own. That was something possible only by the grace of God. But I'd also learned God never tells us to do something without giving us the means to do it.

God strengthened me so that Daddy's awful choices ended with him, and didn't go farther. That was God's victory in my life.

I'll always remember the summer of the penny, the summer of Aurelia and the Six Blue Notes, the summer that my seventeen-year-old sister left home. Now, years later, the summer sunshine seems gentle as I visit the nursing home in Cedar Hill where we visit Daddy now that Mama's gone. They never did get back together. The hurt was too deep in Mama, and she could not face living with Daddy again.

Now that Daddy's health is too bad for him to live alone, Jean and I moved him to Cedar Hill because he needs constant care and this is a hopeful place for people to go. The sun warms the trunks of the nut-colored forest behind the main building, radiates from it, lays over the retirement center like a prayer shawl. Today, I am praying as I walk toward Daddy.

His wheelchair is parked on a concrete patio beside an ornate table with scrolled benches in the shape of half moons. His face is shaded beneath a thick plastic umbrella, the kind they used to have at the hamburger stand near our two-story flat.

"Daddy," I whisper. He is not leering at me; he simply looks up helplessly. In another twenty minutes, a nurse's aid will wheel him to lunch.

"Do you need anything?" I ask him. "Something I can bring you from the store this week? RC Colas? I know you love them."

There are some things I need to say to my father, and I know all too well how futile it will be to wait much longer to speak to him. I run the risk—the same as Miss Shaw ran the risk—of talking only to packed earth, conversing only with vacant sky. I will tell him that God loves him, that he is forgiven, and that he does not need to worry about what will happen to him as he ages because I will take care of him. It is God's will, and God's way of showing love and mercy to those who don't know him. God has called me to honor my father not because Daddy deserves it but because God knows it will mean healing for me. I am also hoping that through my love and forgiveness, Daddy will receive God's love and forgiveness.

I can finally let go of my father's choices without resentment. I am ready. At last. *I forgive you*, I will say. *I forgive you*. I know that as

THE PENNY

I sincerely say those words, a burden will lift off of my soul, and I will move closer toward being the woman God intends me to be.

Here where Daddy lives, all the world is the color of Del Henry's bricks, and it makes me think of Miss Shaw's window displays. I recite the shades in my mind as if I were naming crayons from my girlhood. Sunset pink. Granite grey. Burnt brick. Lemon dust.

All of these colors are beautiful when the light strikes them.

"No." He shakes his head. "I don't need anything. Your being here is enough."

I think, *No, it isn't enough, Daddy. I have been asked to give you more. I have been asked to let go of bitterness. I have been asked to be a part of your life. To stand strong because I know how much I am loved by my heavenly Father and I want you to know his love, too.*

In my skirt pocket, there is a penny. It's a wheat penny, not worth much to anybody else, but it is of great worth to me. I touch it with my fingers, feel its weight, and I am fourteen years old again.

I often reflect on the good things in my past, sorting through them like I'd sort through a postcard collection or stamps or coins or photos. I remember a night in summer when Mama laid wet laundry on us to keep us cool. When T. Bone Finney got a dirty look from Chick Randle because he'd started toe-tapping. "No rhythm with the feet, T. Bone. I'm percussion," he said. "I run the rhythm."

I always felt that penny in Grand Avenue had something to do with my destiny, but it took me a good while to understand how. God puts his love right in the middle of your path. He drops it right there to catch your eye, to show that he can change your life if you'll just let him.

I think that's what he's been telling me every day of my life. Ever since the day of the penny.

READING GROUP GUIDE

Composed by Tinsley Spessard

1. Jenny prayed two heartfelt prayers even when she didn't understand much about prayer or about God. When Jenny prayed the "prayer of salvation," nothing magical happened. She wondered if being saved by Jesus would change anything at home. Again when Jenny prayed for Aurelia, she wasn't sure of the results. Talk about God's faithfulness to answer our prayers, and the answers that may or may not look like what we expect or want.

2. When Jenny decided to pick up the penny, her action began a series of life-changing events. "Then the noise of Grand Avenue went silent. *Go back*, something inside me insisted. *Don't miss this chance*" (p. 9). "I wasn't going to let him use me to hurt somebody I loved" (p. 114). Discuss the difference between deciding on our own to do something, and being drawn by the Holy Spirit into something beyond ourselves. John 6:44 sheds some light on this. "No one can come to me unless the Father who sent me draws him" (NIV).

3. Throughout the story, Grace Kelly was an idol for Jean while Jenny put Miss Shaw on a pedestal. For Jean, going "bonkers over Grace Kelly" was a way to escape to a different world. On the other hand, Miss Shaw slowly became a trusted friend to Jenny. Discuss the pros and cons of having an "idol" versus a true friend who has problems of his or her own.

4. 1 Peter 3:1 speaks of a relationship between a husband and wife when it says, "They may be won without words by the behavior

of their wives" (NIV). Apply this Scripture beyond the confines of marriage and point out ways Miss Shaw, Aurelia, and Aurelia's family lived out the gospel in front of Jenny.

5. Miss Shaw gives a great example of extending grace to others. "But here's the thing with Miss Shaw: she surprised me. . . . When I took my anger out in the jewelry shop, she didn't react the way I expected her to. . . . I waited all day for her to chastise me, but she didn't" (p. 137). Miss Shaw acknowledges Jesus as the source of this grace: "That's one of the things about Jesus. . . . Once you know how to receive the love he's pouring into your heart, then all of a sudden, out of the blue, you start knowing whom to give it to" (p. 71). To whom do you feel God's prompting to extend grace? What is holding you back?

6. The need for forgiveness is huge in this story; the most obvious is Jenny's need to forgive her father. Discuss what it means to forgive someone of such atrocities. C. S. Lewis states, "Christianity does not want us to reduce by one atom the hatred we feel for cruelty and treachery" (*Mere Christianity*). How do you think Jenny would react to that? What does the Bible say about it?

7. As Jenny pushed Aurelia and Miss Shaw away, she was fighting an inner battle. Inside she was crying for help, for someone to see her pain; outside she spewed fury toward her friends. Jean acted similarly toward Jenny. Jenny seemed to realize something was going on with her father: "You probably hurt Jean and me, Daddy, because somebody hurt you" (p. 227). Have you ever been tempted to hurt someone to cover up your own hurt? Explain.

8. Discuss the role of sacrifice in authenticating the sincerity in a relationship, using Jean's sacrifice for Jenny and Jenny's sacrifice for Aurelia as examples. How does Jesus Christ's ultimate sacrifice of his life confirm his love for us?

9. Jenny asks, "Is it different when life gets taken from you moment by moment than when it gets taken all at one time?" (p. 134). Discuss

the difference Jenny was talking about, comparing Eddie Crockett's circumstances and his outlook on life to Jenny's daddy's attitude.

10. Similarly, does a slow revelation of truth have a different impact than a sudden understanding? Jenny's transformation took place over the entire summer through a series of small glimmers of hope—pennies. How do you think she would have responded if she had found a fortune all at once?

11. Jenny says, "I saw the pain behind Jean's words, and I couldn't have felt more betrayed. Mama was supposed to take care of us" (pp. 141–42). How did Mama's lack of intervention increase Jenny's feeling of abandonment?

12. Jenny experienced a shift in her understanding of reality as she began to spend time with Aurelia's family. We measure things by what we know. Do you ever measure God by your meager earthly understanding? How can we come to a complete and accurate understanding of God?

13. A question that comes to mind in light of any abuse is, "How could a loving God allow this horrible thing to happen?" Can you see ways that "in all things God works for the good of those who love him" (Romans 8:28 NIV)? Can you see ways that God took what man had meant for evil and turned it "to accomplish what is now being done, the saving of many lives" (Genesis 50:20)? Discuss how Miss Shaw was uniquely able to minister to Jenny because of her similar experiences.

14. The way her father treated her left Jenny with a damaged and diminished sense of self worth. She said, "I suffered Daddy's reminders in my head. I knew everyone looked at me and did not like what they saw. . . . When wrong happened, it would always somehow be my fault" (p. 97). How did Miss Shaw point Jenny to Jesus as the foundation for her self-esteem? If we are confident in Jesus' unconditional love for us, how will that affect our relationships with others?

About the Authors

Joyce Meyer is one of the world's leading practical Bible teachers. A #1 *New York Times* bestselling author, she has written more than seventy inspirational books, including *The Confident Woman; Look Great, Feel Great*; the entire Battlefield of the Mind family of books; and many others. She has also released thousands of audio teachings as well as a complete video library. Joyce's *Enjoying Everyday Life*® radio and television programs are broadcast around the world, and she travels extensively conducting conferences. Joyce and her husband, Dave, are the parents of four grown children and make their home in St. Louis, Missouri.

Deborah Bedford is an award-winning author whose novels have been published in fifteen different countries and a dozen different languages. She and her husband, Jack, live in Jackson Hole, Wyoming, with their two children. She began her career as a romance writer but now writes women's fiction that stirs readers' hearts and points them toward hope in God. Look for other inspirational stories by Deborah, including *A Rose by the Door*, *A Morning Like This*, *When You Believe*, and *Remember Me*. You can reach her by visiting her Web site, www.deborahbedfordbooks.com, or by writing to:

P.O. Box 9175
Jackson Hole, WY 83001